"The stories in *What Would Elvis Think?* come to life in such vivid detail as you can see each play out like a movie from your younger days. I sensed I knew the characters personally and caught myself laughing at their antics and tearful at times because I had been there, too. This book will have you eager for more and wondering if your story is somehow interwoven in these pages. It's so Mississippi!"

– Barbie Bassett, WLBT-3

"My job as a longtime television feature reporter and the Host of MPB's *Mississippi Roads* has zipped me past every house in Mississippi, I think. In *What Would Elvis Think* we get longer stopovers—long enough to get to know how people think and why they do what they do.

"Pretty much the motive for all of our actions is what the Pastor in 'Home Free' told his congregation: 'Friends, we have a reason to live, and that reason is love.' In *What Would Elvis Think?* love is fragile, puppy, and sometimes twisted enough to disguise itself as something else. But always enlightening in a Mis'sippi sort of way."

– Walt Grayson, Mississippi Public Broadcasting

What Would Elvis Think?

Mississippi Stories

Edited by Johnny Lowe

INK-SLINGERS

First printing: June 2019

"The Garden Club" first appeared in *Eureka Literary Magazine*, Fall 1995. "Ghosts and Grits" was originally published on Amazon Shorts in a slightly different form. "Gone Fishing" was previously privately published. "Jake's Detour" was previously published in a slightly different form in the *Best Short Stories from The Saturday Evening Post American Fiction Contest 2016* All other stories appear here for the first time.

What Would Elvis Think? Mississippi Stories / edited by Johnny Lowe / cover art by Gary Walters

ISBN: 9781096035503

Cover design: Bookbaby
Interior design: Johnny Lowe

Ink-Slingers
P. O. Box 994
Clinton, Mississippi 39060

clintoninkslingers@gmail.com
Facebook: Clinton Ink-Slingers

For Daney Kepple,
and everyone who came out to play.

"Hey, kids—let's put on a show!"
     – Andy Hardy, *Babes on Broadway*, 1941

"I have a bad feeling about this."
     – Han Solo, *Star Wars*, 1977

Contents

Foreword

SOUTHERN LITERATURE. It's as old and colorful as the region itself, and brings forth thoughts of family, tradition, community, religion, and yes, social conflicts.

And any discussion of Southern writing will eventually lead to Mississippi—the state that has more published authors per capita than any other, and boasts a huge number of literary giants: Faulkner, Welty, Hannah, Percy, Morris, Iles, Ford, Foote, Tartt, Grisham, and so on.

Why not, then, create an anthology of stories specifically about Mississippi? Such is the book you now hold in your hand—a collection of tales that are all set here in Elvis Country, and written by veteran writers and newcomers as well. (I predict that any names you might not have heard before will probably be names that you'll recognize in the future.)

Let me make one thing clear: this is not a book of mysteries, or fantasy stories, or romances—although all these genres are represented. It's a book about Mississippi towns and their residents, with stories as varied as the settings. The moods range from gritty to lighthearted, and the plots cover everything from reforming a rebellious high-school student to impersonating a girlfriend at a family reunion to dealing with ghosts that stow away in a traveler's luggage. Some of the locations included are Hattiesburg, Tupelo, Yazoo City, Clinton, Summit, Jackson, Magnolia, and Pearl.

Perhaps the most fascinating thing about this group of stories is their characters: toymakers, accountants, surgeons, cooks, murderers, preachers, socialites, fishermen, adulterers, ghosts, alcoholics, schoolteachers, runners, taxi drivers, gang members, practical jokers, war veterans, seamstresses, coaches, and bartenders. Some of these Mississippians might remind you of folks you know—and others are people you might never want to meet face to face.

What they have in common is that they're all interesting—and unforgettable.

So grab a glass of sweet tea and a MoonPie, stretch out in your porch swing, and get ready for twenty-three offerings of down-home Mississippi entertainment—from the Delta to the hills to the Coast.

I hope you'll enjoy them.

John Floyd
Brandon, Mississippi
January 2019

Preface

"HEY, KIDS—let's put on a show!"

You ever watch *The Little Rascals*? Or the *Andy Hardy* movies with Mickey Rooney and Judy Garland? The characters would utter this familiar line when quick cash had to be raised NOW to get an orphanage or a family out of a sudden financial jam.

And so the kids would, in an amazingly short time, assemble an all-star show. And it *would* be a show—whether they performed in a backyard or a barn, the singing, the music, and the costumes were second to none.

The show would be fantastic, enough money would be raised to get the folks out of their dire situation, and everyone lived happily ever after.

At least through the closing credits, anyway.

This book is our "Hey, kids—let's put on a show!"

Okay, it may not be *fantastic*, but it has been one heck of a ride.

I am a member of a writers' group called the Clinton Ink-Slingers. We've published two previous books, both nonfiction and both sort of their own thing, but this one would be a bit different—an anthology of short stories available in not just a few local shops, but also online.

The idea came about while I was browsing at one of the local bookstores. As I strolled by the Regional/Mississippi section with a fresh cup of overpriced coffee, I noticed a bunch of titles that are what I call "souvenir" books. Books of jokes about the South, books about MSU and Ole Miss, yet *another* book about the Civil War, etc.

Of course, novels and short story collections from authors such as Welty, Faulkner, Gilchrist, Grisham, Ford, Hannah, etc., were just a few aisles over in Fiction, but seeing the "souvenir" books sparked me to make a mental note for some reason. Then, not long after, I read an article about a series of mystery anthologies in which the stories in each book were all set in the same city. That mental note then popped up—how about an anthology of short stories set in one Mississippi town? This later expanded into an anthology of stories set in any town in the state.

To be sure, this is not the first-ever collection of stories related to the Magnolia State—far from it. But there are always more stories to tell, as well as people to write them. Some of the contributors herein are seasoned authors and/or editors, while others are the proverbial "fresh voices" you always hear about. And we wanted to bring them together.

We're not reinventing the wheel here, but we are rolling it down our own path.

I want to acknowledge several individuals for their assistance: John Floyd, for his editorial advice, support, and author suggestions; Judy Tucker for relating her editorial war stories; Meredith McGee, for her suggestions about promotion; Juanita Walker, the head of the Ink-Slingers, for her blessing for this book to exist in the first place; and artist Gary Walters, for his wonderful painting, *Highway 61 Blues*, as the front/back cover to the book.

And, of course, the authors.

This show came together a bit slower than Andy Hardy's backyard extravaganzas—at home at my computer, at coffee places talking shop with authors, and at the Whataburger at two in the morning. But we are finally done.

So come on in and take a seat.

The popcorn's hot and the matinee is about to begin.

Johnny Lowe
Pearl, Mississippi
January 2019

What Would Elvis Think?

Mississippi Stories

What If We Were Strangers

KYLE SUMMERALL

IT'S THE FIRST CHURCH SERVICE I've been to since I was still too young to tell my daddy that I didn't believe in God. I sit where I used to, third pew back from the front and all the way to the left with an empty seat between me and the end. He'd sat there, always had, even before I was born and long after I turned in my verses for a good time.

Nothing has really changed; the place still holds that flickering haze when the sun comes though the lighter panes of stained glass, there's still no air conditioning, and, at least for me, that inescapable feeling of displacement is as real as that living room piano collecting dust in the corner. The young man, who I remember from way back when, now looks like his old man in those robes as he speaks over my father's ashes. Daddy used to tell me stories about how the small church used to be an old barn that he helped convert with Brother Ken's father and grandfather. He'd point to the ceiling and tell me about the strange rafters and wooden peaks that gave the building away.

As Brother Ken says a prayer, I keep my eyes on the telltale signs above us, each one a whisper of the past and a reminder that adults play a much more convincing game of pretend than most children.

Four men are sitting behind Brother Ken in jeans and collared shirts, a choir that looks as if their obligation ended with that final Sunday morning Amen. Aside from them, Brother Ken, and me, the church was just another place.

When Brother Ken is done, and it doesn't take long, he steps down from the pulpit and heads my way, while those four men hit the door. He holds out his hand and shakes mine like a man who shakes little old women's hands for a living. That gives me enough of a grin to not have to force one. He grabs a white rag from his shoulder and blots the beads of sweat racing down his face and white whiskers.

"You know your daddy and mine built this place," Brother Ken starts.

I let him rehash one of the few stories that stayed the same no matter who told it. It was straightforward and he ended by telling me how my daddy never missed a Sunday. What else can be said, though? During my daddy's seventy-seven-year stint on this earth, he managed to destroy a marriage, alienate his only son, and scrape the bottom of every pocket he could. While most men were content to borrow trouble, my father stole it. If God was a lamb and Satan a snake, my father was that slit of cold darkness one could find in the snake's eyes, and by then, if you'd been so unfortunate as to see it, it was too late.

"This was about one of his few constants and I know he didn't do anything he didn't want to, so I guess he wanted to be here," I say, leaving out the part about the drinking and the way he'd treated momma. Some secrets were so much of common knowledge around here, they don't need to be said to be known.

Brother Ken looks like he's about to offer me my old man's place there on the third row, or maybe that's what I see because it's what I expect. Instead, his face changes and the question leaves his face.

"You gunna take him home?" he asks.

I shrug, uncomfortable in these borrowed clothes. I hadn't brought anything worthy of a funeral or church, but I knew there would be a closet full at the house. Momma's clothes were still hanging next to his, absent of any sign that a decade has passed. The rest were his, pressed and folded, even his khakis and slacks on hangers. None of it really fits. It's baggy, heavy on the shoulders where the sweat makes my undershirt cling to my skin like spiderwebs.

"Yeah, I got a place for him."

I know it now like I guess I always have; I carry a piece of him inside me and it's always frightened the hell out of me. I've spent years finding myself traveling down his same path and doing everything in my power to throw this old hunting dog off his scent but my old man left one hell of a stink. He didn't leave me much when he went, he made sure of that, and what he did leave, I didn't want. I'd inherited the side eyes and whispers from those who knew him better than I did. They look at me and see his face. They see the unpaid debts amounting to free drinks, smokes, and a lot more than the few dollars he kept crinkled around the lighter in his pocket. I've never been sure what to do with those looks so I've kept my head down, like I do now.

Brother Ken shakes my hand again and tells me he's sorry. I take it just so that he doesn't feel like he owes me even more. I go, pick up the urn off the podium, and head out to the truck. I don't have to wonder, as I back out of the gravel parking lot, if I will ever be back. We were both leaving together this time.

The cracking leather along the steering wheel is hot from where I left the truck out in the sun, and I'm sure if I had much feeling running along my callused palms, the wheel would be eating me alive. I check the urn, buckled in the passenger's seat, before returning my eyes to the road about the time we cross the Woodland County line where the sky opens and the trees back off the road, exposing patches of land picked clean aside from a batch of white here and there. I grip the wheel harder, feeling that itch I felt as a boy when daddy would take me picking for a dime an hour. I'd open my hands hot with blood and fuzz as if I'd just crushed a dandelion.

Gettin' to pickin' boy or imma just take yours, he'd say. Back then I didn't know he was taking it anyway.

When the trees return and straddle the road up to the sewage ditches, I slow and take the transition to gravel. I drive until the picket fences stretching for miles angle off and are replaced with rusted wire and steel posts. The lines bob in and out of the trees, not following the same straight trends of those white fences closer to town. These fences were hammered in and the barbed wire untangled by hands that didn't know anything but those sharp metal edges and hard living. These fences were started by men who went to war and finished by sons who'd be going sooner or later.

I pass the red gate on my left and drive all the way down to the river before turning around, keeping my eyes peeled for game wardens. I wonder if the McCrairys still own all that land to the right or if old man McCrairy sold his land out from under his kids, too? I'd grown up on those promises about how everything left of the road and from the cotton fields down to the river would be mine. He knew it'd hurt the most when he sold it.

I park on the side of the road next to that red gate and get out. The bolt cutters sit in the back and I take them. I let the woods go quiet after the teeth sit against the gate's chain, listening for that oyster cracking sound of a truck tearing down the road. I crank down and the chain snaps and falls to the ground in a coil.

The urn is heavy in my hand as I hold it close to my chest to keep it balanced. There is no shine to it despite the sun hanging at its noon peak down the ATV trail that didn't use to be here. I'd picked it out with daddy in mind. Among the choices, everything held a shine or a color I didn't think he'd approve of until I saw that steely black cylinder. It had to be every bit of ten pounds on its own and reminded me of the lifeless black that runs along the barrel of a gun.

It's strange to me, after so many years of getting into the woods an hour before the sun hit the horizon, to now be heading into the same trees this late in the day. I wonder if it would still feel so different if this land was still ours and if there weren't so many signs now that it isn't. I close my eyes and find it, a memory like a picture hanging on a wall of what used to be.

Time was one of those things that I came here to escape in my youth and then into my adulthood. Even some Sunday mornings, I'd be up before dad and in the woods listening to the owls preach to the chirping bugs and waking earth. I'd found out more about God through hunting these woods than any man's misinterpreted words could bring and, in a way, as long as daddy thought I was out here, he was okay when I quit going with him. Everything now, though, feels sentimental and I wonder if I'd continued going with him, if it'd have made much a difference.

I make a cut deep into the woods about a mile in. The places where the urn used to feel cool to the touch is hot and slick in my hand. It's all uphill for a while until I hit the gulley where dad and I used to dig for worms before going fishing. It's another thing that's gone. The dip in the earth is dry and the trees that I remember sprouting from the shallow water hold nothing but hanging moss and broken limbs. I walk until I hit a deep running scar snaking between the trees. During hunting season, dad would spend a lot of time out here and he'd haul wood on a homemade sled out to the hunting shed. The wound he left never healed and it led right to camp.

Brown pine needles stick up around the edges of the roof like hair and the cones sit in nests of the clay-colored straw all over the ground. The clearing is small and the trees around me line up heading in both directions if I stand just right. Rust runs down the tin siding like icicles that fade behind the weeds and vines growing up the walls.

I set the urn down and grab a root close to the ground and pull. The vine comes off, pulling away at the loose exterior, leaving the air with a glimmer of that fine dust. I let out a holler as I circle the shed, wait a second, then do it again, hoping not to hear a ruckus from inside. When the only sound that comes is my own returning in echoes, I circle back around for the urn. I think back to all those old tabbies he'd kept fed around here. They'd hear him coming and start piling out of the woods and from under the deck in the back, all hollering. Sometimes, he'd bring me out for the night in hopes of an early start and I would lie on the floor, listening to them howling, fighting, and clawing at the loose screens while he snored in his chair.

The wooden planks that make up the steps and porch bow underfoot and the screen door is locked for what it's worth. I yank hard on it and it pops open, the frame now bent a bit where the lock hung. The storm door on the other side sits open with about enough room for me to fit a finger through. The hinges squeal as the door opens and the stench of rotten mud and mildew escapes from the opening like an exhale.

Darkness crouches in the corners and shadows run long across one another. From the doorway I can see the drapes that cover every window to the point that no light enters. Heat boils from the bowels of the shed and it slicks down my face but if time hadn't had its unjust way with everything, I could swear that nothing had changed. Daddy's recliner still sits in the far corner, the floor still covered in old Falls City beer cans, and his workbench against the far wall stands waist high. For a second, I can swear to be able to smell copper from the animals he skinned.

The boards that lead to his recliner are softer than the ones out on the porch and have the same give as parts of the gulley. I sit the urn in his chair and take a step back, wondering if this is the right thing but when I look around, there is no doubt. Inside his sanctuary, he made sure there was no way for any light to get in and even if it could, it'd never find its way through that shell he's encased in. Even if the wardens ever found this place and tore it down, I'm sure he'd be fine to go along with it.

It was here that he came when he needed time and guidance, when momma would go missing for days or when I was being too much of a handful. It was where he went when he was worried and didn't want no one to see it. He'd slam the door behind him after we spent the last thirty minutes screaming at each other. He'd say I didn't have it bad before rattling off the things his daddy had done to him, each generation of men harder than the last.

I imagine him somewhere in the cramped space finding time to pray right before heading out into the darkness with a shotgun propped up on his shoulder. He was here, with all the things he loved. I'd even spotted that boulder towards the back tree line where he buried his old hunting dog, Juke. The more I let in the atmosphere, the more I feel all that weight he must have carried here with him on each trip. This was and had always been his place to mourn and if time had done anything here, it had allowed the inside to reflect what it always had been.

I pull the storm door to and set the screen door back best I can before tracing my steps back to the truck.

◆

The Motel 6 parking lot is empty when I get there about the time the sky is turning to the color of rusting metal and the sun is so bright, it's white. It's the kind of sunset I never get in the city.

I stand outside my room on the catwalk and smoke until the Winston box is empty and the cars are starting to pile in. I watch couples come in twos and families come in more and wonder what could have been if I didn't carry so much of him with me. I see men who'd hit their wives because they felt helpless while the women kept eyes for men they couldn't keep because they had to come home to get screamed at.

I stand there, thinking and leaning against the rail until the fluorescents kick on and the bugs start in.

Your Life Is Not Over

JANET TAYLOR-PERRY

JOYCE PEARSON stared at the headline: **Guilty! – Yount Gets Life**
Tears trickled from her cheeks and splattered, smudging the newsprint.
Logically, she knew it wasn't her fault. Yet, she murmured, "If I'd only
had a little more time with him . . ."

The high school English teacher sighed. Her former student, Neal
Yount, was guilty of murder. *What could I have done to make a bigger
difference in that disturbed young man's life?*

The divorced mother of twin boys looked up from reading the news
she didn't want to know. She watched her sons play FIFA soccer on their
PS3. They were only six years younger than Neal, and she feared about the
lack of male guidance for her own children.

With their father gone after a mid-life crisis and his affair with a
younger woman, the stay-at-home mother had gone back to work. She
chose to teach in order to have comparable hours to her children.
She sacrificed two nights every week to gain her master's degree and a

renewable teaching certificate. *Will my choice be enough or was it a mistake?* she wondered.

Joyce looked again at the image of the handsome young man who had been in the first class she ever taught. "Oh, Neal," she said with renewed tears the memories brought to the surface.

◆

Two days before classes began, Joyce had landed her first position. An hour's drive one way was taxing, especially when she saw the dilapidated building. The classroom sprawled but was cramped with thirty desks in six rows of five. Boxes of supplies covered the teacher's desk, and the dry erase board smelled of cleaning solution.

Joyce stored the supplies and wrote her name on the board: "Ms. Pearson." She would be teaching oral communications, a mixed age group of tenth, eleventh and twelfth grades.

The bell rang, and twenty-three students sauntered into the classroom of City High School in Yazoo City, Mississippi. The group had more girls than boys, two white students, one Asian student, three Hispanic students, and seventeen African-American students.

The bell was still ringing, but the students' chatter nearly drowned it out. And they weren't moving to their desks.

Try as she might, the five-foot-nothing, one-hundred-pound, auburn-haired teacher could not be heard. She then flipped the light switch repeatedly, but several of the students only laughed at her attempt to gain control of the class. The greeting she had received from a few other teachers played through her memory: *Welcome to the Zoo.*

Then a handsome boy, a good foot taller than Joyce, said, "That don't work at our age." The boy's bitter-chocolate eyes and sassy smirk screamed "Trouble!"

"Sit down!" barked from the depths of the petite woman's gut. A first soprano, Joyce finally projected over the tumult. She locked eyes with the boy, and he cocked an eyebrow.

"Y'all hush." He waved a hand, the pinky sporting a long fingernail. "I wanna see what this little white woman's got."

Joyce realized instantly the young man wielded power and was a leader, if misguided. Her insides quivered.

Bodies finally plopped into chairs. Silence.

Joyce noticed that more than half the boys wore only black and red. She had been told the color combination was to show their gang affiliation. She noticed, too, many of the young men had slits in their eyebrows, another gang denotation of rank. Mr. Trouble had three slits, and that fingernail told her he both used and sold drugs.

Joyce took a deep breath. "What I've got, is your number."

Several students sniggered.

Joyce continued. "Until I get to know all of you, everyone will be seated in alphabetical order." Mr. Trouble watched with curiosity as the teacher arranged the class. Neal Yount, aka Mr. Trouble, took the last seat, skipping a desk between him and the student in front. Joyce pointed.

Neal shook his head. "You don't want me to sit behind him. He ain't one of my homies. I might stab him in his jugular with my pencil."

The smallish boy in the front seat said nothing, but he looked up at Joyce, his eyes begging.

"Fine," she said.

She introduced herself and what the class would cover. She issued textbooks and passed out a syllabus.

When Neal got the pages, he cackled. "You can't be serious. This ain't college." He looked down at the sheet. "You expect us to do this?"

"Yes."

"You got us making a speech on Friday—introduction speech for a test grade with a visual aid. That ain't even a week."

"I'll demonstrate what I want tomorrow. It's time for the bell. When you come back tomorrow, sit in your assigned seats. If you aren't in your seat, you're absent."

The bell rang. Off the second hour of the school day, Joyce sought counsel from other teachers.

Mrs. Franklin, a short, squatty black science teacher who had befriended the new kid on the block, looked over Joyce's rosters. "Oh, you poor thing—Neal Yount first thing in the morning. Better you than me."

She pointed to another name.

"This one, Antonio Ramón, is dyslexic. You won't find it in his file, but he is. Give him his tests on blue paper. He's a good kid, but he gets picked on all the time. Watch Neal with him."

Looking at the roster, Joyce realized Antonio was the "not homie" who sat in front of Neal. That night the newbie to the zoo went home a nervous wreck.

◆

Day in, day out, Neal Yount did something to push Joyce's buttons. Somehow, she managed to keep control, but she wrote several referrals on the boy. He spent more time in detention than her class. And he missed his first speech because he was in detention from another teacher.

He came back to class with the poster for the presentation. "You gonna lemme do my speech today, Ms. Dwarf?"

The class snickered.

"Yes, Neal, as soon as you refer to me by my name."

"Please, Ms. Pearson?" he said, sugary sweet.

She glared at him. He smiled.

The boy was trouble with a capital T, but there was also something devilishly charming about him.

She gestured to him. "The floor is yours."

Neal strutted to the front of the room and displayed his poster. It was red and black.

"I'm Neal. I'm naughty. I cause lots of trouble." He thrust his pelvis. "But the ladies think I'm really nice."

Several girls giggled. Joyce surmised the young women must have experienced Neal's "niceness."

He looked around the classroom and smirked. "I'm egotistical. Rightly so, though, 'cause I'm pretty damned good."

Another thrust.

Joyce took a long breath and glared at him, her mouth a thin, tight line. Neal batted his lashes.

"Sorry. Darn good." Yet another thrust.

More giggles wafted through the classroom. Joyce glowered at the sea of faces.

Neal continued. "I'm adventurous. They ain't much I won't try."

This time he licked his lips.

Joyce covered her mouth to hide her discomfort, but to speak would only add fuel to the boy's fire. Neal went on.

"I'm laid-back." He looked directly at Joyce. "I'd love to lay back for you—I ain't never had a redhead."

The class erupted in laughter. Joyce's face burned scarlet.

"Neal, step outside with me, please."

In the hall, Joyce whispered, "If you think you're going to upset me, guess again. You know that was inappropriate, but I'm not writing you up this time. I'm giving you a 75 on the test because you said 'ain't' too many times and showed me great disrespect, not to mention yourself."

Neal started to speak, but Joyce shot up a hand.

"There is no discussion."

She opened the door and Neal returned to his seat, arms folded across his chest.

◆

Two weeks, three weeks, mid-term—and always trouble emanating from Neal Yount. One morning a balled-up piece of paper plopped Joyce in the back as she was writing on the board. She sighed.

"Neal, I know it was you."

She picked up the paper and dropped it in the trash.

"There is one sentence up here. Class, you have five minutes to write an impromptu speech about the topic. Two minutes in length."

She timed the five minutes with her watch. "Neal, you may begin."

To her chagrin, the one minute, forty-one seconds Neal spoke were nearly flawless and dead on target. He sat back down, smug as he could be.

On the day of the nine weeks' test, Joyce walked into class only to find all the test copies missing—someone had stolen them. She had a good idea who had done it, but not how.

She wrote one question on the board.

After the students came in and took their seats, Neal asked, "Where's our test?"

Joyce pointed to the board. "You have one minute each to answer this question orally. Neal, would you like to start?"

Joyce gloated inwardly at the surprise on his face. She later discovered every student in the class had a copy of the test already completed.

Neal stopped on the way out the door. "You real feisty," he whispered with what almost sounded like respect. Again, his response to the question had been spot on.

The next day, a four-inch rubber-band ball was being passed and bounced around during class. Joyce smiled and began her lecture on persuasive speaking, but never said a word about the "toy." Then when it finally bounced at her feet, she picked it up and dropped it in her desk drawer.

Neal bolted to the front of the room. "Gimme my ball."

Joyce gave him one of his own naughty/nice looks. "It's my ball now. Sit down."

He towered over her, the whites of his eyes showing wide. "You fixin' to get hit."

Whether it was stupidity or bravery, Joyce didn't know, but she stood her ground.

"I dare you."

Neal backed away and sat down without a word, sulking through the rest of the class. Joyce wrote up the incident and took the referral and the ball to the principal.

The next day, Joyce was summoned to the office. Neal was there with the principal—and Neal's mother—who held a document detailing expulsion procedures in her hand. "I know my boy didn't do this," she raged.

The assistant principal came in with Neal's disciplinary file. It was an inch thick.

His mother thumbed through the documents. Then, before anyone could react, the woman, who was not much bigger than Joyce, slapped her son across his face. "You *will* graduate! Yo' brothers graduated, and so will you. I done good by y'all after yo' daddy run off."

Joyce caught her breath as she realized Neal's home situation was similar to her own.

His mother turned to Joyce. "Please, give him another chance. He won't give you no more trouble. I swear it."

Then she popped the boy again.

"You tell her you sorry."

Joyce could not believe her eyes or ears when Neal said, "I'm sorry, Ms. Pearson. I wudn't really gonna hit you. You spunky. I like you."

Having a nightmarish vision of her boys sitting on the hot seat, she felt tears sting her sky-blue eyes.

"Neal," she said, "I'm not afraid of you. You're so much smarter than you want people to believe. You might be a little demon, but you have so much to offer."

"Gimme another chance, I'll be good." His eyes darted to his mother.

Joyce took a long breath. "All right, but if you as much as sneeze without saying 'excuse me,' you're out of here."

"Yes, ma'am." He nodded his head sincerely.

◆

Two days later, Joyce was summoned once again to the principal's office.

What have I done this time?

Both the principal and the assistant principal were there. "Yes, Mrs. Brown?" Joyce asked, her voice shaking.

The principal indicated a chair. "Please sit, Ms. Pearson."

Joyce sat across from Mrs. Brown while Mrs. Temple, the assistant principal, remained standing off to the side.

Joyce felt a reprimand coming.

Mrs. Brown took a deep breath. "Report cards just went out."

Joyce nodded. She had given twelve F's. *Is that what this is about?*

"We are a low-achieving school," Mrs. Brown continued. "We know that. However, half our seniors failed the first nine weeks of English.

"Something is wrong. So I would like for you and Mrs. Dean to trade classes. I want you to take over senior English and give her your oral communications classes."

Joyce's eyes went wide. "When?"

"Today. Right now. We won't ask the students to move, just you and Mrs. Dean. Y'all have the same off period. You can pack up and change rooms then."

Joyce moved the next hour as if in a daze. Mrs. Dean seemed irate about the change and hardly spoke to Joyce.

In the new classroom, Joyce looked through the grade book and Mrs. Dean's lesson plan.

She also saw that she had not escaped Neal Yount.

He was a senior. He had 55 for the first nine weeks in English, although he had eked out 79 in oral communications because he neglected to turn in assignments.

Scanning the lessons, Joyce could not fathom why the students had not read *Beowulf* and *The Canterbury Tales* during the first nine weeks. Her approach to senior English and British literature would have started with the first known piece of writing in English and concentrated on how the language continued to change. Joyce saw the students were supposed to be reading "Ode on a Grecian Urn."

"Geez Louise!" she spoke aloud to no one. "These kids can't even speak modern English correctly and this woman wants them to interpret John Keats's brogue?"

In her first English class, Joyce began the lesson with Shakespeare. Even with that, the students looked dumbfounded.

Neal actually spoke up in a respectful manner. "I don't know what this says."

Joyce tapped the podium anxiously. "Yes, you do." She had a lightning flash in her brain.

"Tomorrow I want all of you to bring a King James Bible to class."

She gave no more explanation. Joyce knew ninety percent of the students went to church—and were familiar with Shakespearean language without being aware. She did, however, have a momentary apprehension of the ACLU knocking on her door—but she rationalized that the Bible could be taught as literature and history.

She used Psalms to introduce King James English, the language of Shakespeare. Beginning with Psalm 100, with Joyce's assistance, the class as a whole translated it into modern English. Then they broke into groups of four and did the same with Psalm 23, this time without her help.

After that assignment, each group received a slightly more obscure Psalm—but one they might have heard—and had to translate it, choosing one member to present their translation. Neal presented for his group.

Finally, each student was given a Psalm they most likely had never heard, and were to translate and present it in any form they desired, even a rap song. Joyce employed the same strategy and kept the groups intact with Shakespearean sonnets.

By the time they read *Macbeth*, the students had translated any number of Psalms and Shakespearean sonnets into rap songs, country music, and just plain poems—and performed them for class.

The first week in the new position brought evaluation visits from the principal. Mrs. Brown's statement read: "I could not believe my eyes. I saw students who never participate working enthusiastically."

After school Mrs. Brown grabbed Joyce. "How in God's name did you get Neal Yount to actually do some work?"

Joyce smiled. "He keeps his word. It's his bond."

She neglected to mention that when Neal challenged her yet again— "You a scrawny little white woman come in here tryin' to change something you don't know nothin' about"—she told him a story about "Jobette," a poor girl who had grown up in the housing projects who got welfare checks, who was nearly killed by her father, and who had been sexually molested, but who still managed to win a full scholarship to college.

When she ended the story—"Guess what Jobette's doing today: teaching your class"—Neal Yount was in tears.

He'd finally seen Joyce as a real person not that different from himself.

Class ran smoothly. Neal Yount flourished. And then graduation time came, with only one student failing senior English.

Neal left her class with an 89 for his year-end average. He'd kissed her on the cheek.

◆

Graduation rehearsal was in progress as Joyce posted her grades for the year. Suddenly the classroom door burst open.

Neal stood in the doorway, fists clenched, breath coming in spasmodic gasps. His nostrils flared, his eyes bulged.

"Neal, what's wrong?" Joyce said, fear washing over her. She hesitantly rose from the chair, not sure what she should do.

"I can't graduate."

"What—why?"

"I ain't passed that damned American history test."

She covered her mouth and took a steadying breath. "Neal. Relax. You can take it again this summer and graduate in August." Anger washed over her as she wondered whether standardized testing might keep this young man who had made such great strides from graduating.

The boy's lip trembled. Joyce had never seen Mr. Trouble so vulnerable, not even when his mother had slapped him in front of her.

"My momma's gonna be so mad," he sniffled.

Joyce hugged the child. Even at eighteen, with a two-year-old son of his own, Neal Yount was still very much a child. He cried like a baby in the embrace of a teacher who truly cared for him.

Two police offers walked into Joyce's classroom. "Ma'am," one of them said, "we're here to escort Mr. Yount from the premises."

Joyce turned to Neal. "What did you do?"

He shrugged. "I sorta threw some chairs across the gym."

"Neal, go home. And do what I said." He nodded, but his eyes showed utter defeat.

Joyce felt the same. The system in great need of its own improvement had failed this young man.

◆

Mid-June, the six o'clock news grabbed Joyce's attention. Neal's face was plastered on the TV screen—the story said he was accused of murder.

Apparently, he had killed Maurice Jefferson, who was the boyfriend of his girlfriend's mother.

During the next year, Joyce made as many days of Neal's trial as she could. Testimony showed that he and the deceased had argued. Neal left the scene and returned half an hour later with a gun. Witnesses said he shot Jefferson point-blank in the face. He died instantly.

Toxicology screens showed Neal was high on cocaine, and Jefferson was a known supplier. The argument stemmed from a drug deal gone bad.

Listening to the proceedings, Joyce had to ask herself if she had been insane when she stood up to this young man who obviously had it within him to kill. She was lucky to be alive; yet, she knew she had touched something inside the boy's pathetic soul.

As the bailiff led Neal away, his eyes caught those of his teacher. His lips formed the words, "Sorry. I love you, Ms. P."

◆

Joyce Pearson glanced from the article in the newspaper to her boys as "GOAL!" resonated from the game system. She looked back down as fresh tears came.

"Life," she whispered. "Parole in thirty if . . ." Her voice faltered.

He'll be fifty years old, his life wasted.

Michael, her dark-haired and dark-eyed son who looked like his father, turned. "Momma, are you okay?"

"Yeah. I will be. I was just reading about that student of mine." She had told her sons about Mr. Trouble.

Although twins, the boys were by no means identical. Richard, sandy-haired with blue eyes, hit the pause on the game. "What happened?" he said.

She passed the newspaper to them. Both boys sat beside her, one on either side. Richard said, "You know, Momma, you don't have to give up on him."

"What do you suggest?"

He shrugged and dipped the corners of his mouth. "Write him. Encourage him to get his GED in prison. I read lots of people do that. There was a program on TV about it, too."

"You can visit him if you want," Michael added. "Just don't forget you have other students now. They're still around for you to make a difference."

Joyce put an arm around each of her sons. "Just promise me you won't ever get mixed up in the kind of stuff he was."

"Promise," they chorused.

"How about Chinese buffet for supper?" Richard said. "It's your favorite."

"Like you don't like it?" Joyce teased.

"Hey!" Michael laughed. "You taught us well."

"Yeah, I did." She tousled the boys' hair. "Okay, Chinese—but first I have something to do. Finish your game and we'll go."

The twins moved back to the game console. Joyce sat at her desk, took out stationery, and started writing.

"Dear Neal,

Your life is not over . . ."

The Tenant

CHUCK MCINTOSH

MARK CAPERS sat at his desk, crunching numbers for his brother's taxes. He worked hard on them because his brother was the first client of his young career. And currently his only client. Business had been sparse in the three years since graduation, which was the reason he was studying to sit for the CPA exam next spring. While small jobs came and went, his brother's tax preparation was the only recurring job he could count on.

Mark's work environment was confined to a twelve-by-twelve office in a building full of identical spaces one block off Main Street in the small town of Tupelo, Mississippi. Its beige, windowless walls and linoleum tiles reflected the hum and glare of the fluorescent tubes in the ceiling. Each morning, he woke up in his one-bedroom apartment, ate his cereal over the sink, and drove his ten-year-old car to the small-business second-floor incubator. On this day he stabbed at the calculator with quick fingers, hoping to finish the project and get paid, on time and in cash.

A knock on his door broke Mark's concentration. He looked up to see two men in dark suits standing in the hallway.

"May I help you?" he said.

The short, burly man marched in first, flashing a badge pinned to his wallet.

"Mr. Capers?" he said.

"Yes?"

"I'm Special Agent John Dorsey. This is Special Agent Thomas Randall. We're with the Federal Bureau of Investigation. May we speak with you a moment?"

Mark motioned them toward the two chairs opposite his desk. Agent Dorsey pulled a photo from his shirt pocket and handed it to him as he sat down.

"Mr. Capers, do you know this man?"

Mark studied the photo.

"Sure, he rents the office across the hall," he said. "But I don't see him very often. He keeps odd hours."

"How odd?" the taller agent said. His voice was high, with a nasal tone that didn't seem to fit a tough G-man.

"Well, he comes in only occasionally," Mark said. "Like, he might open up his office in the middle of the morning, stay a few hours, and then leave right after lunch."

"Uh huh," said Agent Dorsey. "Every day?"

"No, he sometimes doesn't come in for a week . . . maybe two." Mark stopped there. He didn't know why they were asking him questions about his neighbor and he didn't want to know.

"Anything else, Mr. Capers?" The stocky agent stood and the taller agent followed suit. Mark just sat there, looking at them.

"Not that I can think of," he said.

Agent Randall took out his card and pushed it into Mark's face with a bony hand.

"If you think of anything else, please give us a call, would you?"

"Sure," Mark took the card and looked at both sides. He decided the federal government sure spent a lot of money on expensive-looking business cards.

"Thank you for your time, Mr. Capers," Dorsey said, and they pushed through the door into the hall. Mark heard their footsteps fade, then looked at his watch and returned to his books. He was only weeks away from April 15 and he was behind.

Later in the day, Mark looked up to see the shapely form of Jennifer Leyton at his door. Jen had an interior decorating practice down the hall, and at least twice a day she could be found leaning against his doorframe, hand on one hip, sipping coffee and making small talk. Her short blond curls framed an exquisite face highlighted by pale blue eyes and dimples.

"Hi, Mark," she said. Her voice always reminded him of honey on a warm biscuit. "How's your day going so far?"

Each gab session was ten or fifteen minutes that Mark enjoyed, but felt like he should be focused on the tax returns. Being the nice guy he was, however, he always took time to visit with Jen. Besides, she wasn't exactly ugly, he thought. If it weren't for Lacey, I might even—

"Lacey," he said out loud. Mark looked at his watch. "I'm sorry, Jen, I've got to run." He closed his computer and pulled the chain on the banker's lamp.

"That's okay," she said as she watched him grab his jacket. "I was just passing by."

Mark watched her sway down the hall, for a moment transfixed, and then looked at his watch again and headed for the door.

◆

Inside Lacey's apartment, Mark sat on the couch with a beer and watched her move laundry from the washer to the dryer.

"So you say these FBI agents just appeared at your door, asking about the guy across the hall?" she said.

"Yeah, it was pretty unnerving."

The willowy brunette came in, plopped down beside him and, grabbing his beer, took a swig before handing it back. She was the only child to Leo Morton, a wealthy entrepreneur who owned convenience stores, pawnshops, and scrap yards. Despite all his money, Leo was still rough around the edges and proud of it—and he would do anything to make his daughter happy. As a result, Lacey was used to having her way. It was her world and everyone else simply lived in it.

"Well, is he dangerous?"

"I have no idea. I've seen him maybe twice in the past couple of months," he said. "And we didn't speak except to say hello."

"They didn't tell you why they wanted to see him?" She took another swallow of his beer.

"Can I get you one of these? I don't mind."

"No, I'm fine, thanks," she said with a wave of her hand. "It sounds to me like you need to keep an eye on him."

"Yeah, I guess I'd better."

"So," she drained the bottle and jumped off the couch, "where are you taking me to dinner?" Lacey had her jacket and purse in hand before he could get to his feet.

◆

One day closer to the tax deadline, Mark was back at the office crunching his brother's numbers and keeping an eye on the door. If his neighbor happened to show up, he wanted to know about it. He'd already had his morning visit from Jen, and all the while he kept looking over her shoulder, watching the door across the hall.

By lunchtime he needed a break from the debits, the credits, and the tension. He decided lunch at the food truck down the street would give him a chance for fresh air and a fish taco. Strolling down the sidewalk, he eyed every car parked within a block of his building. Were the two agents staked out with binoculars and stale coffee? Did they have walkie-talkies? Mark was beginning to feel like a character in a '50s B-movie.

While waiting his turn at the food truck window, he caught a familiar scent on the breeze. He turned and found himself face to face with Jen.

"Well, hey, stranger," she said. It occurred to him that sunlight made her look much better than fluorescents. That blond hair seemed to take on a glow when out in the open air. "If I'd known you were headed down this way I would have walked with you."

"Sorry, Jen, I should have checked with you," Mark said. While he thought she was very attractive and exceedingly friendly, he also knew that Lacey would have his head if he had lunch with Jen.

"That's okay." She shrugged. "Why don't we sit over here?" The line had moved and it was his turn to order.

"Well, I need to, uh, get back to the office, you know. It's tax season and I'm pretty much stacked up right now."

"Okay, that's cool," Jen said. That smile never left her face. "Maybe after April 15th we can try again." And those pale blue eyes did a flutter thing that he'd never see them do before.

He paid for his tacos and headed back to the sanctuary of his office. It wasn't that he disliked Jen, he reasoned. Far from it. She was attractive, interesting, and easy to talk to. It was just that he was engaged to Lacey and didn't want to give the appearance of impropriety.

As he walked through the parking lot, he was startled to see the tenant from across the hall getting out of his car. They made eye contact, so Mark felt it was too late to change direction. Swallowing hard, he walked up to the man.

"How's it going," Mark muttered—and immediately felt it sounded as if he knew more than he should. To his relief, the man didn't seem to notice.

"Good," he said. "How about you?"

"Uh, good . . . thanks!" Mark's voice went up an octave and he cleared his throat. The man started walking toward the door and Mark kept pace with him.

"Uhm . . . excuse me," Mark said.

His neighbor turned.

"Yes?"

"Do you have a minute to talk?"

The man looked at him for what seemed to Mark like an eternity. "What for?"

Knee-deep now, Mark figured he might as well continue.

"I'd just like to share something with you," he said and gestured toward the door.

The man glanced at his watch. "Sure."

The two men walked into the lobby and up the stairs. Halfway down the hall, Mark took a deep breath and said, "Here's the thing; the other day I had a visit with two guys from the FBI. They showed me your photo and asked me what I know about you."

The man's face never changed, never provided a trace of worry.

"I see," he said. "And what did you tell them?"

"Nothing," Mark stopped in his tracks. "I didn't tell them a thing. Because . . . well . . . you know . . . we've never met." He immediately stuck his hand out. "I'm Mark Capers, by the way."

"Thomas Rayner," the man said, shaking the hand.

"Nice to meet you, Mr. Rayner. So, anyway, these two FBI guys told me if I remembered anything about you to give them a call. And then they left."

The two men stood looking at each other for a moment.

"Well," Thomas Rayner said, and began walking again, "it was probably nothing, but I appreciate you telling me." He stopped at his door. "Is there anything else?"

Mark stopped and stood at his door, as well.

"Nope, that's pretty much it. I just thought you should know."

Rayner scratched his head as he looked at the floor.

"Doggone if I know what they wanted," he said. "Maybe they'll come back by and let us both know. Thanks again, Mark. Very kind of you to mention it." He was into his office and closing the door now. "Have a great afternoon."

"Let's get together for some coffee sometime," Mark said.

Rayner turned and pointed an index finger in Mark's direction, his thumb toward the ceiling. And closed the door.

Was that supposed to be a gun? Mark wondered.

He turned, unlocked his office, and went in.

Well, that was weird, he thought. Get a grip, Mark. The guy seemed okay. I've got my imagination working overtime on this.

He looked at his watch; it was almost two and he still had plenty to do on his brother's taxes. He set to work and focused for the rest of the afternoon.

◆

By the time six o'clock rolled around, he felt pretty good about where he was on the taxes. Jen had come by once but didn't stay long. He was ready to go home, put his feet up, and not think about taxes, the FBI, or Jen. He wanted to just spend some time with Lacey watching an old movie. Mark locked his door and headed home.

◆

It was mid-morning the following day when Mark came in and opened his office. As he turned the key in the lock he heard voices behind him. He turned to see the building manager showing someone an office across the hall.

Suddenly it hit him. This was the office that, until last night, was the office of the guy. *That* guy. The one that Agents Dorsey and Randall were asking about. Mark hurried across the hall and stood in the doorway.

"Mr. Judson?" he said. "Can I see you a minute?"

Judson, who never seemed to change his bowtie, peered at him over round wire-rims. "Hi, Mark. What's up?"

"What happened to the guy who was here yesterday?"

"Oh, Mr. Rayner," Judson said. "He texted me last night that something had come up with a family situation and he had to leave."

Mark gasped. "With his family? He moved all his furniture out overnight because of a problem with his family?"

"He had it written in his lease that he might need to do that one day, so . . ."

"And he used the word 'family'?"

"Yes, he did. Why do you ask?"

Mark was suddenly unsure how much he should reveal about his visit from the FBI. "No reason," he said.

Mark thanked Judson and went to his office, where he sat stunned.

Why would someone leave in the dead of night, sweeping his office clean so that it appeared he'd never been there? What could that mean?

Mark was lost in piecing together a senseless puzzle. He didn't notice the two men standing at his doorway until one of them knocked.

"Mr. Capers?" It was Agents Dorsey and Randall. Mark gulped and stood.

"Yes sir?"

"Mr. Capers, we're Agents Dorsey and Randall. We came by the other day?"

"Yes sir, I remember you."

"Mr. Capers, did you speak with Thomas Rayner in the parking lot of this building yesterday, about 12:45 P.M.?"

Mark could tell they already knew the answer to this. They must have been watching the building. Or maybe they bugged the hallway. Or even his office.

"Yes I did," he replied. "Why?"

"What did you two talk about?"

Mark couldn't think of a reasonable answer. He figured they already knew about Rayner's disappearance.

"Oh . . . not much," he said.

"Did you tell him we were asking about him?"

"Why do you ask?"

"Look, Mr. Capers, we don't have time for this dancing around," Agent Randall said. "You spoke with him yesterday, and today he's gone. What did you say to him?"

"Well, we talked about the weather," Mark answered. "And . . . you know . . . things in general." He stopped talking now. And wondered if he knew anyone who might be an attorney.

"Okay, Mr. Capers," Dorsey said. He must be the "good cop" in this scenario, Mark thought. "Let's be clear. We wouldn't be here if this guy wasn't important to us. If we find out that you told him we're looking for him, you could be an accessory."

Mark looked at Dorsey, then Randall, then back to Dorsey. He gulped.

"Accessory to what?" The room seemed to get smaller as the silence got larger.

"We'll be back, Mr. Capers," Agent Dorsey said, and pushed Bad Cop Randall toward the door. "In the meantime, don't leave town."

Mark heard their footsteps clicking down the hall and fade away just like before, but the roaring in his ears wouldn't fade. He sat staring at the opposite wall.

Accessory to what?

◆

A couple of days had gone by, and it looked like Mark would be able to finish the tax returns in time and get paid by his brother.

Jen continued to drop by on a regular basis, and as the pressure on Mark lessened, he began to look forward to her visits. Lacey even seemed to be in a better mood lately. That suited Mark just fine.

This particular sunny morning while thumbing through prescription receipts, he was once again interrupted by a knock on the door. And once again, he looked up to see two men standing in the hall.

"Excuse me, are you Mark Capers?"

The man speaking had to be on the north side of three hundred pounds. He was dressed in a dark blue tracksuit with white piping and wore a gold chain around his thick neck. It rested on a mat of hair that looked like a toupee taped to his chest.

The older man behind him held an old leather satchel and looked up and down the hall as if expecting someone.

"Yes sir," Mark replied.

The two men walked in and closed the door behind them. "Mr. Capers, you don't know us," the track star said, "but we're friends with Tommy Rayner, your neighbor across the hall."

A light went on in Mark's brain. "Okay . . ." he said. "How can I help you?"

"Help us?" the man said and smiled. "You don't understand. We're here to help you. Bobby?" He extended his hand toward the older man, who handed him the satchel. "Mr. Capers, we represent a friend of Tommy's. And Tommy's friend wants you to have this—as a sort of thank-you for what you did for Tommy."

Mark sat looking at the briefcase in the man's meaty hands. The identical gold rings on his pinky fingers looked tight and uncomfortable. The black onyx on the right ring, in the shape of a knight's helmet, had a small chip in it as if it had hit something hard and broken off.

"There's no need to thank me—"

"Take it, Mr. Capers. You've done our friend a great service, and his friend wants to repay you."

Slowly Mark reached for the bag, and as soon as he had a grip on it, both men rose to their feet and left the office. Mark sat there for a long moment, then carefully opened the soft leather case.

Bills. Large bills, wrapped in rubber bands. Not the crisp notes one gets from the local bank, but dirty, wrinkled, used bills that could easily disappear into circulation around town. Sitting here in front of him was a bag stuffed with money.

How much? He dumped the contents over the tax forms. There wasn't a one-dollar bill in the pile, nor a five. It was tens, twenties, fifties, hundreds. He began to sort them by denomination. It took him a while but he finally got a round number.

Stacked neatly before him on his desk was ten thousand dollars.

◆

Later that afternoon, Mark found Lacey on the phone at her apartment. She waved him to come in while she was looking through her desk in the corner. It was piled with receipts, bills, and who-knows-what. By the way she talked it was obvious what she was looking for in the mound of paper was important. Mark decided to take a seat and wait his turn. He found a magazine and flipped through it mindlessly, instead thinking of the small fortune hidden under the spare tire in his trunk.

"Daddy, I know it's here somewhere, but I can't put my hands on it right now," she said into her phone.

Mark had come to realize that Lacey's strong suit was not organizational skills.

"I know, I know," she continued. "I'm sure it's just . . . I'll find it, don't worry. I'll bring it by first thing tomorrow." She paused. "I said I'll have it." She hung up without another word; not a "goodbye," not an "I love you," just a click.

Typical Lacey, Mark thought.

"Finally!" she said, relieved.

"What?"

She held up some stapled papers. "Something I needed for my taxes. Daddy's accountant almost has my taxes finished, but he needs this to wrap it up. C'mon, let's go drop it off."

"I thought you said you were going to take it over there tomorrow," Mark said.

"Yeah, but I have it now," Lacey said. "Daddy won't mind. Besides, once we drop it off, we can go eat at that new seafood place near there."

Before Mark could ask once again about why *he* couldn't be doing Lacey's taxes, she was already out the door of the apartment and halfway down the hall.

The ride across town to Tupelo's more expensive neighborhoods provided a chance to talk about the two guys in Mark's office earlier in the day. While he told her this, he kept glancing at the rearview mirror.

"Mark, this is great," she said. "Think of what we can do with that much money! We won't have to dip into my bank account for the honeymoon." This reminded him of the economic gap between them, and how it chafed him to have to rely on her wealth.

"I can't keep this money," he said. "I don't know anything about these people—and something doesn't add up."

They drove through the gated entrance and eased past stucco-covered mansions and tall hedges. After pulling into the circular driveway of the early 20th century Italianate home, they stopped at the stone steps leading up to the massive oak double doors.

"Let's not discuss this with Daddy," Lacey said. She was out before he had a chance to shut the engine off. "The less we tell him, the better."

Mark followed her up to the door. The foyer of this house never failed to intimidate him. It was designed to be the opening act of an expensive showcase of power, money and excess. And after 90 years, it still worked. Glistening marble floors, polished columns, and a grand staircase were meant to impress those who had been deemed worthy visitors.

The rich Persian rugs that littered the floor were strategically placed to lead guests into the great parlor. It was in this arched-ceiling room that they found Leo talking to an associate. When the man turned, Mark was stunned to be face-to-face with Special Agent Dorsey. And by the looks on their faces, Agent Dorsey and Leo were both surprised to see Mark.

Without a word, the stubby agent immediately left the room and Lacey's dad sauntered over to the wet bar, as if to distance himself from Dorsey.

"That's him," Mark said. "That's one of the FBI guys."

Lacey looked at her fiancé as if he'd used the wrong fork.

"No, it's not," she said. "That was Buckner. He and Daddy have been friends for years."

Mark looked at Leo. And back at her. And back at him.

"Is that true?"

The older man poured two fingers of Glenlivet into a rocks glass and capped the bottle.

"I think we'd better sit down, son," he said.

Mark sat on the couch opposite Leo's plush wingback chair. "What's going on here?"

"Daddy, Mark told me he was visited by the FBI this week," Lacey said, "and now he's saying it was actually Buckner." She turned to Mark. "How can you say Buckner is an FBI agent? That's just not so."

"I'm telling you, that's the man who came to my office with another guy, and they told me they were with the FBI. They showed me badges! I have his card!"

"And I'm telling you that Buckner is—"

"All right, all right," Leo said. "I'll explain it if you'll let me."

Lacey and Mark sat on the couch and waited. Leo took a sip of his Scotch before speaking.

"Now Mark, you know how important Lacey is to me, don't you," he said. It wasn't as much of a question as it was a statement of fact.

Leo Morton had little interest in the marketplace of opinions; he'd rather give them than take them. "And I believe she deserves only the best of everything: her car, her apartment, her clothes . . ."

"And her boyfriends." Mark was beginning to see where this was going. "Mr. Morton, did you send two guys to my office posing as FBI?"

"Mark, my father would never do something like that," Lacey interrupted.

"I'd like to hear him say that," Mark said. "Did you?"

The old man pondered the ice as he swirled it in his Scotch. He took another sip.

"Yes, I did."

"And the two thugs? With the pouch full of money?"

Leo nodded with a smug.

"Daddy, why would you do that?" Lacey blurted.

"I wanted to see how Mark, here, would handle himself under pressure." He smiled at her. "I did this for you, my dear."

"For me? How is this helping me? What were you thinking?"

Mark stood up, his mind reeling.

"What about the tenant across the hall? Was he a setup, too?"

"Certainly," the old man said, almost gloating. "A man's worth comes to the front when tested by loyalty and temptation. I wanted to see how much of a man you really were when confronted with both."

Mark started pacing. He had been set up by his future father-in-law and was expected to just accept it. How could he trust anything from this family again?

"I suppose Jennifer Leyton is a part of your 'loyalty and temptation program,' too, huh?"

"I'm afraid I don't know anyone by that name." Leo stood, drained the glass, and walked over to the wet bar for seconds.

"Wait a minute," Lacey said. "Who's Jennifer Leyton?"

"Look, how am I supposed to believe anything you have to say to me or to Lacey from now on? What are we supposed to do—just look over our shoulders for the rest of our lives, wondering if you're orchestrating events to make it easier for us?"

"Just a minute, Mark," Lacey said. "My father is not a liar, and if he wants to do something nice for us once we're married, I see nothing wrong with that."

"Oh, really," Mark said. "So you're okay with what he's doing?"

Lacey thought about it for a moment.

"I can understand his position."

Mark stared at her, incredulous. The saying "blood is thicker than water" came to mind but he decided to let it go.

"I guess we all know where we stand now," he said. He started toward the door, then turned. "Leo, I have something that belongs to you in the trunk of my car. I'll leave it out front."

Mark left the satchel, and Lacey, at the oak doors. Without a word he drove away from the house and the manicured lawn and found his way out of the neighborhood.

He felt as if he were being released from prison. A load was lifted off his shoulders and he was ready for a fresh start.

The sun was setting as Mark reached downtown. He pulled in and headed straight for his office. He made a decision to finish the taxes, pack up his office, and start over in another town. Maybe another state. The sooner he could finish those taxes, the sooner he could leave Tupelo, Mississippi.

"Well, hey there, stranger." Jen leaned against his door, coffee cup in hand. "What are you doing here so late?"

Mark looked up from his papers and took in that killer smile and those dimples. It dawned on him that a fresh start might not have to mean leaving town. He dropped his pencil on the desk.

"I was just thinking about dinner," he said. "Interested?"

Home Free

WENDY HARMS

WE LEFT NEW ORLEANS at dawn, neon pink shattering the blue-black silence of the air into which our lazy summer evaporated. Thin as spirits on the currents swirling in and out of the wide-open backseat windows, Sister and I sucked in the humidity as if it were the scent of pine and oranges and peppermint at Christmas, our minds cooling our bodies with the memory of winter air. The ruse continued briefly, not past the light revealing the world to us, not past Maurepas Swamp, not past the Mississippi state line, the furthest we'd ever been away from our home.

"How are you holding up, Ayers?" said Aunt Free.

"Like a bunch of flowers somebody threw in the trash," Mother said.

At the time, I believed it was the impending heat of afternoon; later I learned it was my mother's desperation that forced us to leave so early. By noon, a cloudy sky cocooned us in Aunt Free's cavernous Buick, leaving us with only the monotonous view of a blurred landscape through the rain fanned out in rivulets on the windows. My position compared to the trees and along the roadside was a comet cutting space into halves: the peaceful and the chaotic. I was a parcel, stationary in a spaceship, the tall grass magnified in tiny droplets like planets in an unknown universe.

The language of this new land mingled beautiful oppression with sacred secrets; barbed wire along hay fields strung along for miles interrupted at regular intervals by a gas station, a church, a post office, a cemetery. The revelation of its character was both soft and sudden; its pace forced upon us like a film switched abruptly to slow motion, politely replacing the din of Mardi Gras, streetcars clacking, second line cymbal crashes floating over the beautiful peaks of dilapidated and celebrated buildings.

Ahead, the downpour ended and insects droned, tractors growled, gossip spattered. We glided over narrow strips of slag and tar melted by the fireball sun into a solid mass. Aunt Free drove so slowly the car absorbed the heat of the road like a hearthstone before a broiling fire.

Last night, Aunt Free promised Mother that she would take care of everything: the china and silver, the bed linens, the house. *You three'll be back quick as a wink.* Mother tucked our summer clothes into her suitcase. She brushed the dust from the framed photographs on the sideboard in the dining room and slid them into the round-top trunk that sat unmoved in the hallway as long as I'd been alive. She latched and locked the ornate brass escutcheon before looping the ribbon around her neck. *It'll all stay put, Ayers. Don't you worry.* Aunt Free shooed Sister and me into the nursery where we'd slept since birth. Mother cupped her face in her hands and the skeleton key dangled, heavy with finality, the remnants of our infancy strung on lavender velveteen.

Her given name was Freesia Ayers Walters Mosby, after her grandmother. *I'm free, all right,* she told us that night, *free from home life, free from children, free from shame. So we'll all stay with Granny until you get your head straight again.*

Mother was named after Granny's sister, Lucinda Ayers Walters Mosby. Mother pointed to them in a faded photograph that included her and Aunt Free's mother, who died when Mother was born. The four of us sat around the kitchen table, distracting ourselves from our more recent tragedy, gathering bits of identity to connect us to our next destination.

From the road to the horizon, the fuzzy false ground of a cornfield shimmered in the late afternoon haze. We crept toward the hill in the distance for what seemed like forever; when our car tilted upward, finally climbing the dominating landmark, I spotted a pause in the row of pine trees along the roadside. Branches spanned the space over a path, no wider than the car, which served as the entrance to Granny's land. Around the corner a mansion leaned in upon itself, angled upward to the double brick chimneys, paint clinging to about a third of the cedar planks, a wood and brick marvel lost in its glory days. Granny appeared on the front porch, her round frame smothered in a cloud of calico.

"How long can you stay, Freesia?" Granny said as soon as the engine shut off.

"As long as Ayers needs me."

After supper, Mother and Aunt Free tucked Sister and me into a white iron bed covered in hand-stitched quilts. The second floor bedroom was not so much walls as windows, two on the north side and two on the west side. They stood open, begging for any bit of movement in the solid night air. Sister and I lay feet to head and held hands between us. A gauze of a curtain hung, still as church, sentinel ready if a breeze dared approach. Mother, Granny, and Aunt Free sat on the porch and their voices rose up and cast far out into the dark field beyond the front yard.

"Freesia, you don't have to stay long. Go on when you need to. Ayers and I will be fine."

"Granny, I can take care of my business later. We'll get the girls settled and let Ayers recover," Aunt Free said.

"Ayers can teach in Ripley. It's not too far. The girls can go to school there," Granny said.

"I'm still here!" Mother said. "You two act like I can't speak for myself. I'm not dead. He is!"

"Ayers, I know it. And I'm glad it's done." Aunt Free's voice crackled before a long silence. Only the light on the porch remained, beaconing out across the field. Creaking stairs and bedsprings let me know I was now the lone thinker in the house. I wondered why Aunt Free was glad my father was dead. I was sad, but I couldn't say I missed him.

The next morning was Sunday, so we put on our church clothes and piled back into the Buick. Just to get into the building we had to walk down the middle aisle in plain sight of everyone so we wouldn't miss the stares burning holes in my smocked cotton dress. Granny took us to our Sunday school room and we sat in little wooden chairs. The windows were open, and as the teacher prayed to start the lesson, I stared at men gathered on the side porch just across the yard to smoke and talk. They shook their heads a lot.

"He was caught in the act," a man said.

"She has a lot of nerve walking into church like she belongs here. A lot of nerve," another man said.

"At least she has family here to help her," the first man said.

"Ought to be in jail," the second man said. "Self-defense, they ruled it. Don't believe it."

"Young lady, turn around here and listen!" The Sunday school teacher pushed out a breath. "You need to hear the word of the Lord!"

Sister and I squeezed each other's hands and kept our eyes connected under bowed heads and dared not make a sound. When the teacher stopped talking, the other children stood up and filed out of the room, so we followed out the front door and down the sidewalk to the big church. In a pew toward the back, we found Granny and Aunt Free and let them scoop us up in their arms despite both of us being too big for that.

After church Mother and Aunt Free warmed up the food Granny had cooked early that morning.

"What was the Sunday school lesson about?" Granny asked.

"I don't recall."

"Didn't you listen?" Mother said. "You always liked the stories."

"I liked our church in New Orleans."

Mother held her breath. Aunt Free patted my shoulder. "It might be different here," Granny said. "You'll learn to like it."

"Don't forget to be yourself," Aunt Free said.

In the morning I opened my eyes, fully rested for the first time ever, it seemed. The hum of the morning through the open window, light moving across the field, the grass, tall and busy, accepting the dew as its fate, nature's apology ahead of the afternoon heat, a stillness like the earth had stopped moving while my eyes were closed and had not yet begun to spin again. Sister and I gathered eggs in the hem of our aprons, talking to the hens as the sun lit up the dust through the holes left by knots in the grayed pine boards.

We left the chicken house on wooden steps, latching the rectangular wooden catch on the door. These two places were worn smooth in contrast to the rough surface of the walls. Only with constant human touch will a dead tree become soft and free of splinters.

Mother was mowing grass when a visitor arrived. It was late in the day and we were playing on the porch watching the grass fly up in the air, predicting which way it would go, rocking our doll babies in our arms. Mother stopped pushing and smoothed her hair. There was no breeze to cool, so she turned her back to the car and swiped the drips off her face with the hem of her shirt. A man clicked his shiny shoes along the gravel and waved his arm over his head.

"Thought I'd stop by," he said.

"Carl, hello. Oh, pardon my mess, getting this grass under control," Mother said. She smiled, but the man seemed to be in a hurry and forgot his manners.

"That's not a job for you, Ayers. It's indecent, you coming up here trying to make do without a husband." The man stepped closer to Mother and removed his hat. I gasped. It was the second man from the side porch conversation at church.

"You mean put in my place. We are just fine, thank you. Would you care for a glass of tea?" Mother said.

The screen door slammed and Aunt Free stood on the porch, her thumbs caught up in the belt loop of her blue jean shorts.

"Hey, Carl. How are ya?" she said.

"Fine, just fine, Freesia." Carl stepped toward her. "Just here to rein in your wild sister."

"She won't be bridled, Carl. Let folks think and talk as they will. Ayers is capable."

"Capable of anything, what I heard." Carl spun around on his toes and crossed back over the driveway. He paused and looked over the roof of his car, shaking his head. "Damn near anything."

Aunt Free's fierce glare tattooed the back glass of Carl's car as she sheltered Mother. With her eyes fixed on the expanse of the field, Sister cradled her baby doll and blinked hard with each of Mother's sobs.

"Who was that?" Granny said, rounding the corner of the house. "What in the world has happened?" Folded linens flew up from her clothes basket as she relinquished its weight and rushed to her granddaughters.

"Carl Denson." Aunt Free wiped her eyes.

"What does he know?" Granny enveloped Mother and walked her up the steps. "Girls, y'all go in the house and get a glass of tea for your mama."

I leaned on the wall next to the door to the kitchen and put my finger up to my mouth so Sister wouldn't talk. She sat at my feet with one hand wrapped around my ankle, her head tilted up, eyes red-rimmed and wide with panic.

"Granny, he knows what happened." Mother's sobs drifted down the wide hallway. "He's probably told everyone."

"Carl and his daddy. Always in everybody else's business," Aunt Free said.

"You aren't guilty of anything. Your own husband pointed a loaded gun at you. You were the brave one, with a knife, no less," Granny said.

"He would've gone after my girls." Mother's words were vinegar in my mouth.

That night I decided I no longer believed in time. Years were nothing more than calendar paper pressed together, the days migrating from one page to the next until my story deteriorated into clumps of letters. If I could make sense of anything, it was the heat and insects and hard work inherent in living in Mississippi. Church was also necessary, the stares and the whispers mixed in with candle smoke rising to God. The pastor's warmth and kindness were the only evidence of religion, it seemed, but I prayed anyway, for Mother and Sister and Aunt Free and Granny, their peace of mind, their health. I sent my pleas heavenward on the notes of the piano, the regular progression of chords pulling my feelings from one woman I loved to the next as the congregation sang the ancient words.

Those years were thin and uneventful and lonely, a puzzle with no solution, constantly staring at dirt and trees and sky from the upstairs bedroom, the porch, the church pew. Mother brushing through my tangles with her hand on the crown of my head, the same hand that gripped the knife. Mother's tears when Sister sat at home for the spring dance, the same tears that fell when she forced us to leave New Orleans. Mother on Easter Sunday in the dress she bought on Magazine Street in the fancy shop with gold letters on the display window, the same dress she'd worn the five Easters we'd lived in Mississippi. How subtly the days shifted, like white weightless clouds transformed in a glance to gray and laden with rain.

Before dawn on the Sunday before my sixteenth birthday I heard the clinking of silver and china in the dining room. Mother, Aunt Free, and Granny hushed each other's commands, betraying their secret plans. From the top of the staircase I spied Mother, tacking paper signs over the sideboard, arranging flowers for the table, fussing over details, redeeming her mistakes.

"Don't look there!" Sister's job was to distract me that morning as we left for church. She'd evened up with me in height but surpassed me in the awkward loveliness of a growing young woman. Her unwieldy arms motioned like branches in a storm. "Just quick get in the car!" Her smiling eyes were framed with sun-streaked locks, golden and hanging perfectly by chance.

Most Sundays the sermon never caught my attention. On that day, Sister had a glow that prodded me to listen for something worthwhile. In the pastor's last sentence I felt the burn of truth: "Friends, we have a reason to live, and that reason is love."

The sweet smell of old hymnals and melted wax and hay floating in through the open window fully inflated my lungs for the first time since I last breathed in the delicious funk of the streets of New Orleans. The shuffled cards of my childhood regathered as a complete deck, not in order, but all in one place. Love was my purpose; it had been since the night I realized my mother was more than cake maker and baby doll seamstress. She was courage and rage, tenderness and survival—hers, Sister's and mine.

The Wreath

STEPHANIE SWINDLE THOMAS

W HEN SARAH PASSED, Butch barely cried. He didn't know if men were supposed to cry when their wives died, so he kept what he was feeling to himself. Nothing really changed after that day in January when her car hit that rare Mississippi ice.

Since then, it was as if Sarah had gone on a long vacation. Butch made his way through the spring, summer, and almost the fall pretending she would return and telling everyone he was fine. He thought about how she would go to her mother's house in Tupelo for weeklong visits a few times each year throughout their thirty-five years of married life. "Always a daughter. Never a mother," Sarah would sigh on her way out the door. She had always wanted children, but it never happened.

Doctors gave them plenty of advice, even changing Butch's type of skivvies, but nothing worked. Butch finally convinced her that all of the planning and trying was the problem and that it should happen the natural way. Neither of them believed that, but the hiatus brought relief or, if nothing else, resignation. Butch remembered what people used to say about his uncle who couldn't have kids. Then, he heard it in his head and behind his back.

Every Sunday, as he and Sarah had always done, Butch drove to his sister-in-law's house in Corinth for dinner. She had become a sister to him after his brother died in the war, but he never liked her second husband. He didn't like how her son had called that man "Dad" and let him adopt him, especially on account of his father having been a war hero. But even that husband was dead now, and he and Agnes and the young people were the only ones left.

"We outlived all of 'em, Ag," Butch realized, as he helped put the rolls into a basket one Sunday.

"That we did," she said without looking up from mashing potatoes. "'Cause we're meaner!" she said, laughing a bitter laugh.

"I guess you're right," nodded Butch.

At that moment, Agnes' kids came in, pulling off their coats. Everyone sat down to eat and spent the meal talking about the election and about Christmas. Butch was glad Sarah wasn't there to hear all of the opinions she never liked about them. He could even imagine her fussing all the way home in his truck.

Sitting on the porch, he smoked alone in the cold. He almost didn't want to go inside, but Bear kept scratching and whining from behind the door.

Butch couldn't fall asleep that night. Folding down the quilt and sliding feet into slippers, he got out of bed. He bumped into the nightstand and steadied the lamp as quickly and quietly as he could, only remembering after his hushed response that there was no one to wake. Bear raised his head but went right back to chasing rabbits in dreams. Butch restlessly dozed in his chair for a while and got up to start his coffee.

It was still dark outside as he wandered the house trying to find something to do. His eyes closed in on the blue plastic bulge on the counter—Sarah's Sunday *Times*. He never thought to cancel it, and just kept bringing them in and setting them on the counter. Each week, one plastic bulge replaced the other. Butch thought about how Sarah would spend hours going through that paper and how aggravated he would get sitting in pajamas all morning waiting for her to finish. One day when she was particularly frustrated at him watching her and waiting, she snapped, "Can't you read?"

Butch thought about how mad he got that day, and before he knew what he was doing, he unfolded the paper in front of him.

By the time work was over, Butch was ready to sleep and made up for the previous night. He woke up Tuesday and stood buttoning his flannel shirt in front of the calendar. In Sarah's handwriting was the word "VOTE!" Following orders, he got in his old red truck with the dented side from where the rock had ricocheted off the weed-eater the last time Sarah did yardwork and drove to their polling place at the American Legion.

"Number 278," yelled a young woman, handing him his ballot. She looked at him, sizing him up as someone voting for the wrong guy. Butch had seen that look so many times on the face of his own wife. He knew he would have seen it again this election, had Sarah had the chance to vote for the first woman running for president. Then, Butch did something he couldn't explain. He bubbled in the boxes Sarah would have picked instead. Dazed, he walked out of the church to his truck. He got in and started laughing uncontrollably.

"How'd ya like that?" Butch howled, turning to the empty seat beside him.

He drove down to Abe's, where he and Sarah had lunch every time they voted. When Abe came over, he declined the menu.

"A BLT, extra tomato, light on the mayonnaise, sweet tea with two slices of lemon, and fries," Butch recited, not his, but Sarah's order.

Although he usually hated tomatoes, except fried green ones, the sandwich tasted good. Butch wondered what they would have talked about during all those lunches had they just voted for the same person. Some lemon juice squirted into his eye, and he felt like Sarah was saying hello, like she was telling him that they never would have voted for the same person and that part of what made them a couple was that they were so different. He finished his meal and left a Sarah-sized tip.

A few weeks passed, and Butch kept reading the paper and eating BLTs at Abe's. He knew the holidays were almost there and that he had never spent one alone in his whole life, going from his parents' house to his own house with Sarah. Thanksgiving never meant all that much to Butch, except football and food. Sarah would make a big feast and invite every stranger she'd ever met to join, so Butch didn't know what to do this year. Agnes was going to her son's house in Oxford and halfheartedly invited him to join, but Butch never wanted to be somewhere he wasn't welcome and told her that he just wanted to enjoy his day off this year.

At the Piggly Wiggly, a place Butch still felt uncomfortable on every visit, people were loading carts full of holiday delicacies. As he backtracked to get some lunchmeat, the idea seized him to pull a turkey out of the bin and load it into his cart next to the toilet paper and Alpo. His heart raced, as to his surprise, he continued adding potatoes, cans of corn and green beans, and Stove Top stuffing to his buggy.

At the checkout, the woman asked Butch if he was hosting a big Thanksgiving. He mumbled something, realizing that buying the food was only part of the day. Loading the groceries in his truck bed, Butch wondered how and whom to invite. No kids. He didn't want the stress. No family. He didn't have any to invite. Then, he thought about Sarah's lists from years past. Most of those people had moved, only living there for one reason or another just long enough for Sarah to find them interesting and bring them home to dinner. Come to think of it, that's how they got Bear.

When he pulled into the driveway, he saw the Fishers outside and waved. The old grumps were just getting back from somewhere. The only time they ever spoke was when Mrs. Fisher would exchange her sausage balls for Sarah's fudge around Christmas.

Sarah used to say that they would end up like the Fishers someday, and that's why she felt sorry for them, even though she didn't particularly like them. She said it seemed those two had nobody in the world. Butch realized Sarah was wrong about two things: the Fishers had each other, and she and Butch wouldn't end up like them after all.

With his turkey-filled paper sack in his arms, Butch marched across the street. Mr. Fisher took two steps in retreat and twisted up his face at Butch crossing the imaginary boundary that kept them on separate sides all these years. Mrs. Fisher went around to the side of the car to where her husband stood waiting to find out what on earth Butch Simpson could possibly want.

◆

"Um, hi, Mr. Fisher, Mrs. Fisher," Butch stammered. "Was planning to make a turkey for Thanksgiving, wanted to invite you over."

Mr. Fisher scrunched up his face, and Butch, not having anticipated a negative response, felt a touch of horror and rejection before hearing Mr. Fisher squeak, "Huh?"

He hadn't heard a word Butch said, due to the mumbling and shock of the encounter. Mrs. Fisher heard him, but needed to hear it again to understand, so Butch invited them twice. Although all three were bewildered at the proceedings, the Fishers accepted, and Butch returned to his side of the street with his turkey.

Flipping through old cookbooks trying to figure out how to cook a turkey, Butch ran across his wife's apple pie recipe from her mother and smiled. He knew that he wouldn't be able to make a pie that good, and kept flipping. He found a chocolate pudding pie that sounded easy enough and went back to the store with the list of the four ingredients. The cashier recognized him.

"Back again?" she asked. "You must be having a big party! Makes me glad it's just me and my daughter because I hate cooking. I see food all day here. The last thing I want is to go home and deal with more food."

Before Butch knew what was happening, he offered them to join him. The cashier accepted, and he tried to tell her where he lived.

She laughed and pointed. "It's on your check."

Butch laughed, took his instant pudding supplies, and went home. He spent the next two days trying to find the turkey pan and putting out the nice plates. The extent of his cooking was following the instructions on the backs of boxes or the Post-it Notes on Sarah's casseroles. He always got home first and put dinner in the oven, but Sarah had done all the work for him. When she died, all of these women from the church brought him food for a month. Meal train, gravy train, he couldn't remember what it was called. He wished he had frozen some of it to thaw out for his guests because he had a feeling he was in over his head.

When the big day came, Butch woke up extra early. He shaved and smacked his cheeks with Old Spice before stretching his navy blue sweater over his stomach. Digging under the bed for his loafers, Butch found all the things Bear had whined over and forgotten. Both fellas left the room with their prizes to start the day. Butch picked up and put down every box on the counter, trying to decide which one to open first. Exhausted at the thought of it, he took his coffee and cigarette outside.

Sitting there, he thought about his first Thanksgiving in the house with Sarah. She refused any help and made him stay in the den because she wanted to do everything herself. She even brought him a sandwich on a tray for lunch to keep him out of the kitchen. The later things got, the more Butch had wondered about when the dinner would be ready. He walked in to find her crying at the table. He lifted her chin, and like a scene out of *I Love Lucy*, her flour-covered, tear-stained face looked up at him with a quivering lip.

"I can't cook!" she wailed.

Butch laughed at how hard he laughed that night. He remembered laughing and hugging her, as she tried to stifle his laughter with halfhearted blows until she eventually started laughing herself. She never was a cook, but she got better over the years. Butch had forgotten about that Thanksgiving until now, almost like Sarah was reminding him of it at the perfect moment.

"I guess it won't be that bad," he laughed and went inside.

It wasn't that bad at all. Butch followed the instructions on the boxes, pushing his reading glasses up his nose every few minutes. His guests arrived, ate, and complimented his dinner. Tina, the cashier's little girl, loved his chocolate pie so much that he sent the rest home with her. He loaded up takeaway plates for them and the Fishers, leaving himself and Bear only a little bit of turkey for a midnight snack.

Butch was so tired that he expected to fall right asleep, but he lay awake in bed for hours going over everything he said, all of the things he made, and how nice everyone was to him. He still couldn't believe he did it. He was even prouder of himself than the time he scored the winning touchdown that took Tishomingo County High to the state championship. He wished Sarah had been there to see him, but then again, he only did it because she was gone.

The alarm clock sounded before Butch closed his eyes. He stumbled through the house looking for all the things he hid away in places he didn't remember. Hazy eyes met the pile of dirty dishes, and he knew he would have to get to them before the cleaning lady came on Monday. All his coffee mugs were dirty from his usual shelf, so he reached up to the next one in the back. He pulled it down, looked inside to see if it was clean, and turned it toward him. "I Love My Wife" stared back—an old gag gift from Sarah. Butch smiled and proudly poured the coffee into the old cup that didn't seem as funny as it did true.

The morning at work dragged until Butch's BLT. He was still so happy about his little Thanksgiving, and he wanted to do something special to celebrate. Rather than heading back to the plant, Butch went home. It was a warm day, and he thought it would be perfect for putting up the Christmas decorations.

He dragged out the boxes from the basement and the snowman from the attic. With Bear supervising, Butch made quick work of hanging the lights on the house and moved inside to start putting together the tree. He hated artificial ones, but Sarah loved Christmas and real trees dried out too soon to keep them up until the Epiphany.

Butch fluffed the branches, like he had seen Sarah do, and started unpacking ornaments. It seemed like every ornament had a story, but he couldn't remember most of them. There was the plastic alligator he brought home from his work trip to Florida. He remembered that one because Sarah threw it at him when he gave it to her and knocked off one of its eyes. He turned it so that the good eye showed, deciding that ornament was his favorite. After all, it wasn't the alligator's fault he hadn't called her while he was there. Butch sat back for a minute. He didn't know why he hadn't called her, but he was sorry about it now.

Surveying his decorations, Butch approved but felt like he was forgetting something. He went outside and threw the stick for Bear. He thought about how much he used to grumble about putting up the decorations. He had always waited too late to get the lights up outside and ended up doing it the morning of the Christmas parade, just in time to light them that night.

"Why'd you put up with me?" he asked, shaking his head and looking vaguely upward.

Bear turned his head and dropped his stick at the question. The wind blew just hard enough to rattle the metal door hanger.

"The wreath!" Butch said.

He and Bear loaded into the truck to set out for a real Christmas wreath. He knew Pine Mountain Tree Farm in Walnut always set up their tree lot early and had door wreaths and greenery.

Mike Marolt himself waved the truck into the driveway. "Hey, Butch! Looking for a tree?"

"Nah, just a wreath. A big one, with ribbon!" he said, as Mike headed over to the table of wreaths.

"Like this?" He held up a big green circle with branches, pinecones, and red ribbon trimmed in gold.

"Perfect," Butch agreed. "Load it in the back."

He paid him and drove home to hang the wreath. Butch was excited. He knew it was going to be perfect on the white front door. He and Bear trundled up the steps, hung it on the hook, and went back down to see how it looked. The wreath had been the finishing touch, and Butch knew it.

"Woohoo! Lookee there, boy," he rejoiced, rubbing Bear's ears and pointing his face at the door. "That's the best wreath that door has ever . . ."

Butch stopped. He couldn't swallow and grabbed backward for his truck bed to support him. The wreath that Agnes had put on the door when Sarah died flashed before his eyes, and he felt a jolt of pain. He propped himself up against his truck, trying to breathe while Bear helplessly whimpered. Tears filled his eyes, and he crouched down covering his face and sobbing. He wept, as Bear licked his hands. She was really gone.

Butch didn't remember getting up or making it to the porch to sit down. He clicked his Zippo and examined what was left of a faded quote Sarah had engraved on it long ago.

"Only light can do that," he read.

Smiling, he got up to go inside, closing the door displaying the wreath.

Climbing Mt. Olympus

CHUCK GALEY

T HE FAT TIRE BIKERS call it Mt. Olympus because you've got to be Zeus to climb it. Here I was, Evan Wheemp, trying to run my way up the largest hill in Mississippi I had ever seen.

There were fifteen switchbacks on this hill and I was already out of breath . . . on the third. I stopped and began to hike up to the top of what seemed to be more than Mt. Olympus. It was Mt. Everest.

The path went on forever. It had a series of natural obstacles like jutting roots and huge rocks that came out of nowhere.

I stumbled and almost fell when my toe hit a rock. Where did that one come from? This was harder than it looked.

The sun had been up about an hour. The cool of the morning was beginning to wear off. Sweat soaked through my shirt.

I soon grew dizzy, stopping often to catch my breath. Good grief, I thought. I'm only fifteen. I should be able to do this.

Suddenly I heard a noise behind me. Another runner.

"Nice day for a run," he said as he glided past, running easily, his breathing smooth and even.

He wore a red bandana, which soon was just a spot of color dancing in the leaves beyond the next couple of switchbacks as he moved out of sight.

I stood there leaning against a dogwood, looking down at the trail. How could he just sail up the hill like that? Boy, was I dizzy.

I decided to sit down on a fallen log. My cross-country running coach always said to take it easy early on so I wouldn't pull a muscle.

"It's like lifting weights," he said. "You wouldn't want to try to bench press three hundred pounds the first time out. You start slow. Over time, your muscles become stronger and you can lift more. You build up slowly."

Right now, I couldn't lift a finger.

I kept going, slogging my way up. After every switchback, I stopped to catch my breath. The dizziness wasn't as bad now. I kept my pace slow. Finally curving around the final turn, I saw a flat clearing open up at the top of the hill. A large fallen tree was nearby. I sat on it to catch my breath. I took a drink from my the water bottle.

My thoughts began to wander. What was I doing up here? Coach had told me there are college scholarships available for cross-country athletes. It would be a good way to take care of some college expenses. But three years to graduate seemed a long time away. It will take a lot of work.

Coach Karing was an old guy who had seen his better days. Sometimes I thought that he didn't have a clue about what kids like me were going through. The only future I had after high school was to work in the local locker factory. Yep, the factory was the maker of quality lockers for all your school's needs. Except mine.

The sun had moved through the trees and it was time to return the way I came. No way was I going to try to make it down the other side. I didn't know where I was! I picked up my water bottle and screwed the top back on. It wasn't fancy like the running store bottles. It was a Walmart brand, fresh out of the cardboard packaging.

I felt depressed because it was so hard for me to get up the hill. Maybe going down the hill was easier. Coach always said that life isn't always fighting uphill. Sometimes you find you're running downhill, too. I wasn't sure if that was a good thing.

The trail zigzagged down the way I had come up. It looked different from this viewpoint. The big boulder-size stones looked different from the other side. I began an easy jog down the trail. This was a lot easier than fighting uphill.

My foot slipped in the dirt when I tried to avoid a tree. My speed kept increasing. I was skittering like a dog on ice.

I stumbled over a root and a rock outcropping. I had to slow down. A tree branch swiped my face. Was it there when I came up this way?

Mt. Olympus was throwing me forward. The roots and rocks seemed bigger . . . and lethal.

Hurling down the hill, I tried to keep my balance. I checked my speed while slipping on the loose dirt. I didn't notice that I was on the last switchback.

When the ground flattened out at the bottom, I found myself breathless.

I staggered over to my old beat-up Toyota and pulled a paper sack out of the trunk. The banana and water inside were a welcome relief.

This was not the greatest start to my cross-country career.

◆

The next day the boys' cross-country team met in the gym after school. Coach Karing came out of his office. "You guys run a few laps around the track to warm up. I'll be out there in a minute. Evan, I need to see you in the office."

I followed him as he waddled back into his office with his clipboard and dropped into his desk chair. Fading photos in dusty frames covered the walls of his office.

I sat in a metal chair that had Choir Room stenciled on the back. Coach leaned back and gave me a curious look.

"Did you run the mountain bike trail the other day?" he asked.

"Yes sir," I said, fighting back panic. I crossed my feet and pulled them under the chair.

"Well, that's not a regulation course for cross-country. You do know that, don't you?" He moved a few papers around on his desktop.

"No, I didn't. I figured a trail is a trail, no matter where it is." Stupid answer.

I took a deep breath. Had I done something wrong? There was a long pause before he asked his next question.

"Did you trip any? You know, fall?"

I thought back over the time on Mt. Olympus. "I almost did. Stumbled a few times."

The phone on his desk rang and startled us both. He answered it and talked as he looked for a file.

I looked around the room at the photos. The color shots were more recent, but the black and whites were taken years ago. In one, I thought I recognized a face looking back at me through the years. It was a group of boys in cross-country kit underneath the large mascot painted on the wall of the gym. The skull and crossbones flag of the Pelahatchie Pirates. Directly under the skull was a boy with a bandana on his head. He looked vaguely familiar.

Coach Karing interrupted my thoughts when he placed his hand over the phone and nodded toward the door. "This is going to take a while. Let's do this another time."

◆

Later that week, I felt better about trying the mountain bike trail again. I drove my old Toyota to the trailhead, got out and stretched to get into the right mindset. The air was cool, the shadows long and stark.

At the bottom of the trail was a flat meandering section. I liked that because it let me warm up and mentally prepare before I hit the switchbacks of the climb. Today, the goal was to go all the way up and then down the other side. With all the slips and slides the other day, I felt a little nervous. I sensed a harmful presence hovering in the trees.

The switchbacks came soon enough as the ground rose in front of me. As I looked up the hillside, I promptly stumbled over a root and fell into the wet leaves. My water bottle came loose and slid into the brush.

The fall reminded me to keep my eyes on the path. It will catch you, I thought, if you don't pay attention.

I found the bottle, brushed the dirt and leaves off my wet shirt, and started up again.

I counted off the switchbacks, noting all the roots and rocks I saw the last time. A fresh set of leaves had covered the roots on the dirt course.

I was rounding the last switchback when I remembered the photo on Coach Karing's wall. The boy the young coach was standing next to. He was the same kid I saw on the trail the first time I had run these switchbacks. But something was different—or should have been. That guy didn't look any different than in the photo.

For the moment, I pushed that from my mind.

Finally I reached the summit of Mt. Olympus. I felt a wave of excitement; running up all the switchbacks had been easier this time. I was still exhausted and out of breath, but not as bad.

I sat on the fallen log throne, basking in my achievement. I sipped some water, and my breathing became steady.

The photo. Was the boy I saw on the trail an older brother?

The sun was lower in the sky now and the wind had picked up. Overhead, crows cawed as if laughing at me.

After a while, I was ready to head down the other side. I crossed the clearing and began my descent. The wind was blowing harder; the leaves rattled in the trees. The trail became steeper. My speed was picking up.

Somewhere in the noise of the wind, I thought I heard footsteps coming down the trail behind me. Suddenly a branch caught me under the chin, and a sharp root punctured the top part of my shoe. I pitched forward and crashed into a tree trunk.

I lay dazed with my foot still hooked to the root. A fuzzy shadow covered the low sun as the sound of the wind retreated and the night came in. I lost all sense of time and space. Darkness settled over me.

◆

At last, I opened my eyes to a blurry world of dark spidery forms. As the surroundings focused, I realized that I was sitting up against my car, at the trailhead. Bare trees silhouetted a purple sky. My head was throbbing.

I reached up and felt a cloth—a cloth tied around my head over a bloodied wound. I tried to piece together what had happened, but other than falling on the trail, that was all I could remember.

I pulled off the cloth and looked at it. A bandana. But where had it come from? I didn't own a bandana.

Somehow I managed to drive myself home. My parents bandaged the gash and took me to the doctor, who said I had been knocked out by the tree trunk and was very lucky there were no broken bones or, worse, a broken neck.

The next day at school, I dropped by Coach Karing's office. He was shocked to see my head bandaged and asked what happened. When I told him about the trail run, he shook his head.

"I should have warned you." he said and looked at the old photo on the wall.

A chill rippled down my spine.

"Who is that?" I said, pointing to the boy in the red bandana.

He leaned back in his chair, still looking at the picture.

"That photo was taken twenty years ago, when I first started coaching here. The boy next to me was Jim. He was a good little trail runner. Big heart. Kept going all the time. He loved that mountain bike trail.

"One day he was running by himself and tripped on one of the rock outcroppings on the descent. He hit his head on a rock and broke his neck. A couple of mountain bikers found him the next day.

"There was a big ruckus about the whole thing. Folks blamed me for what happened. An inquiry found that John was running on his own and not under my supervision. They declared that it wasn't my fault. Still, the situation wasn't good."

He paused a minute and said, "I always felt that he was always running by himself because he was running away from something. Something to do with his family life. Never could get it out of him, he would never say. I think it finally killed him."

He stood up and walked over to the photo, studying it with his hands on his hips. "Yep, he was a good little runner."

Then he looked at me. "In a way, I see a lot of him in you. You need to be careful. You need to know what you're doing out there on the trail. It'll kill you if you don't."

◆

A few days later, I was feeling better, and asked one of my training buddies to run with me on the dirt trail. The switchbacks were still tough, but we managed to get up the hill in good time. I was getting stronger.

We rested a while on the flat open area at the top. Before we went down the other side, I pulled the red bandana out of the pocket in my running shorts and tied it to a tree limb a few steps off the trail.

I was giving Jim his bandana back. And I thanked him for his help the day I fell.

As the weeks went by and cross-country training got into full swing, I was careful on the trail and grew stronger on the switchbacks. Each time I ran past the bandana, I always touched it to acknowledge the one who went before me.

One day, I climbed Mt. Olympus and the bandana was gone.

The Stars and the Saints

BRENT HEARN

<u>Day One</u>

NELSON WAS ON HIS WAY to work when he saw the dog.

It looked like a German shepherd, maybe even purebred. It was on the left side of the on-ramp to 55, must have been hit and flung there, but it didn't look it. No twisted legs, no guts spilling out, none of the usual telltale signs of roadkill. Nelson slowed down and had to look twice to make sure it was dead. It looked like it had wandered onto the side of the road and curled up for a nap, its utter stillness the only evidence of its untimely expiration.

Nelson found his thoughts returning to the dog throughout the day. He worked in IT for a large auto insurance company headquartered in Jackson, and he was good at his job. Except for the occasional legitimate crisis—a clueless agent in the field doing something idiotic while uploading a quote or a hacker trying to make a name for himself (Nelson thought there must be farms in Eastern Europe where they grow them in rows)—

he operated on autopilot for the majority of his workday. He liked it like that. It gave him plenty of time to think.

Nelson wondered if the dog had been abandoned. Didn't seem likely. It was a gorgeous animal, clearly well fed and, other than the fact it lay dead on the side of the interstate, in excellent condition. Maybe something had spooked it and it had run away.

Did German shepherds run away? Were certain breeds more or less likely to bolt when frightened? Nelson couldn't say. He'd always thought of shepherds as fearless dogs, rushing into danger, but it was possible he'd been overly influenced by cop movies featuring canines that took bullets for their washed-up partners.

Lo texted to ask him to pick up a milkshake and some cashews on his way home. The baby had her crazy for sweet and salty these days, and the bed seemed to be making the cravings stronger. *Makes sense*, Nelson thought. *Not much to do but eat and read and watch TV and sleep.*

He almost mentioned the dog but for some reason didn't. He didn't think about it again until that night in bed. The last thought he had before sleep came was to wonder if the dog had seen it coming and if it had been afraid.

<u>Day Two</u>

The dog was still there the next morning.

Nelson checked his mirrors to make sure nobody was behind him and then slowed down as he passed. It hadn't been moved, and it didn't look to have been further molested by traffic. Maybe, like him, the other drivers had been struck by what a fine-looking dog it was and had taken care to avoid further disturbing it. It was off to the side of the road mostly, with only its hind legs in the road proper.

It looked much the same as the day before, except for its lips, which were curled back into a tight rigor mortis snarl. It looked like it was dreaming, like someone had taken its photograph while it slept, caught it between paw twitches as it chased some imaginary squirrel.

Nelson wondered if someone would remove it. He'd seen hundreds, probably thousands, of animals in the road over the years and he'd run over plenty himself—you couldn't do much driving in Mississippi without mowing down your share of possum and armadillos—but he didn't give much thought to what happened to all of them. He guessed most were eaten by scavengers or just run over until they disappeared, but he thought he remembered reading something once about disposal crews. He didn't know if that was still a thing, though, or if it ever had been in Mississippi.

Either way, Nelson thought *somebody* ought to move it. Even tossing it into the trash would be a nobler end than the one it was facing. A shame for a dog like that to become just another splatter on the blacktop.

He found himself getting angry at whoever was responsible for it ending up the way it had. The more he thought about it, the more convinced he was that it hadn't just up and run off. But what kind of a person owned a dog like that and just abandoned it? Maybe it had been stolen and dumped, the driver slowing just enough to boot it out. Payback for some wrong, or perceived wrong, perpetrated by its owner.

Maybe the dog had been loved and was missed. Maybe its owners would drive by on their way to work or to get groceries and see it and wrap it up in a blanket and take it home and tell their kids that Bo or Sarge or Lady or whatever its name was had been in an accident. Or perhaps they would soften the blow with a lie, say that the dog had likely gotten lost and had been taken in by someone else who needed an animal to love or to be loved by.

Maybe they'd tell them they could have a new dog—*Yes, sweetheart, it can be a puppy.* Or maybe the kids would be in the car—maybe they'd even be the ones to see it—and cry out for their parents to pull over and pick up Champ or Lizzie, and the parents would do so, silently cursing their luck at having passed *that* particular spot at *that* specific time when their kids were in the car. Or maybe they loved the dog just as much, and the family would be on the side of the road, bawling and holding one another at the loss of their beloved whatever-its-name-was. Their Rin-Tin-Has-Been.

Nelson wondered if Lo would let them get a dog after the baby came.

Not immediately, of course, but maybe when he or she (they'd decided to be surprised) was old enough to crawl or at least turn over. Lo had always been more of a cat person, but he thought maybe if he asked her real sweet when she was in a good mood or maybe if a stray came along. The cats they had now had both been strays, and Nelson had been a little bit, too, he guessed. He looked at the dog in the rearview mirror, figuring it would be gone by the next day.

<u>Day Three</u>

It had come a quick rain the night before, and the dog was still there, looking smaller with its fur drenched and flattened. It was only when Nelson had almost passed it that he could see it was starting to bloat. Not much, though. It was still remarkably well preserved for being in the road for a few days, but it had finally started to look like something dead.

> *Time, it marches on, my friend, even when you're dead,*
> *And if you don't believe me, put a bullet in your head.*
> *They'll drop your body in a box and that box down in the dirt,*
> *A waiting room for Judgment Day's the trade for all your hurt.*
>
> *You'll be dead and gone, with your bones down in that box,*
> *While some asshole in a Goodwill counts out pennies for your socks.*
> *No more second chances, "maybe later," no more "someday,"*
> *But the stars keep shinin' on and the Saints still play on Sunday.*

The words came to Nelson clear as the Lord's Prayer, but he couldn't think of where he'd heard them. A song? A poem? He couldn't remember.

He turned into the parking lot at work and realized he still had some time yet. He pulled up his "White" playlist and put it on shuffle. After three tracks by John Paul White and one from Whitesnake, Nelson closed his eyes while Jack White sang about all the things he wanted love to do and what he wouldn't let it.

He kept them closed until two minutes before he was supposed to be at his desk and then grabbed his ID badge from the console before stepping out of his car and walking toward the building.

Day Four

When the alarm went off, Lo jumped. Nelson turned it off, kissed her on the forehead, and got out of bed. He hardly ever worked Saturdays, but the company had been putting off updating its website and had set aside this weekend to make a dent in it. It was technically voluntary, but Nelson felt like he should be there, especially since he would be out for a few weeks when the baby came.

He put some coffee on and then showered and dressed, opting for a T-shirt and jeans. If he was going to be at work on the weekend, by damn, he was going to be comfortable. He filled a thermos and got on the road. If it looked like things were in good shape, maybe he'd only stay half the day.

The dog was still there, but something had hit it; there were skid marks. Looked like somebody had damn near flipped their vehicle to make sure they ran over it.

Its head still looked like a head mostly, but its jaw had been broken and unhinged and was gaping, frozen in a hideous forever-yawn. One of the lids was gone, pecked away by birds probably, and the socket was mostly empty, too. It wasn't pretty anymore, but if you looked at it right—looked real fast and then looked away—you could still tell that it had been once.

Not the rest, though; it had exploded like some overfilled balloon. Meat and guts trailing out of it, sticking all the way out into and almost across the road, some of it already flattened from early-morning traffic. It was starting to look like just another piece of Mississippi roadkill now, and it pissed Nelson off that nobody had bothered to take it out of the road before it got to looking like that.

Somebody should have; there'd been construction on this part of the interstate recently. Seemed like there always was in Jackson, but the roads never got any better; there were always barrels and signs and potholes and mounds of red dirt, gritty manifestations of bureaucratic indifference and incompetence. Any one of the workers could have taken a shovel and disposed of it or even just moved it out of the road. How long would it take? It wasn't some squirrel or skunk or rabbit; it was a German shepherd, for fuck's sake, and anybody who had eyes—didn't have to be a dog person, even—could have seen, before it had been turned into this, that it deserved better. Hell, if not based on the dog's breeding, then their own.

Nelson passed the exit that led to his office and kept driving until he reached Canton. He pulled into a parking lot, somewhere away from what little noise there was from the sparse Saturday morning traffic, and called in sick, said he'd eaten something that didn't agree with him. He could tell his boss wasn't happy, but since he didn't technically have to be there in the first place, Nelson didn't much care. Even if attendance had been mandatory, he had plenty of sick days saved up—more than he needed, really—for when Lo had the baby.

He stopped at a little gas station and picked up a couple of sausage biscuits, a link for him and a patty for Lo, and almost left before going back in and getting a couple of different candy bars, too, both for Lo. He turned back around and drove home to crawl into bed with his wife and eat breakfast, leaning over her and dropping crumbs on her distended belly. She was glad to see him and rubbed his neck, her sitting there knocked up and miserable. He got to feeling bad about that, so he rubbed her feet, and she moaned like she did when he went down on her, and then they both felt a little better.

He spent the rest of the morning paying bills, and after lunch he tinkered some with his motorcycle—or, rather, what would eventually be a motorcycle—in the garage. He and Lo played board games that evening, and he went to bed glad he'd played hooky and wishing he didn't have to go to work the next morning.

Day Five

So he didn't. Instead he called in again and spent the day giving Lo back rubs and making her laugh by reading tech manuals in his best faux-sexy voice, something he'd first done just to be goofy while they were dating. Just being there with her and listening to her cackle, with no work and no boss and no dead dog, was exactly what he'd needed, and he felt something tight inside his chest let up for a little while.

<u>Day Six</u>
Nelson took the long way to the office Monday morning, drove down 80 all the way through Brandon and Pearl so as to avoid the interstate entirely.

He'd had dreams, bad ones, and he remembered all of them. Most consisted of him hitting the dog, hitting it and dragging it all the way to work. In the dreams, the dog didn't die, just whined and cried and yelped the whole way, but for some reason the car wouldn't stop, and Nelson could see it in his rearview, dragged by its entrails, bouncing and rolling and flipping behind the car like it was on a long bungee or a ski rope, steadily getting flayed by the asphalt.

Eventually he'd moved to the couch so as not to disturb Lo with his tossing and turning, and what had started as a mild crick in his neck had spread upward and was now threatening to burst through his skull. After he parked, he walked over to the coffee shop across the street, hoping the caffeine would join forces with the off-brand Aleve he'd taken before leaving the house.

It didn't. It was one of those days that was full of the most miserable kind of busy, the kind that, instead of making the day go faster, seemed to grind it to a near-standstill. Another guy on his team, a junior programmer under him named Kyle, had jacked shit up over the weekend trying to fix something that wasn't broken. Nelson had to alternate between putting out fires with agents and patching together a temporary solution until he could figure out what exactly Kyle had done in his ill-fated attempt at "optimization."

Truly fubar days like this were rare—maybe one or two a year—so Nelson knew he shouldn't let it get to him, but between dealing with the work itself, the wannabe 10x-er's excuses, and the 808 that had taken residence inside his skull, the only thing he could think of when he finally left the office at 9:30 that night was a hot bath and a bourbon, preferably at the same time.

When he got home and walked into the bedroom, he didn't have to say anything—Lo could see it on his face—and when he got out of the tub, she lay a cool washcloth across his head and ran her fingernails lightly up and down his arms until he fell asleep, dreaming nothing, thinking nothing, feeling nothing.

<u>Day Seven</u>

Nelson left the house in a better state of mind. He had awoken next to the best kind of woman, had a baby on the way, a roof over his head, and a beat-to-shit drum set and half a motorcycle in his garage. He took his usual route to the office, barely looking at what remained of the dog as he passed by.

Work was better. Nelson had a talk—more gently than he could have and maybe should have—with Kyle, and the guy had the decency to look properly chastised, mostly just nodding and seeming relieved to still have a job.

Nelson walked out at five on the nose, and when he got home, Lo had a list waiting for him. Their hospital bag was already packed—had been for weeks—but in one of her few real nods to nesting, Lo liked to inventory and change out the contents periodically. Lo called it her bug-out bag. When Nelson had told her that maybe she'd been watching too many shoot-em-ups and cracked a joke about canceling Netflix, Lo had given him a sweet smile and cracked a joke about chopping off his balls. He'd added subscriptions to a couple of other streaming services just to be on the safe side.

After spending a couple of hours helping Lo remove all the contents of the bag, refold them, and listen to her debate what to take and what to leave behind, they ended up switching out an old beat-up pair of slippers for a new fuzzy pair she'd ordered online. She changed her mind and went back to the ratty ones before finally deciding to take both pairs.

Other than adding a tube of hand cream and a few hair ties, that was the only significant change.

It had surprised Nelson when Lo had said she wanted to take at least a year off for the baby. She had been a public defender for nearly a decade now, standing in the gap for precisely the kind of little bastards he'd once been. He liked to joke with her that she liked delinquents so much, she'd married one.

He knew she must be going out of her mind spending most of the day in bed. It had to be hard for somebody who was so used to moving. Doing. Helping. If rearranging her bug-out bag made her feel better, he'd do it every night if she asked him to.

Day Eight

Traffic was backed up the next morning. Nelson figured there was an accident up ahead, maybe at the Waterworks Curve, which had played host to more daisy-draped crosses over the years than most churchyard cemeteries.

Whatever the holdup, the on-ramp to 55 was stop-and-go, and Nelson couldn't help but see what was left of the dog. It was recognizable as such only to someone who'd seen it when it still resembled one. It didn't look like anything special anymore. Just another pile of spoiled meat and matted fur. Nelson felt that tightness again, more in his gut than his chest now, but he pushed it down and started up his "Clear" playlist. "Father of Mine" gave way to "Bad Moon Rising" and Cybertron, and then he was at work.

The hours passed, devoured by tedium, until quitting time. Nelson made stops for Chinese takeout and a couple pints of Ben & Jerry's on the way home. Lo had had a rough day and was hurting—hurting badly enough that Nelson suggested calling the doctor—but she said she'd be okay, and she cried when she saw the ice cream.

Day Nine

Lo was still sleeping when Nelson got up, and he eased out of the bed so as not to wake her. He fumbled in the dark for some clothes and took his shower in the guest bedroom. It was raining, and he hoped the steady rhythm of it would help her sleep a little longer.

When he went back into their bedroom later to grab his wallet and keys, she was awake and said she felt a little better. Nelson sat down on the edge of the bed, kissed her, and promised to call and check up on her in a little while.

When Nelson arrived at work, he barely remembered driving there. He didn't remember the road or the dog or taking his exit or even pulling into the parking lot. He'd been thinking of baby names. They were in agreement on Emma for a girl, but they were split between Howell and Aaron if it was a boy. Aaron was his pick, but he knew he wouldn't put up a fight about it.

Nelson answered emails and fielded agent phone calls for the first couple of hours. After that, he walked over to HR for what he thought would be a two-minute sit-down; he had some questions concerning his leave when the baby came. Instead he was there for almost half an hour, and he eventually had to cut the lady off so he could make his department's weekly meeting at 10:30.

He realized when he sat down in the conference room that he'd left his phone in his cubicle, thinking he'd grab it when he got back from HR. He didn't think the meeting would take too long, though—several people on his team were at a conference—so he figured ten or fifteen minutes without his phone wouldn't kill him.

After sitting through an hour of discussion that could have been handled just as easily over email, Nelson headed back to his desk. He picked up his phone and saw a voicemail and a dozen missed calls: a couple from Lo, a bunch from Lo's parents, and another from a number he didn't recognize. He dialed his voicemail, grabbed his keys, and nearly mowed Kyle down on his way to the door, leaving a ". . . the hell?" and spilled coffee in his wake.

When Nelson got to the hospital, he went to the front desk and there was some whispering, and someone was leading him down a hall. Doug and Diane, Lo's parents, were already there, huddled in a ridiculously tiny room with a lady who had the biggest red hair Nelson had ever seen. When he saw the looks on their faces, he knew, and his legs went out from under him and the lady said she was *so, so sorry*, and he asked about the baby and he heard a sound—a strangled, croaking sound—that he realized was coming from Doug but then it was coming from him, too.

It had been a boy, and they needed a name for the death certificate. Nelson told them it should be Howell, and when they asked for a middle name, he said he didn't know because they hadn't decided that yet. They said it was okay, that they would hold off on the paperwork, and then he went to see Lo.

They said he could have as long as he liked, but he only stayed in there for a minute because he knew that wasn't her, didn't even look like her. They asked if he wanted to see the baby, and he said he didn't think so right now. Doug and Diane had left to make calls, and he said he'd be back in a little while and would that be okay and they said it would be.

He turned off his phone and drove. He considered going to the house, was headed that direction, but he thought people might be getting there before long, Doug and Diane and maybe other people, too. Instead he took the Crossgates exit off 20 and went to Walmart and got what he needed. When he was done, he headed back toward Jackson, and when he hit the on-ramp, he put on his hazard lights and pulled onto the shoulder.

There wasn't much meat left to the dog, and what was had been flattened to where it was practically part of the road. Nelson thought maybe he could see an ear, but mostly it was just matted hair. He had expected it to stink, but it wasn't too bad. Nelson thought the hard rain earlier might have helped.

He popped the trunk and took out the shovel. He slid it underneath the dog's carcass and scraped, feeling goose pimples rise on his arms at the sound of the metal on the asphalt. He managed to work some of it off the road, but when it started to tear, he stopped, took out a pair of gloves from the console, and started, little by little, peeling it off the road by hand.

There was a collar. Or had been, at least. Most of it had been torn off, but Nelson felt a little piece of metal on the dog's underside, and it came off in his glove when he tugged on it. He couldn't read what it said; it had been run over too many times, and the writing was scratched away.

When he was finished, Nelson wrapped the dog in Visqueen. He was afraid it would get jostled and come unwrapped in the trunk, so he laid it on the floorboard on the passenger side next to him.

He was hot and sweaty and dirty. He hadn't realized it until he was finished, but he felt it now, his long-sleeve button-up sticking to his neck. He took it off and threw it in the passenger seat, leaving him in khakis and a white T-shirt. He got in the car and started driving, thinking on where he could bury the dog. There were a few parks around that would be nice, but he figured he'd probably get hassled by somebody if he started digging a hole in a public park in the middle of the afternoon.

After driving around for a while, he decided he'd bury it in the backyard. The decision made, he pulled over at a convenience store to get something to drink. He really wanted a beer, but he wouldn't want to stop at just one, so he settled on a plastic bottle of sweet tea instead.

Before he got back in the car, he popped the trunk so he could move the dog. He'd gotten to thinking, and he'd decided if anybody was at the house when he got there, he didn't want to answer anybody's dumbass questions about what that was in his car.

An older black man—maybe early 60s, Nelson thought—watched him as he pulled the lug wrench out from its cheap plastic casing and placed it on one side of the Visqueen and the shovel on the other, hoping it would keep the dog from moving around too much while he drove. The man didn't say anything, just smoked his cigarillo by the ice cooler and watched.

"Those things any good?" Nelson asked the man.

"They alright. You want one?"

"I can go in and get one. I'll get you another one, too, if you tell me what the best flavor is."

"This one here's the best. They cheap as shit and I got plenty, so ain't no need of you buyin' one."

The man handed him one and lit it with the end of his own. Nelson nodded his thanks and the two men smoked in silence. Nelson hadn't so much as puffed on anything since college. The smoke smelled sweet and it scratched his throat some, but not too much.

Nelson wondered if anybody would be at the house when he got there and if he should go ahead and try to bury the dog if there wasn't. Once people started coming by, he figured it would be a few days, maybe even a week, before he would have the place to himself. He took another drag on the cigarillo and felt that tightness he'd been feeling inside let go, replaced now by something different.

He wondered who Doug and Diane had already called and who all he would need to call. He thought about what middle name he should give his dead son, and then he remembered that those lines he'd thought of a few days ago, the stars and the Saints ones, were from something he'd written for a band he'd played drums for briefly in college, verses from a song he'd never managed to find a chorus for.

Setting Sail

SHERYE SIMMONS GREEN

A JUBILANT CHEER rose from the crowd assembled on the main deck as the massive ship slowly pulled away from the dock. Gulls swirled overhead as though swaying to a Caribbean samba. Long hemp ropes that encircled iron pilings the size of tree trunks were cast off into the sea by dockhands. Magically, they disappeared through large portholes like they were being pulled by some unseen massive hand within the belly of the ship.

Alana Jacobs had booked the trip on a moment's notice, driving down from Laurel to New Orleans. A tip gleaned from a conversation overheard between two co-workers prompted her to conduct an Internet search of last-minute cruise bargains. A call to her boss obtaining permission to lay claim to her last vacation days of this otherwise miserable year confirmed her spot on the *Windward*. At least for the next five days, Alana might begin to sort out the broken pieces of her life.

The Crescent City's listing as the *Windward's* point of embarkation only hastened her urgency to secure passage on this last voyage of the year. New Orleans had held a special place in Alana's heart ever since a weekend trip she had made with her parents on her ninth birthday. She remembered chirping excitedly like a little bird during the drive from their hometown of Laurel, Mississippi, asking her parents countless questions about The Big Easy. Memories of strolling hand in hand through the French Quarter with her mom and dad were still some of her favorite.

Alana remembered sitting as still as a nine-year-old possibly could while a hopeful artisan sketched her likeness in pastel chalks. The portrait now hung proudly in her own guest room. The highlight of that birthday celebration had been experiencing the sticky, powdery sweet goodness of beignets at Café du Monde.

Alana stood alongside the port rail of the ship's main deck. The wind tousled her hair and lifted the collar of her silk blouse. She pulled the fitted ankle-length wool reefer close around her. Throngs of passengers were scattered in small groups from bow to stern across the deck. While the ship completed its purposed turn in the wide Mississippi, the city rolled by. For all the excitement buzzing in the ship's atmosphere, New Orleans couldn't care less. Just another ship. Another day.

Alana was mesmerized by the expanse of water glistening far below. The mighty river rippled and roiled. Currents and eddies tumbled over each other, making the channel look like a liquid, wrinkled sheet under which mysterious sea creatures writhed. The glassine surface at times appeared to be a dull gray and at others as shiny as mirrored glass.

Glancing back for one more look at the skyline, Alana noticed cars passing lazily across the bridge upriver, seemingly unaware of the great distress that raged within her. Remarks made by the ship's crew during the recent muster call and security briefing warned all of *Windward's* passengers that fire was the greatest safety threat aboard a ship. Alana whispered a silent prayer that the late-December chill would be enough to douse the embers of anger and hurt glowing on the hearth of her heart.

Like scenes from a movie, the events of the last four months of Alana's life played out in her mind—especially the promotion to assistant vice president and the sudden need to move her widowed father to an

Alzheimer's-friendly facility. For three weeks she had survived on four hours of sleep each night. Eight to ten hours of daylight were spent learning the ropes of the new position at the mortgage company; seven to eight hours of darkness were consumed with boxing up the contents of her parents' home. At least for now, Alana was assured that her dad was safe and well cared for, which was more than she could say for herself.

Jenny, her sweet friend from church, had been a lifesaver. A married, stay-at-home mom with older teenage children, she had gobs of time to spend as she pleased, and Jenny was pleased to lend three days to the packing project. She served as the liaison for the pickup by Goodwill of household goods and assorted pieces of furniture, and even volunteered to meet the realtor for the walk-through sales appointment. Alana just wasn't up to it.

Ever since her mom's death due to a heart attack eight years earlier, Alana had resigned herself to the fact that she, as an only child, would someday be left to dispose of her parents' estate.

Alana was grateful she still lived in Laurel, although she'd been tempted to move away several times. Living in a place that wasn't familiar, while having to cope with all the life changes she'd faced recently, would have proven too much to bear.

Her father's symptoms first appeared with a vengeance three years prior to his wife's death, and probably were a contributing factor to her early demise. Alzheimer's had stolen her dad away from both Alana and her mother much too soon. Now the damage caused from Rob's painful and sudden departure from her life only four short days ago was threatening to upend her world again.

The small farms lining the banks downriver from New Orleans caught Alana's attention as the *Windward* chugged lazily toward the sea. Their serene simplicity seemed to beckon her. After all she'd been through, simple sounded perfectly charming to Alana. Nagging thoughts of her string of bad luck made her wonder if anything in her life would be uncluttered and uncomplicated again.

According to her watch, Alana knew the dining room would soon be open. As she was traveling alone, she knew all too well that no one would miss her or even fail to notice were she not in the dining room at the appointed time. *Good thing I don't drink*, she thought, *or I'd be well on my way to a bender.* Five days at sea would be a sufficient amount of time to drown her sorrows in the waters of the Gulf of Mexico. With depths of over ten thousand feet, the dark lapis waters would be deep enough to hold all the hurt in her heart and then some.

Darkness gently pulled itself down over the horizon of south Louisiana while the *Windward* neared the mouth of the Father of Waters. Stars that earlier might have been mistaken for streetlights now moved higher into the night sky. The embarkation boarding period had given Alana time to deposit her two small suitcases in her cabin, retrieve the freshly folded beach towel from the stool in front of the dressing table, and make her way to the highest observation deck of the ship.

The lounging chaise was comfortable enough. Alana reached down to tuck in the long folds of the woolen trench around her ankles. Inside the coat's left pocket her gloved hand located the small ribbon-tied packet within. This dark night would provide the perfect opportunity to free herself of her burden.

Rob had been a totally unexpected entry in the thirty-second year of Alana's life. Ten years her senior, he seemed confident and comfortable in comparison to how timid and awkward she felt. What had started as a conversation over coffee during a break in a program of a regional business conference ended up in what Alana had hoped would be happily ever after. Destiny had other plans.

Alana knew she'd fallen too hard too fast, but she couldn't help herself. Rob's six-one physique standing next to her lithe five-foot-eight frame lent her a confidence she'd never found with a man. Not that there'd been many. During the high school and even most of the college years, Alana had focused on her studies. The first in her family to attend college, she'd promised herself that mastering love's lessons would have to wait until she'd secured the all-important sheepskin.

Her fingers curled around the letters in her coat pocket. The relationship with Rob had lasted almost eight months. Since he lived in a town two hours from Alana, the relationship had consisted mainly of emails, texts, phone calls, occasional lunch and dinner dates, one or two long drives in the country, and these cursed letters. Rob's strong, bold script written across the light blue pages was what had captured the imagination of Alana's heart.

Marshall, Alana's affable employer, wasn't quite old enough to have been a father to his protégé, but was certainly advanced in age enough to see the promise and potential tucked away behind this young woman's reserved demeanor. The kindness and mentorship of many along the path of his career had benefited him greatly. Now he wanted to return the favor. Marshall had also known Rob's secret and suspected if he didn't intercede, Alana might be ruined forever. He correctly surmised she was not savvy enough in the language of true love to spot an imposter.

A sweet, unsuspecting wife and three late elementary-age children were Rob's first responsibility, no matter how many times he tried to pass himself off as available. Earlier this week what Alana thought was to be a ten-minute daily briefing with Marshall extended into a two-hour conversation, the employer carefully breaking the news of the cruel deception to his favorite employee. Alana's eyes smarted with tears as she berated herself for her naiveté.

Turning the face of her watch toward the moon gleaming overhead, Alana saw that it was almost midnight. She gathered up the beach towel draped over her feet and rose from the chair. Across decks, down stairwells, and along galley ways Alana strode determinedly to the back deck of the ship. Once her leather pumps made contact with the floor of this level, she knew exactly what her next move must be.

Thankfully, only two or three other of the *Windward*'s passengers were still milling about. Alana waited patiently while one by one they made their way inside. Sounds of live music and light laughter floated out into the night air each time the door opened and closed. Now all alone, Alana moved to the center of the back rail.

Always a rule follower, Alana smiled to herself as she remembered an onboard announcement earlier that afternoon reminding passengers not to hang out over the rails or to throw items overboard. *This is one time,* Alana thought as she withdrew the packet of letters, *rules are meant to be broken.*

Totally unsure of what lay ahead on the horizon of her life, Alana Jacobs knew that clinging to Rob's farce would not be part of her future. Reaching as far out over the railing as she safely dared, Alana stretched out her hand. As the ship's bell sounded the stroke of midnight on this New Year's Eve, Alana let go of the creased papers that had bound her soul for far too long. Once she did, her heart immediately felt cool and light like a tall glass of lemonade on a hot summer's day.

"I'm setting sail," she whispered to the moon hanging overhead. The rolling foam of the Gulf's deep waters welcomed her offering.

Ghosts and Grits

JANET BROWN

IT WAS A ROUGH DAY when Neva Clare and Sistuh brought the murder-ghost home. At least, that's what Daddy Roy said later. That didn't mean much, though, because Daddy Roy wasn't ever quite right when it counted. He was always having a rough day. He slept rough. He even ate rough food. When he had grits, he put on old work gloves. "Can't get no rougher," he'd say with a wink and a grin. "Grits is bleached. Boiled up. Ground down. They even got husks if they ain't ground good enough. Hate husks."

Mama Little never laughed at him. "Daddy Roy knows a thing or two," she'd claim while the man sat sopping eggs and grits with her biscuits.

Still, all the grits in the world couldn't keep the murder-ghost away when Neva Clare and Sistuh pulled into the driveway early that afternoon.

"So how's New Orleans? As sinful as ever?" Mama Little waved her spatula at the girls as they came into the kitchen. "Watch you don't get used to that sort of thing."

Neva Clare shook her head while Sistuh lugged the hanging bag upstairs. "I gotta leave," Neva Clare said. She twiddled with the car keys, but she waited for Sistuh to come back down.

"What's the rush? Coffee won't hurt you." Mama Little put a full cup on the table.

"Can't. Harry's leaving this afternoon. I got to go service him."

Mama Little laughed and shook the spatula hard.

"Not that kind of servicing, Mama." Neva Clare frowned. "I meant I got to pack his suitcase."

"Pity. He'd probably stay home more if you did the other."

"He's got a job. Harry's got this traveling job. Daddy, tell her how it is."

Daddy Roy waved his gloves. "It's a rough job, Neva Clare. Your mama knows that. She just wants you and Sistuh to have the best. Harry wasn't your best choice."

Sistuh walked back into the kitchen and slumped into a chair. "Here we go again. It's all about choices, huh, Daddy Roy? You two didn't appreciate Elvis because he got fat. But he could still sing. I know. I've watched him on YouTube. Hell, he could even shake and wiggle, too."

"Watch your tongue, young lady." Mama Little pointed the spatula at Sistuh's mouth. "I can still slap as hard as when you was two."

"But she's not two any more, Mama." Neva Clare palmed the car keys and squeezed them until they began to cut into the skin. "She's twenty-two and I'm twenty-five and we're grown women. You can't keep putting us down."

"I can do whatever I want as long as you're in my house. I deserve some respect in my house."

Neva Clare rolled her eyes. "And that's why I'm fixing to go," she said. She paused in the doorway. "Sorry to be leaving you with this, Sistuh, but we had our fun, didn't we? We'll stay longer next time." She slammed out the door and onto the gravel and into the car, but she could still hear Mama Little screeching her ideas on respect at Sistuh and Daddy Roy.

Neva Clare wondered when Sistuh would leave. Ever? Never? It was tough trying to please old folks. Tougher to leave them. She knew that well enough. Her grandparents had raised her and Sistuh after a drunk driver killed Mama and Papa on the way to Vicksburg. Ten years ago. A long and protected ten years. But the way her grandparents saw it, neither of their granddaughters was going to get into the foolishness that their only daughter had. Drunk drivers were way too many in Mississippi. The fact that Neva Clare's parents had also been crazy drunk at the time of the accident only reinforced the idea.

Neva Clare sighed and drove home. She was tired and her head hurt, but she and Sistuh had had a great time in New Orleans. The business with the murder-ghost at the hotel still put her off some, though. It was one thing to believe a room was haunted. It was quite another for the ghost to show up.

Room 639 was small and jammed into a noisy corner overlooking Bourbon Street. Neva Clare had immediately walked to the window and watched the people and the traffic blur by. The room cost them far more than they'd planned, but they'd decided it was worth it. They were smack dab in the middle of the French Quarter. It was *the* place to be.

But when they first entered the room, the smell of cigar smoke was everywhere. "Must be coming up from the bar," Sistuh said.

"Six floors? Well, seven actually, if you count that mezzanine-thingy between the lobby and one." Neva Clare shook her head. "Something's wrong here. This was supposed to be a non-smoking room. We paid for a non-smoking room."

"It's the ghost," the porter said, holding his hand out for a tip.

"Ghost?" Neva Clare held a five just out of range. "Tell us."

He fidgeted. "I shouldn't ought to have said that. Hotel management wouldn't approve. It spooks the guests. Ha ha. No such things as ghosts." He laughed nervously and moved his hand closer.

"There is if you say so. You said so."

He frowned, realizing now that there would be no tip unless he spoke up. "Okay, okay. Some guy killed his girlfriend over at The Grand on Canal Street in '69. People heard him screaming at her late at night. Something about how she didn't know how to love or maybe she didn't appreciate his love. Makes no difference because he hacked her into little pieces. Tried to flush her guts down the commode, and when that stopped up, he bundled the rest of her in the sheets. Maid came in the next morning and caught him standing in a mess of gore."

"The Grand? What's that got to do with this hotel? This isn't The Grand."

He smiled and his black eyes popped. "No, it ain't and that's a fact. But people were slow on the uptake in those days. Not use to all the murdering like we got going now. The maid, she went running and told another maid, who told a porter, who told the manager, who finally called the police. By that time, the guy had checked in here. He smoked cigars."

"And?"

"And nothing. They never found his girlfriend's body. Figured he slid her into some concrete. They were doing some big construction work around here at the time. Lots of wet concrete. Just shove and go." He grimaced.

"I still don't get it. If she's dead, how come we smell his cigar in here?" Sistuh asked, coming up beside Neva Clare.

"Because he pushed a dresser up against that door over there and swore he'd never go to jail. Then he blew his head off. Folks who stay here always say they smell cigar smoke. It's a non-smoking room, and it's been that way a long time. And yet . . ." He shrugged and she gave him the five.

"Maybe he's still smoking," Sistuh said with a laugh. "You know." She aimed her finger at the floor.

"Hmmm. I reckon so. Anything else I can do for you before I leave." He wiggled his eyebrows.

"No," Neva Clare said.

He shrugged. "Can't say I didn't try."

"Yes," Sistuh said. "You're very trying." She slammed the door in his face.

When she turned to Neva Clare, she was laughing. "Mama Little would have a stroke if she'd heard all that."

"And a haunted room. Daddy Roy would swear we are bound for the devil." Neva Clare laughed with her.

They smelled the cigar smoke off and on the next few days, but it didn't bother them. Neva Clare woke up late the second night and thought she saw the shadow of a tall, big man standing by the window near the bathroom, but then she remembered Sistuh's hanging bag, and she yawned and rolled over and dreamed. *Or she thought she dreamed.*

It didn't come to her until the fourth morning when they were getting ready to leave with their packages and suitcases, that Sistuh had kept the hanging bag in the bathroom. Steam always helps to lose the wrinkles.

The man's shadow had spooked Neva Clare and she told Sistuh, but by then they were leaving and there was nothing they could do.

"You're saying you might have seen the ghost?" Sistuh said on their way back to Pearl.

"I saw something. Felt something. Probably a dream."

"Well, a ghost is better."

"Yeah. I'll be sure and tell Harry that. He won't appreciate it, either. Let's just drop the subject, huh?"

"Why? You scared?" Sistuh squinted at her, and Neva Clare decided that Sistuh always had a squinty look about her, even when she wasn't looking.

"What's there to be afraid of? Like Daddy Roy always says, 'Ghosts and grits don't mix.'"

"Yeah, I've heard him say that. Sometimes he doesn't make sense, though. And that makes him sound even more senseless. What's it mean?"

"Oh, just that grits are for daylight and ordinary things. Ghosts? Well, they're for places like haunted rooms and nighttime and dreams. We're back to the grits, Sistuh. Make no mistake about it. Pearl, Mississippi, is not New Orleans."

Still, after Harry left later that afternoon and Neva Clare was home with just Beau Nell, their golden retriever, she thought about the ghost. She knew she'd been awake that night when she'd seen darkness in the shape of a man move to her, and she'd thought—oh, only briefly and maybe even hopefully—that the thing had touched her, had rolled her over and kissed her and held her for a long time. But she'd thought it was a dream. What else could it have been in the middle of a night filled with shadows?

She took a bath at ten. It was a relaxing bath, and not having Harry in the house made the bath even more relaxing. They'd been married two years, and she knew she'd made a mistake. He didn't really love her, not the way she needed to be loved.

She stepped out of the tub and began to towel off when the room went cold. She could hear Beau Nell whine from the bedroom, and she yanked open the door. "Darn air conditioner," she said, stomping to the thermostat in the hallway. "You were supposed to fix it, weren't you, Harry? But no, you always put things off. And you put me off, too. Always."

She was shaking with anger as well as with the cold by the time her eyes adjusted to the dimness, but the thermostat was set on seventy-five and that's exactly what the thermometer registered. She noticed, too, that it was warm enough in the hallway and the bedroom, but the bath felt like a deep freeze.

"Air ducts. Cold air returns. All a lousy mess in an old house," she told the dog, who cocked its head from side to side.

She slipped into her nightgown—the one Harry thought was indecent—and padded to bed. "Indecent! We're married, aren't we?" She yelled at the dog again because there was no one else there. "Harry was more fun when we weren't married. That's what I think." Beau Nell, of course, didn't talk back like Harry. She just whined, so Neva Clare picked up a magazine and began to read.

A half hour later Beau Nell bristled and jumped off the bed, then stood at the bathroom door and sniffed. Her nose went up high as if it could point and touch the thing it smelled.

"What's the matter, girl? You have a bad dream?" Neva Clare spoke softly now, and all the while she watched the shadows gather at the bathroom door.

The dog crept across the threshold and snuffled more carefully this time, edging back a few steps before finally entering the room. It was almost as though the dog could see something that Neva Clare could neither see nor smell.

"Dumb dog," she said, swinging her feet over the side of the bed and touching the cold floor. "What's with you, Beau Nell? Can't you . . .?"

Her voice dwindled away as she felt the rush of cold from the bathroom surround her. The dog leaped backwards, flopped a bit, then scrambled up on the bed where it lay half-whining, half-barking.

Neva Clare sat back and shivered. "Hush," she told the dog. "And you in there. You—you—whatever you are. You're scaring my dog. No need for that. But you're scaring me, too. You know, you shouldn't do that. It ain't right. Not fair."

Then she smelled the cigar smoke. It came with the cold and the darkness, seeping across the doorway and spreading into the room. The dog whimpered.

There was a long sigh from the shadows, and then the room began to fill with heat. Neva Clare continued to shiver, but she was getting warm now. Maybe far too warm.

The telephone rang the next morning. It pulled her from a shadowy slumber and drew her into the light. She blinked and fumbled for the phone. Her gown was askew, and the last thing she'd remembered was a dream she'd had about warm, loving arms wrapping around her and holding her for a long time.

It was good to be loved like that.

"Neva Clare? Neva Clare, that you?" Sistuh's voice was tinged with fear.

"Well, it surely ain't Beau Nell."

"Neva Clare, something's not right here at the house. I been smelling cigar smoke since early this morning."

"What time is it, Sistuh?"

"Almost eleven."

"Daddy Roy and Mama Little, are they around?"

"I dunno. Haven't looked. Guess they're down in the kitchen where they always are. But the upstairs reeks of cigar smoke. Neva Clare." Sistuh began to cry. "What're we going to do?"

"Listen to me," she said, her voice firm. "Just do what I tell you. Get the hanging bag and take it to the barn, Sistuh. Leave it there. Do you hear? Leave it there."

"Do you think . . .?"

"I don't know what to think," she said in a whisper now. "Just do it and call me back."

The phone jangled ten minutes later, and Sistuh was sniveling on the other end. "I did it, Neva Clare. The bag's in the barn. Do you believe we brought that ghost home? Did he come back with us?"

"Maybe."

"He did. You know he did. Something's happened to you again, and you're not telling, are you?" Sistuh snotted into the phone.

"You're not telling me, either. It didn't take you all morning to smell cigar smoke," Neva Clare said.

"It was just a dream. Like you said. Only a dream."

"Well then, there you have it, Sistuh," she said.

"Will he go away? Will the dreams stop?"

"I don't know, Sistuh." Neva Clare fluffed her hair and tugged at her gown while Beau Nell whined. "Maybe he won't go." She frowned a moment, then began to smile.

"Who knows—maybe we don't want those dreams to stop. In fact, we might want them to stay with us always." Neva Clare frowned again. "But if we get tired of this—this thing, we can just take all the suitcases and burn them. Or pass them on to somebody else. That'd be easy."

"Even the hanging bag?" Sistuh's voice was tinny over the phone.

"Especially the hanging bag," Neva Clare said.

That was when the bedroom turned cold. The dog whimpered and ran from the room, but Neva Clare sat rigid and listened to Sistuh, "Hey, Neva Clare, you there? You there?"

The ugly cold bit into her flesh as if she had been forced into a freezer. Strong, frigid arms held her hard and her skin was so cold that she felt as if she were being burned. The shadow's arms tightened even more and she vaguely recalled that severe hypothermia can cause death in ten to fifteen minutes. Maybe even less—*depending.*

It hurt to breathe now. "Run, Sistuh," she whispered.

Then to the coldness she wheezed. "I promise. Sistuh and I will always love you. Always."

Soft laughter was at her ear and the cold increased. "That's right," the shadow said.

"Always. Always."

She dropped the phone.

I Can Take Care of Myself

FREDERICK CHARLES MELANCON

S AL'S WIFE got the results of her PET scan yesterday evening. He was almost certain it'd be fine. At least, he hoped it was. It was the nature of their relationship. Tragedy happened, and they survived. Peg might need chemo, but he'd take care of her. It didn't matter that she'd found a new lump on her left breast. Peg didn't seem all that concerned. She even insisted he go to his dinner with his Romeos, Retired Old Men Eating Out.

When he got home that night, he checked on his wife. She'd closed their bedroom door and locked it.

Sal could've forced his way in. After all, he was the youngest member of the Romeo bunch, but he'd been married to Peg long enough to know not to. She dealt with heartache alone, and he'd get more from her tomorrow than he'd ever now. She was probably just overreacting.

Sal clenched the doorknob and pushed one more time. It didn't open. So he spent the rest of the night worrying about her and trying to sleep on the couch, and sometime, in the early morning, he finally did.

When early afternoon resounded with the barks of the neighbor's dog, Sal, stiffed back and sore, rolled off the coach. Staggering toward their bedroom, he found the room and the rest of the house empty. He would've called her, but Peg never cared for cell phones. She worried the things would give her brain cancer or something. With no other way to get in touch with his wife, he swallowed two pills for his back and left for Saturday lunch with his granddaughter.

◆

The waitress filled Sal's water again and asked if he wanted an appetizer. As he finally ordered the spinach dip, his granddaughter flung open the restaurant's glass doors. Blocking the view of City Hall across the street, she didn't move from the threshold until she saw him.

His soon-to-be college-bound granddaughter, Diane, was his favorite. Not that Sal announced it to anyone, but he didn't have to. The rest of the family knew and bore their second-class status quietly or only sniped about it during birthdays and holiday get-togethers. Wanting to be fair, Peg worried over how this perception started so that she could fix it, somehow. Sal didn't worry. In his own way, he loved all of them. It was just that Diane constantly needed help in a way the others didn't. In fact, Sal knew her personality better than any of the others, and he could tell right now that she was upset.

As Sal scooped spinach dip, he asked, "So what's wrong?"

Diane flicked her head as if removing an imaginary strand of hair from out of her eyes. "Nothing. I have a report due for History class."

The flick was key. It told him that she was lying. "A report on what?"

"Clinton. Family history." She brushed her hair behind her ear.

"Really, you remember the bookstore?" he asked.

The bookstore right next to City Hall had been their favorite place to go. There was a small room in the back behind the register that had children's books. On weekends, the owner let him take his granddaughter back there, and they read book after book. He was a pretty good reader, and it wasn't surprising to find him back there with three or four children listening attentively.

"It's closing."

"Sad," he said. "You could use it in your report."

"How you used to take me there?"

The two sat in silence until the waitress put their lunches on the table. Diane poked around her salad, finally settling on a tiny piece of lettuce. She usually inhaled her food right away.

"Remember the time you broke the toy crane in the back," he said.

"You got mad."

"At them."

"You wanted to pay for it and save the day." Diane ran her fingers through her hair, putting a lock over her left shoulder.

"I did."

The crane had been fifteen dollars, and he'd refused to leave until he paid for it. After all, she was his granddaughter. It was his responsibility to clean up her messes. There'd been a fight about it between the college kid working the register and Sal. The kid even threatened to call the police, but Sal paid for it, though he suspected that the kid pocketed the money.

"I never gave you trouble about it," he said.

That's when Diane started crying. It wasn't her normal tears that trickled off her cheekbones. It was a dry heave that made the waitress and other people stare. Sal's back popped as he stood up, forcing him to waddle over to comfort her.

"Sorry," she said between sobs.

It wasn't her fault. It was Peg's. Obviously, Diane had eaten breakfast with his wife, and the private old broad divulged everything. Sal just needed his granddaughter to tell him in case he was wrong.

"You've been with Grandmother."

Diane shook her head. It wasn't going to be that easy. Sal returned to his side of the table, and Diane composed herself.

"I didn't break the toy crane," she said.

"What are you talking about?"

"It was already broken. You threw such a fit that I never got to tell you."

Sal's back hurt. "I wouldn't call that throwing a fit. That why you're crying?"

"You threatened to punch the cashier."

"But I didn't. Not like he didn't have it coming. And I didn't see him put the money in the register either."

Diane wasn't eating, and Sal wasn't hungry anymore. The waitress asked, "Is everything okay?"

The woman stood a table away, and Sal hadn't noticed her until she called out to them. Both he and his granddaughter smiled and nodded at her.

"If you need anything, let me know," the waitress said.

When the woman was a safe distance away, Sal continued the conversation. "It's what I'm supposed to do. I took care of you, so one day you'd want to take care of me."

"But it wasn't broken."

This time tears trickled out of her eyes. What was Sal supposed to do about this? "Your grandmother told you about the scan?"

Diane nodded. Strands of her hair fell in front of her face, and she didn't touch one of them. That told Sal enough. He didn't need to ask for any more details. He signaled to the waitress for the check.

"Why didn't you tell me about the toy crane?" he asked.

"Don't tell Grandma."

"I think I'm smart enough to figure it out."

"She meant well. She just wanted to make sure you were taken care of."

At Sal's age, he knew when to disengage. He didn't want to get into a fight with his granddaughter. His wife would be another matter. How dare she presume he needed help? Sal would've preferred to have found out from Peg instead of Diane. As the waitress placed the paper check on the edge of the table, Sal focused on the bookstore and the toy crane.

He wondered if it was too late to get his money back.

Joy in the Morning

JUDY H. TUCKER

AT TEN O'CLOCK Friday night Ben Gilbert sat at his desk and stared at the blank page on the screen in front of him. The dining room table, which doubled for his workspace at home, was thick with dust.

He needed to get started on Sunday's sermon. His deadline had long passed. He pursed his mouth and stared at the baby bottle half full of rancid soy milk, a bowl encrusted with dried oatmeal, a pair of scissors, and a ragged scrap of a head scarf—all lay between him and his Concordance which he sorely needed at that moment. He reached one arm through the mess and across the table and removed a topless jar of peanut butter off the heavy, worn book and set it on the thesaurus. His elbow hit the cereal bowl, which rolled off the table and caused a great racket as it smashed on the floor, bringing Kate running from the kitchen.

For a few seconds she stood still, estimating the damage. Then she picked up the peanut butter jar and ran her finger inside and pulled out a lump of the good stuff. "Ummmm," she sighed. "Good!" She paused and looked at her husband who was stretched half across the table. "Have you pulled your back out again?"

"No, the back's okay. But I can't come up with a subject for a sermon. It's been like this all week. I just can't think." He couldn't think, but he did pause to wonder what it would be like to live with some order in his life. Maybe his thoughts would be more orderly, come to him more readily, if his surroundings were more—well, orderly.

"Writer's block?" Kate asked, as she handed him the heavy book.

"You might say that. My sermon—I can't get it off the ground. I want to wake 'em up. Jolt their souls. Get 'em thinking."

"Well." Kate rolled her eyes. "You know you're not asking much, don't you? You gotta remember, nobody hits a homerun every time at bat." She nuzzled his neck and nibbled an ear lobe. "Why don't we just go to bed? LiliBeth's asleep, and I've read *Yertle the Turtle* to the Benster three times, and tucked him in."

Ben pushed his chair back and stood up. She took his hand and led him through the door.

◆

Ben had felt the call to the ministry ever since he could remember. His father had been a preacher, more a preacher than a minister. Ben didn't choose the same path because of his father, but in spite of him. The old man didn't ever write a sermon. He just opened The Good Book, dropped it on the dais, and preached whatever jumped off the page. The oratory sprang from a well inside of him, ran off his tongue wild and loud, and his congregations loved it, but he never stayed with them for long. He kept moving, always moving on, taking only his family; leaving only a cloud of dust in his wake.

Ben had tried to deny the call to be a preacher, but it wouldn't leave him alone. And finally he'd promised, down on his knees, that he'd do it better than his father. Ben had tried to explain all of it to Kate, but his need couldn't be described in words. He simply had to do it, but she married him anyway.

Early on, before they took their vows, this good woman had told him:

"You don't have to do it better than your father did it, just do it. You need to be a pastor. He was a preacher. You'll be both."

◆

So here he was, Saturday at the breakfast table gulping coffee—his daughter in her mother's arms, his son in the high chair—without even the idea for a sermon in his head. Outside his kitchen window the sun bounced off the steeple of the church and raced through the huge oak trees and played in the autumn leaves that fell along the brick streets of Old Towne.

"Maybe I wasn't cut out to be a preacher," Ben said. He looked at his son, how he'd placed his dish on top of a worn book. "What you got there, Benster?" Ben reached over and touched the boy's shoulder.

"He's going to be a scholar like his daddy," Kate said. "He's already got his head stuck in a book." She bent and kissed the top of her girl-baby's soft hair.

"Yertle. Yertle." The boy slid the book out from under the bowl, spilling his milk in the process.

Kate grabbed a napkin. "He can't be separated from that book," she said. "Let me have the book, Benster."

"No! no! no!" The Benster set up a howl and his little arms pawed the air. LiliBeth started to fret, like she was abetting her brother's side of the matter.

"I read it to him four times last night." Kate pushed back her chair, stood up. "Now he's begging for it first thing this morning." She began to stack the dishes. "Why don't you go to the church to work on your sermon," she said. "It'll be quiet over there."

◆

Ben stared out the church window and assessed the weather, another golden autumn day. Another Saturday with Sunday morning closing in without a wisp of an idea of a sermon in his head. He leaned forward and pulled the pictures of his wife and children up front and close on his desktop. He leaned back in his chair and studied their faces.

That's when he noticed the dust and got out his handkerchief and wiped the glass over the picture. He cleaned his desktop, then stared at the floor. It really could use a broom.

When he looked up at the clock again, it was almost noon and the office was as clean as a whistle. The bookshelves were in order by subject, the cushions on the couch plumped, trash can emptied, the lavatory shining. The windows were opened to let in that cool, fresh fall air. He could hold a deacons' meeting in there and be proud of it. By golly, he ought to host an open house!

He'd been so busy, the thought of why he had come to the church on Saturday morning—it never crossed his mind, though he remembered as soon as he stepped over the little ditch that separated the church grounds from the parsonage. He still didn't have a sermon.

Ben took a deep breath of the crisp air, which blew in on the front of a high-pressure system. He heard the honking of geese and looked up to see the giant V of the flock spread across the blue sky over the town of Clinton.

Kate came down the back steps to meet him. He pointed at the sky. She took his hand and they stared up at the spectacle of the geese winging their way south to the marshes. They climbed the steps to the stoop and she moved ahead of him and swung the kitchen door open for him. "Well?" she said with a smile.

A pan bubbled on a back burner of the stove. The room smelled like cinnamon. LiliBeth cooed on a pallet in the corner. The Benster came out from under the table with his book in hand. "Yertle. Read Yertle, Daddy."

Kate looked at Ben and begged with her eyes.

Ben reached for his son. "Let me spend a few minutes with Ben." He took the book in one hand and the child's hand in the other. "And then we'll talk," he said to her as he gently urged the Benster out of her path.

"Ben," Kate called after him, "Why don't you take one of those sermons you wrote while you were in seminary and use it tomorrow? You've got some good stuff in that file."

He turned and smiled at her. "Love, when I wrote those I was just a young and callow fellow. I can do so much better."

"You were a poet and didn't know it." She teased.

His heart swelled up when he saw her impish smile. He gathered her into his arms and whispered into her hair, "And you, you are my pearl of great price."

Suddenly he knew what he would preach tomorrow. He would do as his father had done. He would open the Good Book lying before him on the dais, and tell about the joy that comes unbidden just when you need it.

Have faith and wait, and it will fill you.

The Crossing

LOTTIE BRENT BOGGAN

"ALL DEAD. Every one of them," Frank Aden repeated. His voice sounded like an out-of-breath child who had been playing outside in the night air and hollered too much. "I tried to tell—but they wouldn't listen."

Mr. Aden held a rolled newspaper to his chest. He tilted his head back and took a long swallow of Old Charter from a full shot glass. His La-Z-Boy popped as he stretched it back a notch. The elderly man wore a satisfied air of "I told-you-so." He took a deep sniff of his whiskey before he drank it again.

There was no one in the room but Mr. Aden. The only sound was the noise of a TV. An old black-and-white episode of *The Fugitive* was playing. Every now and then he mumbled, "All dead. I told them to watch out for that train. They wouldn't listen. Dead."

Pushing his recliner all the way back, he settled into the center of the overstuffed chair. Mr. Aden's legs were stiff and sore from arthritis and inactivity. He stretched his legs in a tentative movement, then slowly straightened them. He'd found it didn't hurt as much that way. A feeling of drowsiness crept over him. It seemed as if a bright light swung back and forth in front of him. Still holding the newspaper, he closed his eyes.

◆

The sky that day was the color of a blue jay's wings. The little boy Frank and his father were walking to downtown Summit to pick up their weekly newspaper, *The Summit Sun*. Mr. Aden sold shoes and nails at the S and S Mercantile Store on Main Street during the week. Even now, out in the open air, his hands smelled of nails and polished leather.

Sunlight washed over Frank's straight, light-brown hair. His hair was combed with a precise part in the middle and slicked down with Vaseline. The Vasoline had softened in the heat and his hair was beginning to ride up and fall across his forehead in uneven strands.

Every now and then Frank glanced up at the sky, heavy with puffy clouds that were easing slowly from view. He tugged at his father's arm. "That cloud's a long, straight line. It has a fluff on the end, like a cow's tail."

His father didn't answer. They had stopped in front of Addkinson Hardware. The smell of fresh ground coffee beans drifted through the open doors. Two men in wooden ladder-back chairs sat out front playing checkers. And when it was time to make a move, each in turn would lean his chair forward, move a black or red checker, spit brown spray on the ground, then ease back. Their movements were slow and deliberate.

Stopping in front of them, Mr. Aden pulled a pocket watch from his plaid shirt pocket. "The eleven-fifty's a little late today. Most days you can set your time to it."

"Does that sometimes on a Saturday," one of the men answered, without looking up. "I hear the engineer takes a long stop at Brookhaven. Got him a girlfriend there."

The little boy made quick side steps. He was barefoot, but his feet were summertime tough and he didn't feel the chunky reddish-brown gravel as he tried to get his father's attention.

"Goin' to get your paper, Mr. P.E.?" one of the men asked Mr. Aden.

Mr. Aden nodded and put his watch back in his pocket.

"Papa, look." Frank was pointing toward Main Street. "I hear the train." Frank tugged at his father's arm, "Look at what's coming, Daddy—they don't see it."

"Be quiet, son."

Frank stood stock-still. Children were to be seen and not heard. "But Daddy," he tried again. "Watch out!" he screamed, pointing toward the train snaking around a curve. Moving toward it was a black Model-T Ford filled with people.

The train came around the bend slowing down at Summit only enough for the mail pouch to be quickly thrown and caught on a large metal hook. The signal blew as the train approached the station. It shrilled out a high note on the scale, over and over, as if something was caught in its stack and the engineer was fiercely trying to blow it out.

The driver of the car had seen the train too late. The car's rubber tires made a pitiful sound as the driver frantically pumped its brakes.

The car slid toward the tracks as if it had a mind of its own and couldn't be stopped. There was a terrible grinding; a metallic thud crashed the still summer day.

"The train's run over them! The train's run over them!" Frank screamed.

The men in front of Addkinson Hardware popped their chairs forward, hitched up their overall straps, and walked hurriedly toward the carnage on the tracks.

Parts of people were scattered all over the ground like a leftover meal flung out for animals. The monotony of a Summit Saturday was broken. Men and women hurried from Fly's Drugs, S and S Mercantile, and the doctor's and dentist's offices.

"These people from out in the country—they ought to know better," somebody in the crowd said. "Just going in to McComb to window shop probably, and look." Whoever said this had accusation in his voice, as if the people had done something wrong.

"All dead. Every confounded one of them." A stout lady wearing a long black skirt and a white blouse, sleeves pushed up to her elbows, hollered.

A little shiny speck of something pink had stuck to the hem of her skirt. "The good Lord called them to His precious bosom today. If people would stay on the straight and narrow, things like this wouldn't happen." Two raggedly dressed children danced excitedly beside her.

Dr. Goodman had walked out of his office, stethoscope dangling from his neck.

Looking around, examining the corpses, he said, "No need for me to do anything here. Somebody ring the operator and get her to call the Sheriff and the Hartman Funeral Home."

He shook his head. "It's almost like that old train chewed 'em up and spit 'em out."

Frank and his father joined the crowd of somber-looking people standing around the track.

"Shame somebody didn't warn them. Bound to happen someday." One of the men who had come from Fly's Drugs pulled out a piece of thin tissue paper. He poured tobacco from a cloth bag tied with a drawstring. He rolled the paper and tobacco, then spit on the edge of the paper to make it stick. The man pulled the drawstring together with teeth stained the same brown color as the tobacco. He flared a large match with his thumb. "Hard to tell, but must have been four of them."

"Five, not four." One of the round-faced men who had been in front of the hardware store pointed to a pair of Brogan shoes. They were sticking out from under the train and turned at an awkward angle. "Musta bounced off the engine, then got throw'd up under. Busted him to smithereens."

"A horse woulda shied. This never woulda happened," Mr. Aden said. "Not with a horse. Another good reason not to drive one of those contraptions."

The Sheriff had arrived in a horse and wagon, and a few minutes later the Hartman Funeral Home hearse drove up.

"Y'all go on home now. They're all dead," the Sheriff said. "If you want to help, tote one of these stretchers and help us load up."

Frank didn't look. He had walked step-by-step next to his father, but he never looked at the dead people. "Papa, I think I see something."

"Hush, son." Mr. P.E. walked over to a small crowd of men standing in a clump. Several of them had stretchers, but none wanted to touch the bloody mess scattered all over the tracks. Bodies lay in a line like a load of red, brown, and black wash that had been whipped off a clothesline in a high wind. In the full glare of an afternoon sun, the vivid colors slowly faded and lost their sheen.

"Daddy, I see something," the boy called again. Frank ran to the train, climbed up on the front, and stood on the cowcatcher. "Looka here," he hollered. He bent over, held out his arms, and in a scooping motion gently lifted, then raised a baby up, as if he were making a love offering to the machine. The baby lay still—only his eyes moving—then he opened and closed his fists, clutching for something he could no longer grab.

The baby's lips began trembling, followed by an awful wailing. The child cried as if the anguish of all those who had been killed came from his own little mouth. The woman in the long black skirt snatched the baby from Frank's arms, and with a hard push, shoved him out of her way. Frank fell, stinging his hands and knees on the rough cinders. He closed his eyes and sat alone and motionless on the ground.

◆

The Fugitive had gone off. Mr. Aden dreamed he'd heard the voices of his children, Frank Jr. and Jewel. He didn't want to wake up. It was easier not to think about them. If he did, he sometimes wept for the missing of them. On the few occasions when they did come to visit, he carried the sound of their voices with him for days, a gaping wound that was slow to heal over. It was easier for him if they just stayed away.

"What do you think he'll do?"

Mr. Aden slowly opened his eyes; for a moment he was disoriented and felt as if he had slept for a long time.

His daughter Jewel was standing by his recliner, his son Frank Jr. right behind her. Jewel bent and kissed him. "You're pale as death." There was an evasiveness in the way she brushed her lips across his cheeks.

"Dad," Frank Jr. said. He shook his father's hand, but there was no warmth in the handshake. "It smells musty in here. This room is a wreck."

Mr. Aden put the newspaper down, rubbed his eyes, then poured himself another shot of Old Charter.

"Don't you think you've had enough?" Frank Jr. asked.

Mr. Aden held up the newspaper. "You're dead. All of you. I didn't get there in time to warn you." His voice sounded rusty, a heavy catch seemed to come from the back of his throat. A thin, teary mist covered his brown eyes. "They picked up your pieces; they carried them away."

The brother and sister looked at each other.

Mr. Aden patted his hands up and down, up and down on the arms of his chair. "Sonny, your face is blanker than that closed-up depot." He reached for his drink, took a swallow, then patted the chair arms again.

"Dad!" Jewel said. "We need to make some changes. That's why we're here. We've come to help."

"You can't help me. You're dead."

"No. We're all right," Jewel answered.

"Don't argue with him," Frank Jr. said. "Dad, it's hotter than a steam engine in here. Why don't you turn on the A/C unit we gave you?"

"You must have left my door open. It's chilly now you've come in." Mr. Aden picked at a scab on the back of his dry, scaly hand.

"That scab looks nasty," Jewel said. "You're irritating it, Dad."

Mr. Aden dug a little deeper. A small drop of blood spurted out, then tracked across the top of his hand and down his fingers. "You're thin as a rail, girl." He pushed his upper false teeth forward. Against the black hole of his mouth, they looked like a string of bones left out to bleach.

"Dead . . ." But the word blew against his teeth and came out in a garble. Realizing that he couldn't make himself understood at all, Mr. Aden took out his teeth and put them in his suit pocket. He looked hard at his two children.

Jewel looked away first.

"I warned you not to sell the Summit house out from under me. I said I would see you in hell, and now that's where we are."

"We're right here," his son answered sharply. "At your apartment in Jackson."

"Now that everybody's dead, I guess the two of you are satisfied. I'm supposed to warn everybody about those tracks. I was told to."

"You have. All our lives. Ad nauseam. We never left for Summit that you didn't harp on it," Frank Jr. said.

"I remember that day like it was yesterday." Mr. Aden picked up his drink again.

"Fate," he said. "I always knew it would catch up. It all runs together. Just like that clickety-clack train. I didn't get a chance to warn them this time either. But I can next time, before my thinking gets completely off track."

"Finish your drink, Dad," Jewel said. "We've come for a reason. We're going to take you to a nice place."

"With no warning signal?" he asked. "But I'm not ready."

The elderly man turned his head toward a small patio. Outside, a white dogwood gently spiraled in the late afternoon sun. "Puts me in mind of a cow-tail cloud." There was a calm smile on his face, as if he were looking at something familiar. "I'm done studying the here-and-now. But I haven't warned everybody yet. People who don't do like they should are not worth their weight in salt." He glared at his son.

"Dad, I can't understand your thinking."

Jewel turned to her brother. "We want to make this as easy as possible. I feel like a mean old woman trying to tell a child things he doesn't want to hear."

"Don't say it then," her father said. "A weak-chinned woman shouldn't have any gumption."

"Why don't you be quiet, Dad?" His son's lips barely moved when he spoke. "You could make this easier."

"Don't tell me to shut up, or what to do. I'm rounding that corner ahead of you." Mr. Aden's voice carried an implied threat. "If you're not going to help, go away and leave me in peace." For a few moments, he felt like he was in control; he had his hand on the throttle. His La-Z-Boy grated as he snapped it forward. He unrolled the newspaper, his eyes gleaming like lumps of fired coal as he pointed to an article. "I told you. I told all of you. Read this and see what happens."

"You read it, Frank." Jewel held the article out to her brother.

Pulling out a pair of half glasses and pushing them up on his nose, Frank Jr. began to read from *The Summit Sun*.

"Mr. and Mrs. J.P. Aden, formerly of the Holmesville Community, failed to stop at the railroad crossing on Main Street. Husband and wife were both killed instantly."

Frank Jr.'s words rolled out in a dull monotone.

"They had recently purchased the old Aden homeplace on East Robb Street from a cousin, Mr. Frank Aden, who now resides at Shadylawn Apartments in Jackson."

Mr. Aden looked hard at his son.

Frank Jr. raised his eyes and looked over his glasses. He shook the newspaper at his father. "My selling that falling down old house against your wishes has nothing to do with what happened to those people. This means nothing to me."

"They were dead set to go for the mail and this is what happens," Mr. Aden said.

Jewel went to her father and put her hands around his thin shoulders. "You didn't do anything wrong, Dad."

"Just get me out of Jackson and back home to Summit, so I can warn everyone about the train coming. You can't see, until it's around the bend." His voice was strained, sentences choppy as if he had rocks under his tongue. "This is a matter of life and death."

"Dad—we're going to have to take you somewhere. For your own good." Impatiently tapping his feet, Frank Jr. cut his eyes away. Crumpling the newspaper into a ball, he threw it in the trash can.

"I'm plumb wore out, but you've done it now." Mr. Aden jerkily stood up. "Somebody has got to stop them. I didn't do my duty once." He walked toward the bathroom.

Frank Jr. picked up the telephone and dialed. "Is this the Care In Nursing Home?" he asked.

Jewel turned away when she heard her brother.

"Yes. I think we can get him in without too much trouble. He's not violent, but just in case, you might have an attendant at the entrance."

"I can't sit here like a bump on a log and let it happen again."

Mr. Aden was standing in the doorway. Silence heavy as a black quilt covered the room. A gun hung from his hand.

His voice came out in a feeble wail: "All dead!"

Jewel and Frank Jr. both saw the gun at the same time. Frank Jr. put his hands over his ears and closed his eyes; Jewel gave a high scream and rushed toward her father.

The explosion broke the stillness of the afternoon.

◆

There was a sharp pain when he breathed. Air was being pressed from his lungs.

At first he saw only a hazy outline, then a bright sun glistening on the smooth, silvery rails.

"I hear something," the little boy cried. He jerked away from his father and ran toward the tracks.

Homecoming

NICOLAS SMITH

Hanson sat in the back seat of the cab and looked at the driver's eyes in the rearview mirror. They were fixed on the road ahead. Hanson leaned back and looked behind him as the Jackson Municipal Airport receded into the distance.

"No family to pick you up?" the driver said.

Hanson turned back around. "I want to surprise them."

The driver nodded. "That's nice. I'm sure they'll be glad to see you. How was it?"

"How was what?"

"You know. Vietnam. That's where you came from, right?"

"Oh. Yeah." He glanced down at the Silver Star and Purple Heart on his uniform but didn't say anything else right away.

"You don't got to talk if you don't want to."

"It's not that. I'm just trying to get my thoughts together."

"I got it, man. You say what you want when you're ready—or don't.

Ain't my business. Just trying to break the ice a little."

"I appreciate it," Hanson said. He wanted to talk, but he couldn't find the words. All he saw was the image of a boy with his legs gone. He lay in the middle of a crater created by the landmine he had triggered. The memory of the boy walking, then flying high in the air, his body going straight up then down while his legs flew out of sight, then hitting that smoking hole like a sack of gravel dropped out the back of a truck bed.

He doubted this man would want to hear a story like that.

Instead he looked at his hands and wiped them on his pants. He tugged at his collar, trying to cool off. He wondered why they built this car with such a low roof and doors far too close. He reached over and rolled one window down and closed his eyes and let the breeze flutter against his face. He shivered despite the heat. The sheen of sweat on his face and neck cooled in the air. He breathed Jackson, Mississippi, in and cleared his throat several times.

"Hey, you okay, man?" the driver said.

Hanson wiped his face and neck with the back of his hand and rubbed it against the seat. "Can we stop for a minute?"

"Sure thing, buddy. Let me find a spot real quick."

"Thanks . . ." Hanson paused and looked at the driver's dashboard and saw an identification card displayed by the radio. He read the name. "Mr. Fields."

"Don't mention it. Hey, what's your name? You can call me Thomas."

"Hanson. Hanson Blair."

"Good to meet you properly. Here's a place."

When Thomas pulled to the curb and parked, Hanson noticed him shut the meter off. Thomas turned around and faced him. "What's wrong?"

Hanson rubbed his eyes. "It's so different here. I mean, being home. It's hard to explain. I guess it's all starting to sink in. That I'm actually out. I suppose that's normal after being gone for a while. Nobody shooting at you. Nobody yelling at you, telling you what to do all the time. None of that."

"I don't doubt it," Thomas said. "Hey, you need something to eat? Maybe coffee or something?"

"I'm good." He listened to the people walking down the sidewalk next to them for a few moments, then took in a deep breath and let it out. "Yeah, I'm good now. I just need to get home."

"You got it," Thomas said. "Be there before you know it."

Hanson just sat back and looked at the city as Thomas drove on. The advertisements on the billboards were different. He glanced up at one as they passed and felt himself catching Dodge Fever when he saw the new model. The movies playing at the theatres were unfamiliar to him. *Rosemary's Baby* and *Bandolero!* But most of what he saw was like what he remembered before he left. He was glad for that.

As they pulled onto his street Hanson looked for his house. They passed the Malcolms' and the Jacksons' and the Petersons' and then he saw his house at the corner.

"That's it at the end there," he said, pointing.

Thomas pulled up to the small starter house Hanson's parents had lived in ever since they got married twenty-seven years prior. "Nice place."

"Thanks," Hanson said. "How much do I owe you?"

Thomas tapped his fingers on the wheel a couple of seconds then reached over and reset the counter. "Welcome home, soldier."

"Why did you do that?"

Thomas looked at him. "I been seeing how a few of y'all have been treated coming back. I had me a boy in Korea that didn't come back. Whichever way the world turns, I didn't want to make anyone willing to get killed feel like a loser in his own country."

"I'm sorry about your son."

"Hey, I'll see him again one day. You go on now, see your folks."

"Thank you, Thomas."

"Same to you, soldier. Go on and get out. Let me get your luggage."

Hanson stood on the sidewalk, looking at his front porch. He saw movement behind the curtain next to the front door. Then the door opened and his mother stepped out onto the porch, eyes wide. She slowly sat down on the porch steps with her hands over her mouth, her face aching with joy. Hanson walked up to the steps, slipped the cover off his head, and crouched next to her. "Hey, Mom."

She looked up at him and smiled, her eyes wet, finding her voice. "I thought for a minute that you were those men that only come with the bad news. Why didn't you tell us?"

"I wanted to surprise you."

She laughed and wiped her eyes. "Well, you sure did."

"Come on, let me help you up."

Hanson helped his mother to her feet as Thomas walked up with the luggage. Hanson turned to him and said, "Thank you, Thomas."

"Don't mention it," he said, setting down the suitcase. "I got to get going. Take care now, okay?"

"Sure," Hanson said. "You, too."

Thomas went back to his cab and waved as he drove away. Hanson watched him go, then turned back to his mother when he heard the door open again. He looked and said, "I'm home, Dad."

Hanson's father stood in the doorway, his expression the usual hardness, but his eyes showed something akin to relief. Hanson's mother stood by him. He seemed older. They both did.

"Welcome home, son," he said.

Hanson shook his father's hand. Then he hugged his mother, grabbed his suitcase, and they all went inside.

While his mother called family and friends, he went to his bedroom, set his suitcase on the bed, and sat down next to it. He looked around at all the things he had left behind. Everything was exactly the same. The model B-52 still unfinished on his desk. The high school track trophies on the top shelf of his bookcase.

He pulled out his senior yearbook and opened it to the graduating class and found his picture. In the bathroom down the hall he held it up to the mirror and compared his reflection to how he looked then.

He saw the other students in his class. Other friends. Jack Godwin. Robert Forrester. Ted Michaels, and others. He wondered what they had all been up to.

Then he came upon another familiar face. Pete Jackson. He thought back to the last time they had spoke, then set the book on the bed and went into the kitchen.

His mother was chatting on the phone, back to her animated self. He looked around and saw his father reading the mail. "Dad?" he said.

His father looked up at him.

"Have you heard from Pete recently?"

His father sighed. "He was killed two weeks ago."

"What?"

His father removed his glasses. "We didn't tell you because we didn't want you to worry. You needed to be focused on surviving. Not about your friend. I'm sorry."

Hanson looked at him, blinking. "How? What was he doing?"

His father put down the mail again. "I don't know the details. You'll have to ask his parents. Killed in action, I heard."

"Oh," Hanson said. He turned away and leaned against the doorframe and looked out the front door to the porch. He thought back to when he and Pete had first met in kindergarten. He turned back to his father and said, "He was going to be a dentist," but his father didn't seem to hear him. So he just stood there and looked out the window.

After a while his mother finally hung up the phone and said, "We're having a party for you tonight, Hanson. A welcome-home party."

Hanson turned from the doorway, his thoughts far off. "What?"

"A party. For you. Tonight. Won't that be nice?"

"Oh."

His mother took his hand. "You just go relax. Take a little nap, get your energy back. The trip must've sapped your strength."

Hanson just nodded and shuffled back to his room. He shut the door and lay down on the bed. He stared at the solid white ceiling that replaced the olive green canopy he was used to. He rolled over and faced the wall and cried until he fell asleep.

He awoke to an explosion roaring in his ears and jerked himself up, his eyes wild. He grabbed for his pistol but found only mattress and pillow. Then he looked around and remembered where he was.

It was dark now. He swung his legs over the side of the bed. Listening. Laughter.

He peeked out the door. He saw Miss Maxine a few seconds before she moved out of sight. The talking was louder. Had the party already started? He made his way to the living room.

Neighbors and friends were there, standing and talking. A few were picking through his mother's record collection. Several noticed him and he felt hands on him, faces close, too close. Hugs, slaps on the back, hot breath, and the occasional waft of cigarette smoke filling him. He eased through the congratulations and welcome-backs and stepped into the kitchen.

His mother was stirring something in a pot. Food covered the dinner table and the counter, all wrapped in various dishes and tinfoil. People were filling paper plates and cups. He looked at his mother. "What are you making?" he said.

"Turnip greens. Your favorite. They're not quite ready yet. Want to get something to eat? There's plenty here."

"Maybe in a little bit," he said.

"Betty is waiting for you."

"She is?"

"Outside. On the porch."

Hanson turned and went outside to the porch. Betty stood in the yard, her back to him as she looked up at the evening sky.

"Hey, Betty," he said, standing behind her.

She glanced at him without turning around. "I'm glad you're back," she said.

"Did you hear about Pete?"

She nodded. "I did. I'm sorry, Hanson. I know you were good friends."

Hanson frowned and nodded. He cleared his throat and said, "I wrote you two or three times. About us starting where we left off once I got back. But I guess they got lost."

"They didn't get lost," Betty said, turning around.

She looked like how he remembered her. The only difference was the bulge of her belly. Hanson looked at it, then met her eyes again.

She raised her left hand and showed him a wedding ring. "Bill Wallace and I were married back in February."

Hanson could only look at her.

"I'm sorry, Hanson. I didn't tell you because I didn't want to hurt you. The same thing with Pete. My mama and your mama got together and told me not to tell you. About me and Bill. And what happened to Pete."

"I'm happy for you," Hanson said. His jaw was hurting as he clenched his teeth.

"Hanson, please understand I—"

"I hope you're happy and I wish you the best. Now please leave. I'll see you later."

"Hanson—"

"Goodnight, Betty."

Hanson turned away and stomped back up the porch steps. He threw open the door and went inside, slamming the door behind him.

The guests turned at the sudden noise as he stormed toward his room. He shut himself inside and paced for a while. Then he turned off the light, took off his uniform, got into bed, and tried to sleep.

After a while he heard the doorknob on his door turn and the door squeak open slightly. He kept his eyes shut, and the door closed. The house was silent, the guests all gone, and he was alone again. He tossed and turned, then finally found asleep.

His slumber was marred by dreams, one after the other. Images of dead men and fire. Every time he would wake he felt less rested than before.

The next morning he awoke to the sound of his dad opening his door. He sat up as his father stood in the doorway.

"When are you going to get a job?"

Hanson looked at him, then over to the open yearbook on the nightstand. All those familiar faces, so alien and young. He looked at the model airplane and the trophies and the other testaments of memory. Then he looked at his father again.

"What happened here?" he said.

Road Trip

MARION BARNWELL

MOST NIGHTS, Damon Chastain comes in around nine and orders a Coke. Not the usual order, but then Saints is not your usual bar.

It used to be St. Michael's Catholic Church in the New Orleans French Quarter. Ernie, my mother's brother, came up with the idea of converting it to a bar and calling it Saints, a nod to the church and our beloved pro football team.

St. Michael's was about to be razed due to a dwindling membership, and, as luck would have it, Ernie had just read about an architect who'd transformed a Catholic church in Philadelphia into a beer parlor. So he jumped right in and bought the property.

He hired me on my twenty-first birthday not quite a year ago. There's still a lot I don't know but intend to find out. I like learning about drinks like absinthe with its checkered past. I like getting to know the customers. Melissa, for instance. Eighty years old and she comes in every day at five wearing bright red lipstick and a proper lacy blouse or silk jacket. She has a sherry or three and then regales us with stories of her own checkered past.

Back to Damon. He's a good-looking guy, tall, well dressed. Mid-thirties. His nose is bent, takes a slight left turn midway down, whether from a fight or a wreck I don't know. You forget about his nose once you notice his deep brown eyes.

When he came in tonight, he talked to a couple of acquaintances, took his seat at the bar, and introduced himself to the man sitting next to him. Nice manners. Friendly.

After I poured his Coke, he said, "What's going on, Katie? Make any A's today?" and I gave him a thumbs up. I'm crawling my way toward a degree in social work. He motioned me closer and said, "I need a favor."

"You got it." I leaned in to hear him over the noise. "What?"

"I've got to go up to the Mississippi Delta for a couple of days to see some people." He paused, took a breath. "I want you to go with me, pretend to be my girl."

"No way," I said.

"You turning me down? Just like that?" He snapped his fingers dramatically and gave me his most charming smile.

I looked away, massaged my neck, and wiggled my foot out of my shoe to stretch my toes. I thought about how nice it'd be to get away. I was strained to the max, trying to keep up with my classes and stay upright till closing time at two.

"You want me to pretend to be your girlfriend?" I said, incredulous.

"I'm not putting the make on you." He held up three fingers like the good Boy Scout I'm sure he never was. "Promise."

"Where and how long?"

"Hotel. One night. You'll have your own room."

"Why me?"

"Blonde. Nice figure. I need you around to make me look good."

"You don't need me to make—" I stopped when I realized I was about to return the compliment.

He smiled again.

"Can't you take a real girlfriend? You're bound to have plenty of those."

He looked to his left and then to his right. "Yeah, well, I seem to have run out."

If he was on the make, it was one of the more original propositions I'd heard. I'd give him that. And since it's not my first rodeo, the world wouldn't end if I had sex with him. Charlie and I broke up a month ago, and a fling might be just the thing to put him behind. That is, as long as we used protection. As long as he didn't get rough.

Besides, it was perfect October weather.

"You a good driver?" I said.

He laughed. "Yes. But if you don't believe me, you can drive."

"We won't go through Covington, will we?"

He tilted his head. "Pardon?"

"We don't have to go through Covington, do we?"

"That's my preference, but we don't have to."

I shrugged. "It's okay."

"What you got against Covington?"

I looked away, said nothing.

"Did they beat your school in football or something?"

"Something like that."

"So you'll go?"

"I might not be able to get off work."

"Hey, Ernie," Damon called.

Ernie splashed some vermouth in the martini he was making and placed it in front of the customer who'd ordered it. He came over and leaned on the bar. "Damon, my man. Whatcha need?"

"I need for you to let your poor, overworked niece off for the weekend. She's agreed to help me with a project."

Agreed? I started to protest, but sure that Ernie would say no way, I kept quiet.

"'Bout time she took off," Ernie said, smiling at me and kneading my shoulder.

On the drive home Ernie said getting away might do me good, give me a new perspective. Perspective about my mother was what he meant. Not for the first time, Ernie said she's forgiven me and wants me to call her. I didn't say anything as he saw me to the door of the garage apartment I rent from him.

"What if I haven't forgiven her?" I said before taking the stairs.

Damon made his proposition Tuesday night. On Friday at ten A.M., he knocked on my door. He was wearing tan cords and a black tee shirt under a black-and-white checked shirt, rolled at the cuffs.

I'd stayed up studying after work, so my eyes were crusty, my body was in slow motion, and I hadn't started packing. Damon paced my living/bedroom while I threw some things in an overnight bag.

Carrying it, he listed a little. I guess it was heavier than I thought. Everything else was too: my eyelids, the humidity hanging in the air, his mood. He looked grim. I didn't know what to think. At Saints, he's always so cheerful.

He stopped at a red Jag. He punched his key fob, and the doors unlocked. I tried not to show my surprise. Not that I cared, but until I saw his car, I didn't know he had money. "You want to drive?" he said.

"No. I want to sleep."

"There's a pillow on the back seat."

I reached for it and put it between my head and the passenger window, but I couldn't keep my eyes closed, not even when he finally got out of the uptown congestion and onto the interstate with its smooth drone. I'll admit I felt a little excited to be riding next to him in his fancy car. And awkward. It was one thing to shoot the breeze with him on my own turf at Saints, another to be alone with him in his car.

"So . . . tell me again why we're going to the Delta."

He was changing lanes and didn't answer right away. Then he glanced over at me and said, "Family business."

I sat up in the seat and made a show of dropping my jaw. "Family? You need a girlfriend to see your own family?"

"See my family on business," he corrected.

"Okay. But why do you need a girlfriend for that?"

"A long story."

"We've got time," I said, gesturing toward the windshield and the road beyond. It was a four-hour drive.

He slumped—as if my prodding him had made him extremely tired. "There's nobody left but a bunch of cousins. They've all made something of themselves."

"And?"

"They make me look bad," he said, shrugging.

I've wondered about him. Wondered how many times he'd been married. (More than once, I'd heard.) Wondered if there'd been another kind of addiction before Cokes. (A safe bet there, I'd heard.)

"What do you do?" I said.

"Unemployed." He looked at me as if daring me to make something of it.

"Temporarily?" I said hopefully.

He shifted in the seat and didn't answer right away. "Nah."

I'd never known anybody who didn't work. My own mother didn't miss more than a handful of days at the laundry each of the five times she'd given birth. "What do you do all day?" I blurted.

He laughed through his nose. "Take care of my cats and watch the stock market."

"How many cats?"

"Two."

"That doesn't sound like a full-time job."

He sighed. "Go to jazz joints. I'm a music a-fic-i-o-na-do," he said, stretching the syllables to suggest that it was a job of sorts that took up a lot of time. "And I go to churches-turned-bars, yours being my favorite because I get to see your pretty face."

I'm sure my "pretty" face flushed. "It's the *only* church-turned-bar in New Orleans."

He ran a hand through his hair. The ends stood out, giving him a cool edgy look that I liked. "So it is."

"What else?"

He thought a minute, scratched his beard—it too was heavy this morning. "I'm a Saints fan?" He knew he could derail me with that one.

"There you go!"

We both hooted. His laugh was something to behold. He'd scrunch his neck, lift his chin, lean forward, and let out a low *heh, heh, heh.*

After we replayed the third quarter of the last Saints-Falcons game, I asked him about these cousins who'd made something of themselves. "Ned manages the farm. Gayle's a rep." He waved a hand. "Blah, blah, blah."

He reached for the radio dial and fiddled with the knob until he found the jazz station he'd been looking for. I was disappointed. I didn't know a thing about jazz and liked hearing his voice, a rich tenor. I wanted to hear one of his wicked stories, always told in present tense—"And this old guy *knows* something's up." Like that. His stories were inspired by the usual sightings—a mime on Bourbon Street, a woman trying on hats in a fancy shop, an old man giving Tarot readings. Amusing stories, full of rich detail unless he brought himself into them and they turned sinister, usually because somebody was out to get him for reasons that weren't clear.

We stopped for gas at a Shell station. He bought a Coke for himself and a cup of coffee for me. "You're going to have to tell me about your cousins, you know," I said when we got back in the car. "As your girlfriend, I'd know something about them."

He frowned and shushed me. "Listen." He turned up the radio. "Art Blakey."

I tried to listen, but now we were on the causeway, a twenty-three-mile bridge over Lake Pontchartrain, which led smack dab into the town of Covington. I watched the water through the railing. It seemed to flow backwards. I leaned my head against the window and tried not to think about Marshall . . .

He was one of the cool guys. His dad, from North Carolina tobacco wealth, had added to the family fortune as a successful New Orleans corporate lawyer. Marshall's future was mapped out. Yale, like his father, and his father before him. After that, a law degree from Harvard.

In my family, I was the only girl and the baby, so my mother was as strict about boys as she was about germs and intended to protect me permanently from both. In high school, I wasn't allowed to date, but I'd "gone with" four football players in succession, meaning I flirted with them by the lockers and made out with them in dark corners of supervised dances.

When I started working on the school newspaper in eleventh grade, Marshall was the editor. He was tall and lanky—his build a little like Damon's, come to think of it. Indifferent to clothes and haircuts, he looked like anything but the heir to a family fortune. He knew a little about everything—history, politics, travel. He'd been to Greece and Brazil. He'd seen *Phantom* on Broadway.

The summer before, I'd fooled around with my next-door neighbor, Marty, while my parents were at work. We hadn't "done it" but came close a couple of times. After a few weeks, I ended things because I felt bad about myself and didn't like the feeling.

With Marshall, it was different. When he said he liked my hair or sent me a rose, I felt cherished. Since I didn't feel the shame I'd felt with Marty, I thought Marshall was The One, and he might've been if I'd met him later. I got pregnant in November of our senior year.

Such an old story. Such a cliché. I'd heard it from my customers hundreds of times, same story, different verse, mostly from guys who'd walked away and still felt guilty. Marshall had walked away too. (Did he feel guilty? Still?)

When Marshall's dad found out about the pregnancy, he offered to pay for an abortion. But since I'd already done the first worst thing a good Catholic girl could do by having unmarried sex, I couldn't do the second.

On a Friday night, after my two brothers still at home had left for the evening, I told my parents what had happened. Mama went to her room. Daddy retreated to his corner with the newspaper. After a while, Mama came out and started fixing supper. Total silence at the dinner table while we tried to eat her meatloaf and mashed potatoes. After supper, I could hear them talking in low voices while she washed the dishes and he dried. They came and sat down on the sofa. I was sitting sideways in the big armchair, my knees drawn up to my chin. Mama didn't look at me. The room was thick with her disapproval. She reached for Daddy's hand.

Daddy said since the horse was out of the barn, there was no sense in giving me a lecture. And besides, since I'd just advanced myself into adulthood, that's the way they would treat me. As an adult, on my own. He looked at Mama, and she looked at me like she smelled a decomposing corpse.

I learned from a girlfriend about a place in Covington that ran a home for unwed mothers, with an adoption agency conveniently located next door. I arranged everything. I had to call Marshall's daddy to ask if he'd be willing to pay my room and board when I started showing.

A month before graduation, I left for Harbor Home. I had a baby girl at 9:02 A.M. at the St. Tammany Parish hospital in Covington on Tuesday, September 18, and at 9:04 I gave her up to the couple waiting for her.

End of story. End of the causeway as well. I took a sip of cold coffee. As we drove through Covington, a beautiful little town, lush with live oaks and late-blooming azaleas, I felt the pain all over again of having my child ripped from my arms.

When Covington was finally far behind, I nudged Damon and said, "Where'd you say we're going?" I meant it to be funny.

"To the Delta," he said, looking straight ahead. "To a funeral for my cousin Lindy."

"Whoa," I said. "You didn't say anything about a funeral."

"Thought you might not come."

"I didn't bring anything to wear to a funeral."

"You'll be fine."

"Yeah, right," I said, looking down at my most comfortable jeans, stylishly holey, and my silver-spangled top. Good grief. What had I gotten myself into? I hugged the pillow to my chest.

"What's the matter?" he said.

"First you tell me we're going to see some people. Then I find out they're your kin. And now you tell me we're going to a funeral."

"It's not what you think. It'll be casual. Poolside."

I sat back and looked out the window, trying to imagine a poolside funeral. Before long, the hills flattened out and I could see the horizon.

"Where are we anyway?"

"The Delta, silly."

"You can call it that if you want to, but technically the Delta is where we came from."

"Technically, you're right."

"What town did you say we're heading for?"

"I didn't. Magnolia."

"You say the funeral is poolside? Explain, please."

He sighed. "Ned inherited the family home. When Lindy got a divorce, she told Ned she wanted to live in the pool house, and he said fine."

"How'd she die?"

"Breast cancer."

"How old was she?"

"Fifty-three."

"Jesus." I rubbed my ear. "How many cousins am I going to meet?"

"Three or four."

"Oh my God. You'd better fill me in."

He heaved another sigh. "Grandmother and Granddaddy had two girls and two boys," he said like he was quoting scripture. "Ann and her husband James had two daughters, Lindy and Gayle."

He drummed his fingers on the wheel. "Claire and her husband Mark had Helen, Ned, and Elaine. But Elaine may be in France."

"Lindy, Gayle, Helen, Ned, and Elaine who may be in France. But Grandmother and Grandfather also had two sons."

"Right. My daddy, Roy, and his wife Catherine had me."

"Only child?"

"Yep."

"And the other son?"

"Uncle Richard never married."

"Gay?"

"Maybe. But we didn't talk about it. And then there's the wives and husbands."

"Oh, shit." I sank in the seat. "Thank God Uncle Richard was gay."

"Did I say he was gay? So Helen is married to—"

"Enough! For now." I looked out the window at fields of half-picked cotton stretching to the horizon. "What about your parents? What about theirs—these cousins' parents?"

"Mine are in Peru, or at least I think they are. The rest are scattered. Or, in Lindy's case, dead." He said he was raised by his grandparents in the house Ned lived in now. He'd told me that before. Surely his parents hadn't been in Peru during his entire childhood.

"Don't you like these cousins of yours?"

His knuckles whitened on the steering wheel. "I liked Lindy."

We came into the Magnolia city limits. Damon turned off the highway into a down-and-out neighborhood that could've been any ghetto in New Orleans. Ramshackle houses, cars parked in the yards, junk littering the porches. When we turned onto a downtown street—different story. Pretty shops painted hot pink, bright aqua, pale yellow, or mint green with imaginative window displays that made me itch to get out and browse. Damon wheeled into a parking lot in back of The Preston Hotel.

Inside, we were greeted by sparkling chandeliers above us and flowers everywhere. Peonies, roses, lilies. Damon registered and then introduced me to the bellboy, Justin, who whisked us into the elevator to the second floor.

"How's school?" Damon said to Justin.

"Hell, man. I've still got three more semesters."

"Tell me about it," I said. "I've got six."

Justin shook his head. "Sucks, right?"

When I saw our suite I had to touch the doorframe to keep my balance. Could've been a living room out of one of those architecture magazines: Two sleek chartreuse sofas artfully arranged next to a couple of designer chairs covered in a geometric black and white. Justin showed us the two bedrooms. "Which one do you want?" Damon said to me. Technically, he'd delivered on his promise: I'd have my own room, but he hadn't said it'd be in his suite.

I thought I should act a little picky so I said I'd take the first one.

Justin led me back and put my bag on the luggage rack. I tipped him to let him know I was my own woman. I closed the door, opened my bag, and took out my long purple skirt and white woven top, the most subdued clothes I'd brought, and put them on. They would have to do.

I stepped into the living room. Damon was looking out the window. He had changed into a crisp yellow shirt and dark slacks.

I joined him. "A luxury hotel in the middle of nowhere. How'd that happen?"

"Granddaddy reinvested the money he made in the cotton business into the town." He pointed to a building directly across the street. "That was his bookstore. And over there," he said, pointing the other way, "was his four-star restaurant."

"I never knew anybody who owned a town."

"Not all of it." Damon looked at his watch. "Let's go."

After three downtown blocks, we crossed Tippah River Bridge and came onto a wide boulevard lined with majestic trees and palatial homes. I asked Damon to slow down so I could look. To no avail. He took the corner too fast as he turned into a tidy neighborhood and then onto a lane of seashells bordered by a tall hedge on either side. His knee jiggled as he wiped his hand on his slacks. A house of glass appeared on my right sporting white wicker furniture inside piled with pillows in hot shades of red, pink, or orange and bold paintings. "The pool house?" I said.

"Yep."

In the distance, a crowd had gathered at one end of what looked like an Olympic-sized swimming pool where a bartender was serving drinks. "And there's your party," he said, like I'd instigated it. When I opened my car door, the sounds of Bobby Blue Bland drifted from a five-piece band playing beneath the low limbs of a live oak strung with glowing paper lanterns.

Damned if Damon hadn't been right about my clothes. They *were* fine. On this unusually warm night, most of the men were in shorts, and the women wore gauzy tops with jeans or mini-skirts. He guided me straight to the bar and introduced me to the bartender, Jake, a black man with white hair. He was as string-skinny as Damon but not as tall.

"Jake of all trades," Damon teased, extending his hand. He turned to me and explained that Jake had been his granddaddy's chauffeur, handy man, and procurer of hooch during Prohibition. "How long you been with us?" Damon said, punching him on the shoulder.

Jake grinned. "Fifty years, but who's counting." He took our orders, a gin and tonic for me and a Coke for Damon. I longed to be on the other side of the bar.

"Damon!" a woman called out. Tall with shiny platinum hair, she came over and gave him a full-frontal hug.

"Mary Louise," he said. "Still beautiful."

Mary Louise. Not a cousin.

"What will we do without her?" she said, blinking back tears. "Let's get a drink."

Another woman appeared. She wore her dark hair long and straight and a giraffe-print tunic. "Aren't you going to introduce me?" she said to Damon.

"I thought I'd get her a drink first," Damon said, the atmosphere suddenly chilly.

Her. I felt invisible.

The woman made a face at Damon.

"Hi, I'm Gayle," she said to me and stuck out a hand.

Lindy's sister. "A rep," Damon had said, only I'd find out later that meant a Representative—in the Mississippi House.

"I'm Katie," I said, shaking her hand. She didn't look like a politician. She looked like a celebrity.

"I'm going to the little boy's room," said Damon, pointing to the bushes.

A young man with a blond ponytail came up and introduced himself.

"I'm Ned," he told me.

I'd been staring at the glass pool house. "I'm Katie. So that's where your cousin Lindy lived?"

"Yes."

"What holds it up? Invisible beams?"

He laughed. "Magic."

"What was she like?"

He adjusted his ponytail. "Gregarious. Loved everybody. She's the one who kept in touch, got us together."

Gayle had drifted away to speak to somebody. Now she was back. "What do you do?" she said.

I saw what Damon was up against. I tried to figure out how to explain that I was a bartender but that the job was temporary and tried to think up a major more glamorous than social work, but before I could come up with something, Gayle had lost interest. "You met everybody? All the cousins?"

"Yes, except for, um, Elaine and Helen."

"Elaine's in France. She teaches English at a school for kids of diplomats. Helen's over there by the bar. The tall one in white. Go introduce yourself. I have to check on the food."

The clouds had roosted among us. Through the mist, I heard a scream. I froze. My thoughts reeled as I tried to identify the sound. I tugged at Ned's arm. "Somebody's hurt. Come on! It sounded like a child."

He laughed at me. "It's okay. It's just a peacock."

I stopped, mid-motion. "Peacock?"

"Yeah. Grandmother used to raise them, so I keep one in her honor."

The peacock screamed again. I turned toward the sound and saw a massive stone house several hundred feet away, ghostly in the mist. "That's yours, right," I said.

"What I hear. My grandparents built it."

"Nice."

He snorted. "The upkeep is killing me, but nobody else would take it."

"So that's where Damon grew up."

"Correct. His parents are travel writers. Gone a lot." He looked around. "Come on. I'll introduce you to Helen."

We made our way to the pool.

"Hey, you're Damon's girlfriend, I hear," a woman yelled from several feet away. "I'm Ned's wife, Diane," said a petite woman with red hair and a loud voice. "Have you met everybody?"

I was catching on. "Everybody" meant the cousins. The rest of us were extras.

"She hasn't met Helen," said Ned.

Diane took me by the hand and led me to the crowded bar.

Helen was leaning against the back of a very tall man as if he were a tree. She held a cigarette in one hand and a drink in the other and was wearing white shorts, a transparent white shirt, and a low-slung belt of turquoise and silver.

"This is Katie," said Diane. "Damon's new girlfriend."

Helen boosted herself off the back of the man behind her. "Hi," she said. "I'd shake your hand, but . . ." She held up her drink and cigarette. "Malloy," she said to the man. "This is Damon's new girlfriend." Malloy turned around, raised his glass, and went back to his conversation.

"Your husband?" I said.

"Ex. Now I'm married to, um . . ." She looked toward the band. "Henry. The one in a striped shirt that looks like an awning." She took a drag off her cigarette. "So how long have you and Damon been going out?"

Oh, God. Damon and I should've worked this out. "Six months."

"Oh, really? Then it must be serious. Most of his girlfriends don't last that long." She dropped her cigarette and ground it out with the toe of her silver sandal. "If that sounded rude, I didn't mean it to."

"No offense," I said.

"Where is Damon?"

"Somewhere over there," I said, waving vaguely. "So what do you do, Helen?"

"Fashion designer."

"Where?"

"New York."

Figures.

Gayle hurried over to us. "Crisis. We're out of ice," she said to Helen.

"Not to worry," said Helen. "Annie and Skeets are on their way. I'll call them." She took a phone out of her pocket. "Let's check Lindy's freezer."

They turned and headed to the pool house. Alone, I tried not to look as awkward as I felt. I finally spotted Damon on the other side of the seashell lane. I started toward him but then stopped. Propped against another lantern-lit tree and wearing his shades, he might as well have hung out a sign, "Don't tread on me."

I made my way to the buffet. The main attraction was an array of crabmeat, shrimp, and oysters artistically displayed on heavy pottery. I wondered how fresh it could be this far inland and picked up a ham biscuit.

"Here they are. The icemens cometh!" somebody yelled, as a truck pulled up. An actual truck, not a fancy car, and I thought they might be my kind of people until they drove the pickup onto the grass and up to the very edge of the pool. A man and woman got out and unloaded several sacks of ice from the back.

"Try the oysters," said a man who'd introduced himself as Chester. He speared three with a toothpick, squeezed them with lemon, and downed them in one gulp.

"I'll see how you fare."

He laughed. "They're fine. Brought in from the coast this morning."

I didn't say anything, just made my way around the table to the grilled squash, tomatoes, and mushrooms. We ate and chatted awhile about nothing, and I was relieved that we didn't have to talk about what we did for a living. He asked me to dance and led me over to a pavilion where three or four other couples were dancing.

Unlike the cousins, Chester was not conventionally attractive and not much taller than my five-five. But he was easy to be with and turned out to be a great dancer.

"Have you met the cousins?" he asked.

I nodded and smiled at the familiar question. "So is it a Delta thing, this funeral?"

"No. It's a Lindy thing," he corrected. "She always wanted everybody to get along and have fun."

The mist had turned to rain. I heard someone yell and figured it was the peacock, but then recognized the voice. Damon was yelling at Ned.

Then he pushed him. Ned pushed him back, and then Damon thrust a fist into Ned's face. Ned fell backward but was soon up and taking a swing at Damon. Damon stayed on his feet, but blood spurted from his nose onto his yellow shirt. I got there just before he swung again. When I tried to step between them, a man grabbed me by my waist and pulled me out of the way. I heard a crack. Damon's fist on Ned's jaw. Ned took another swing at Damon, missed, and fell backward.

Diane screamed, and I realized she'd been screaming for some time. And so had the peacock. Diane knelt beside Ned and everybody crowded in. His eye had swollen to the size of a tennis ball, a bleeding gash above it. When I looked up, Damon was gone.

The rain had stopped. Diane and Henry helped Ned across the yard to his house. Helen and Gayle examined my face. When the guy pulled me away, I'd fallen sideways against a tree and grazed my cheek.

"I'm Bill," said the guy, stepping up. "Sorry, but if I hadn't done that, you'd be in the hospital right now."

"Damon just hauled off and hit Ned for no reason," Gayle said. "I saw him."

"What did Ned do to him?" I said.

"Nothing."

"Damon hates us," said Helen. "Didn't he tell you?"

"No," I said. "If he hated you, he wouldn't have come."

"Whatever," said Helen. "I'm going to get a drink? You want one?" she said to Gayle.

"No," said Gayle. "I'm going home."

"He doesn't hate you," I called to Helen's retreating back.

I touched my stinging cheek and took out across the lawn to look for Damon. Near the hedge, I stopped and blinked. The Jag was gone.

I wandered back to the pool. Helen was dancing with a man in a safari hat. Her husband, Henry, grabbed me and tried to kiss me. "Whoa, now," I said and pushed him away. I looked for Chester, hoping for a ride home. I finally saw him. He was in the pool with a woman I hadn't met. Both were fully clothed, but her legs were wrapped around his waist. *Whatever.*

I wandered from one circle of strangers to another. They hardly noticed me, and I decided to turn it to my advantage. I sat in the shadows and listened to their conversations. To my right, a woman pulled a pink shawl around her shoulders and told a couple of other women that Damon's parents had treated him like an orphan, so what could you expect. A man in a lounge chair to my left smoked a long cigar and told a trio of men that Damon must've fallen off the wagon, simple as that. One of the men leaned back in his chair and said maybe, but then Damon had always resented Ned for living in the family home. Another one muttered something about too much money.

"Only one thing to do," said the woman in the pink shawl. "Have another drink."

"Let's get a drink," said the man with the cigar.

The two groups converged on the already crowded bar. I planted myself behind it and started taking orders and fixing drinks. Jake eyed me curiously but was too busy to argue. When things slowed down, he asked me where I'd learned to tend bar, and I told him about Saints.

"Why do you think he did it, Jake?" I said at the next lull.

"Who? What?" he said, his face a conscious blank.

"Why'd Damon start the fight?"

He shook his head and pitched an empty fifth into the trash. "I don't know nothin' about that."

"You've been here fifty years? Come on."

He shook his head again. I opened a beer and handed it to him and then opened one for myself.

"I'm only asking because I like him. You like him too. I can tell."

He took a sip of beer and nodded. "Listen," he said, stroking the beer with his thumbnail. "Like most of us, he's been hurt, only Damon, he holds onto it. The rest of 'em, 'cept for Damon and Lindy, they lost in they own world. Lindy could handle it, but Damon . . .?" He shrugged.

I finished my beer and told Jake goodbye. When I reached the hedge, I looked back. A man and a woman were balancing on paddleboards, trying to knock each other off.

The rain started up again, came down in torrents. I took off my sandals and strode barefoot back to the hotel. Fueled by rage, it didn't take me long. I thought about how it had been—how it had really been—riding in the car with him. The few times I'd volunteered to say something about myself, he'd nodded, sniffed, and said, "Yeah," like he was thinking about it but I knew he wasn't. If he could just have gotten out of his own way for one full minute and asked me like he was truly interested, I might've told him about myself, my past. Then maybe he'd have seen that other people, even his cousins, have problems and make mistakes.

When I finally got back to the hotel, we spoke our last words to each other since we didn't speak at all on the long drive home. When I opened the door to our suite, he was at the window, staring out. I can't remember what I said, but he turned around, still wearing the yellow shirt spattered with blood. "I couldn't come back for you," he said.

I glared at him.

"Not after what he did."

"Ned? What'd he do?"

He shook his head. "It wasn't so much what he did. It was the way he looked at me."

I thought about how Mama had looked at me when I told her about the baby and softened. But I decided right then that if he tried anything, I'd stop him. At the door to my room, all he did was touch three fingers to his head in salute and turn away.

◆

Monday night back at Saints, it was hard to believe that road trip ever took place. Except that my perspective had done a 360. I wasn't about to move back home, but what was left of my grudge against my mother had dissipated like the rain, so this morning I made the phone call she seemed to need from me.

Now it was well past nine and Damon hadn't come in. I wasn't surprised.

I was making a Pimm's Cup when my cell phone vibrated. After serving the drink, I took out the phone and looked at the text: "Letting you know in case you give a damn, I'm leaving town for parts unknown so you can forget about me. If anybody asks where I am, tell them you don't know. D."

For several seconds, I held the phone and stared at the empty spot at the bar. Then I shut it off and put it back in my pocket.

Gone Fishing

DANEY KEPPLE

RUDY TAYLOR reached me on my cell phone before I even got to the church this morning and filled me in. "It all happened so fast, they didn't have a chance to call you, Liz. They just headed for the Memphis airport, which is where they are now. Their flight is delayed for at least two hours, so if you could come . . ."

"Of course. I'm about twenty minutes away." I actually made a U-turn on the busiest street in town and headed back toward the airport.

"I'll meet you at Security in the main terminal," Rudy promised. As president of the Airport Authority, he was probably the only mortal who could get me to the gate without a boarding pass. We arrived at almost the same minute, and he talked me through as though he performed such miracles every day. Maybe it was part of his job. I didn't have time to think about the duty roster of the Airport Authority.

Jake and Molly were huddled together in a corner of the boarding area, as far as they could get from the blaring television. If I hadn't already been fond of them, this would have done it. I knelt down in front of them, but not to pray. "I'm so sorry."

◆

After they had given me the facts—heart attack while running, the greatest unfairness of all, it seemed to me—Jake looked at me. "You've been through this, haven't you, Liz?"

I nodded.

"How was it for you?"

To my surprise, I said, "When I learned of my father's death I immediately sank into a reverie about the last time we went fishing rather than grappling with questions about his immortal soul." In response to Jake's surprised look, I added, "That may seem odd for someone in my line of work, but it's true."

◆

I was fourteen and had just learned that my dad was engaged to my Aunt Min before he went off to war. When he came back, he married my mother instead. Having heard my mom's version, I was eager to get his side of the story so I asked him to take me fishing. Once we had taken such outings often, but lately I usually had better things to do.

His answer was immediate. "I can't think of anything I would rather do. You just say where and when."

"Alligator Beach." That's what *we* called the place we always went. I loved the snaky old swamp because it was on a road so deserted I could sometimes pester him into letting me drive. "Any time you can get away from the store," I added.

"Hell, we own the place. I'll go whenever I want to!"

My mother met my eyes across the table and smiled at my dad's rare display of boastfulness. "You see how excited he is to be spending time with you?" is how I read her look.

"No time like the present."

I couldn't believe he would play hooky from the store on a Saturday, his busiest time, but it was a glorious day, the first of the season. Maybe he had spring fever. So we decided to go right after breakfast. He was already in the garage stowing fishing gear in the trunk by the time I got my clothes on and joined him.

"You can drive as soon as we get out of town," he promised before I even asked.

He was as good as his word. We had just passed the Indianola city limits sign when he pulled over and opened the door. "You can take it from here, Liz Beth."

I scooted over to the driver's side and had the seat adjusted by the time he circled around the car and opened the passenger door. I waited for him to get settled, then pulled away carefully and concentrated on steering straight.

"You know, when you were a little girl, you asked for a doll for Christmas for several years, then you stopped. Do you remember why?"

I almost took my eyes off the road to stare at him. My dad wasn't big on probing questions or, for that matter, conversation of any kind. I tried to think of an answer but nothing came, maybe because I was watching so hard for the gravel road that angled off to the right. I shook my head. "I just don't remember."

Out of the corner of my eye, I saw him nod. "You know, Liz Beth, it's always hard to remember endings. Things just seem to slide into something else so gradually a body doesn't even notice."

My mother had probably warned him that he was in store for an interrogation. At the time, I just thought he had handed me the perfect opening and I grabbed it. "Is that the way it was when you stopped loving Min and started loving Mama?" I blurted out the words just as we pulled into the bait shack, giving him the opportunity to bolt. Or, to be fair, to open the door and head inside, telling me over his shoulder that he wouldn't be a minute.

I promised myself, while he was buying worms in case our feathery wooden lures failed to entice the fish, that I wouldn't push him for an answer, but by the time he returned he had his statement prepared. "It was never a matter of loving one sister and not the other," he explained carefully. "I just realized I loved them in different ways."

I couldn't stop myself. "How?"

My dad busied himself clamping his ten horsepower trolling motor to the back of the wooden boat he selected from the pile on the bank. I had pulled the car down near the edge of the dock and we ferried back and forth with paddles, tackle boxes, rods and reels, cushions, and the metal basket we hung over the side to hold the fish we caught. I still remember the smell of the place, a cross between fish and snake.

He didn't answer me until he had cranked the motor and headed toward our favorite spot, a cove about half a mile from the dock. I pictured the place in my mind before we got to it, the weeping willows that shaded it, and the underwater roots and snags where fish apparently loved to nest.

I was surprised when his voice emerged above the drone of the motor. "Min and I are friends, always were, and always will be. My feelings about your mother are more—complicated."

"I understand," I told him, even though I didn't. But I didn't stop probing either. "Why do you think Min left?"

His face didn't change. Maybe he didn't hear me. While I was trying to decide whether to repeat the question, he cut the motor and the boat glided to a stop just before slipping under the willow branches.

"Way to go, Dad!" I almost always said that.

He grinned. "Practice." That was his usual answer.

He handed me my rod, then took up his own, unhooking the fly from the cork handle and pulling line from the reel until it was the length he wanted. He tipped a paddle toward him and with his foot, picked it up with his left hand while with his right he flicked the fly over his head and, with a perfect wrist movement, planted it exactly where he intended— directly above a submerged tree trunk. All the while his left hand operated the paddle to keep the boat steady.

He glanced at me. "Aren't you going to fish?"

I began to unreel my line. "I was enjoying watching you."

He smiled again.

I was concentrating so hard on my cast, his voice surprised me. "I reckon I've never come up with a satisfactory answer to that."

He was trying to answer my question about Aunt Min leaving.

"Me either," I told him.

"Maybe we're all trying too hard."

That was a knack he had, of diminishing problems effortlessly. I relaxed and quit thinking about Min or the fish or the fly on the end of my line. Then my arm, wrist, and fingers started to function automatically.

"Atta girl," he said.

Still waters run deep is what people always said of Charlie Haskins, and I suspect that was true, despite my dad's description of himself. *I'm just a simple guy with simple tastes* is the way he always put it.

"Do you ever think about the war?" I have no idea why I said that.

He didn't look at me. "Not if I can help it."

So I let it go. Instead of badgering him I let my thoughts drift through the facts I knew about him. He grew up right in Indianola, the son of a farmer and his hard-working wife. Perhaps his "people" were below my mother's on the social register, if there were such a thing around there, but that part of the state was never much concerned with caste.

"We're all the same in God's eyes," as my grandmother put it.

She meant only the white ones, of course.

She would describe my father's family as good, simple folk and she would be accurate. My grandfather Haskins was as quiet and even-tempered as his son. Grandmother Haskins died before I was born.

My dad admired both of my grandfathers for different reasons. One was larger than life; the other took life as it came.

◆

We caught a lot of fish that day, cleaned them at the stand near the dock, and took them home to my mother who served them with hushpuppies and slaw for our supper. It was just delicious.

Before we left the lake my father said something that surprised me. "You're a lot like Min."

I nodded. People were always saying that.

"You have a lot of your mother in you, too."

I turned around and looked at him. Nobody had ever said that to me. "What do you mean?"

"You have Min's drive, but you've also got a large measure of Callie's patient goodness," he pronounced. "The combination will take you far."

I almost cried when he said that. Remembering it brings the same rush of feeling, even after all this time.

◆

Jake squeezed my hand. "Thank you for telling me that, Liz. It helps."

I squeezed back. "Thank you for asking, Jake. I haven't thought of that day in a long time."

Decisions

DIANE THOMAS-PLUNK

ANNABEL stood in the spare room, cluttered with boxes and assorted junk, and struggled for inspiration to help transform the mess into a snuggly nursery. She absent-mindedly stroked her burgeoning baby bump. The monotone of MSNBC was white noise in the background—that is, until the key words blared clearly: Camp Leatherneck, Helmand Province, Afghanistan; shooting; Afghan police trainees fire on Americans; two Marine instructors down mortally wounded; walking wounded Marines rounding up the trainees; all names withheld pending notification of families.

Annabel found herself in the living room, seated on the coffee table, fixated on the news. *That's where Josh is. That's his assignment. He and others from here at Twentynine Palms are instructors.* MSNBC reported that, upon being handed a loaded weapon as part of the training exercise, an Afghan police trainee turned the weapon on the Marines, wounding several, killing two.

Annabel thought that she was grateful to be on base at Twentynine Palms. All the affected spouses would be on or near the base, and they could support one another. She knew she had frightened sisters even in her apartment building. She knew that it wouldn't be Josh, but, just the same, she was immobile in front of the television news for more than an hour when the knock came at the door. Thank God, it was Pamela, red-eyes brimming with tears.

"Come in here and stop that, Pammy. If you cry, I'll have to. It's too early to cry."

The young women hugged, and Annabel brewed tea. The phone rang, and Annabel startled.

"They don't give bad news over the phone. They come to the door," said Pamela.

It was Josh's mother, who lived in a plantation home near the river in Vicksburg, Mississippi. It was one of the beautiful handful that had survived the Civil War's river battle and siege. She was the first to call. She tried not to sound terrified and hoped that Annabel had more information than the TV news. Of course she didn't. Spouses from around the base began calling each other, trading rumors, offering support, telling pretty lies. The CO's wife sent out a message inviting the spouses from that assignment to her home for coffee and mutual comfort. She was a good woman. Annabel and Pamela appreciated the invitation, but declined. They didn't want to be in a big group. There was no news forthcoming.

"We need to go to the commissary," announced Annabel.

"You want to buy groceries?"

"Yes. We'll need to take casseroles to a couple of homes tomorrow. We should get them ready now. It'll keep us busy."

Annabel was only twenty, but she'd been a Marine wife for two years and a good Baptist for all her life before that. Casseroles were always in order.

Later, when two dishes were in the oven, Pamela made sandwiches for them. The phone calls had stopped.

"I can't go home," said Pamela as darkness settled over the base. They heard taps being sounded as the base flag was lowered.

"What if . . . well, what if your neighbors need to know where you are?" asked Annabel.

"I left a note on the door with your address. And really, everybody here knows everything anyway. They'll know I'm with you. Annie, the television and newspapers get these things faster than the Casualty Officers can make contact. No one's going to come looking for us yet."

"No one's looking for us, period. I feel it. Tomorrow we'll know the awful news and we'll comfort our sisters. Breaks my achin' heart, but we'll stand tall for them," said Annabel.

The girls curled up together in Annabel's bed, but slept restlessly listening for the terrible knock at the door. They woke up earlier than they wanted and surfed all the news channels while they ate a skimpy breakfast. Annabel took her prenatal vitamins while tea brewed.

"For God's sake. Don't they know they're torturing us? You know they have the names now, and they know where the spouses are. Damn them to hell!" Pamela threw the remains of her breakfast in the trash.

"No one's going to make any announcements for a while," she said. "They're not through tormenting us. I'm going home, clean up, and come back. Is that okay, Annie? Will you be all right? Will you be all right, too, little baby?" She leaned down and whispered to the baby bump, gently stroking Annabel's belly.

"Go home, Pammy. It could well be tomorrow before we know anyway. But I sure want you back for handholding. Don't you suppose that the others are buddied up, too?"

"I know they are. You do worry about everyone, don't you? I'll be back soon, really soon."

Before getting in the shower, Annabel turned up the TV volume to its highest level so the television noise and rushing water would drown out any knock at the door. She was sure it wouldn't be her door, but she dearly wanted Pamela to return for both their sakes.

Smelling of peach-scented soap, Annabel dug through her snack stash. She'd not anticipated how hungry she'd stay during pregnancy, but she indulged every yearning. Dried fruit sounded good right now. But she dropped the plastic bag when the knock came at the door. She froze, but quickly relaxed, telling herself, "Annie girl, you are such a dumbass. It's just Pamela coming back. I should really give her a key."

So Annabel was smiling when she opened the door and saw the two Marines in dress uniforms. She screamed NO and tried to slam the door shut. The enlisted Marine shoved her leather pump between the door and the jamb before it closed. The corporal stepped back for the officer to lead them into the living room. Annabel backed away from them, trembling, wailing, occasionally articulating words: No. Go away. Don't talk to me.

The two Marines gently guided her to the sofa. "Who shall I call to be with you, Mrs. Gardener?" With no response, the officer sent the corporal out of the unit. "Go knock on doors. Find out who her friends are. Get someone here."

Annabel cried so violently that the officer called for a base doctor. Pamela arrived, wept softly, and held Annabel in her arms.

"I'll call her mother-in-law. I know she'll come quickly."

The officer handed Pamela an information sheet with guidelines and telephone numbers.

"When she can, we'll help with transport of the Lance Corporal to the burial location and with the other aspects of the funeral. Of course, the Corps will provide a military funeral with honors. There's assistance available for her."

"Thank you. I'll go over this when she's ready. I need to ask—where do you go next? My last name is Worthington. Am I your other stop?"

"No ma'am. You're not on our list."

They left and Pamela felt guilty relief. Her best friend was sinking into a nearly catatonic state of denial. Pamela grieved for Annabel, Josh, and the baby, but sent up praises that it wasn't her Tony. She disliked herself for that, but maybe all Marine spouses feel that conflict right now.

Pamela bore the weight of sharing the news with Josh's mother who choked back a scream and regained her composure, asking about Annabel, the baby, and what Annie might need. Pamela stayed with Annabel until Paulette Gardener, Josh's mother, arrived the next day. Pamela, afraid to leave Annabel, had another friend gather up Paulette at the Palm Springs airport and bring her to the apartment. Pamela and Paulette exchanged information in whispered tones while Annabel existed only as a shadow. Paulette remembered Annabel's sparkly, turquoise eyes which now appeared deep indigo.

Paulette took over care for Annabel and tried to engage her in the decisions that had to be made to return Josh to their home in Vicksburg for a proper Marine funeral and burial. He deserved those honors and, no doubt, medals.

The base doctor was cautious in prescribing medication for Annabel due to the pregnancy. With the help of Pamela and on-base sisters, they packed up the young Gardener's possessions and readied them for shipping. Once back home, Paulette made a comfortable room for Annabel. James, her husband, did his best to welcome Annabel and his forthcoming grandchild, but he buckled in his own grief. The sight of Annabel and her round, baby belly only prompted painful memories of his only son.

There would be a time when Annie would be grateful for all that Paulette did, but that time hadn't arrived.

Annabel didn't remember much of the funeral. There were flowers everywhere. Kind words were spoken. Hymns were sung. At the cemetery, someone handed her a folded American flag that she pressed to her heart. There was a mournful tune from distant trumpets and a gunfire salute that was a disturbing reminder of Josh being gunned down.

There was no discussion about the permanence of Annabel's move into the Gardeners' home. She had no close family and was clearly in need of tending. So she stayed. Though Paulette loved her sweet daughter-in-law, she confessed only to herself that it was Josh's baby she desperately wanted in the home.

She took Annabel to the best OB/GYN in nearby Jackson and cleared out a small junk room near Annabel's for conversion to a nursery. She tempted Annabel with splurge shopping at Babies R Us, but Annie declined. "Too soon," she would say. Paulette fretted over barely touched plates that she removed from Annabel at the end of meals. She heard Annabel pacing in her room at night.

For her part, Annabel was aware in some part of her consciousness that Paulette was extending extraordinary care and love to her. She was vaguely aware that she should be grateful. Problem was that she hadn't the energy to care. When she sat at the breakfast room table, the vision she saw through the lens of her depression was, instead of Paulette's carefully tended flower beds, a backyard splotched with garish floral colors all stacked rudely on Josh's fresh grave. Foreign men with guns stood guard. When she could, she chose a chair facing away from the window. The vision was always there.

Paulette ignored Annabel's ambivalence and marshaled her to obstetrician's appointments. In ordinary times, Annabel would have liked Dr. Gooding, a round, middle-aged woman who simultaneously exuded skill and sweetness.

"Mrs. Gardener . . . Annabel, I know you're still grieving, dear, but you need to start taking better care of yourself and that little one growing inside you," said the doctor. "What can I do to help you do that?"

"Yes, dear, it's not just you that you're hurting," said Paulette. "I know you want the baby to be healthy, don't you?"

"The baby!" snapped Annabel. "The baby's father is a ghost, and I'm already dead, too. Can't you tell? You two have no idea."

There wasn't much to say after that. Paulette took Annabel home and continued to gently encourage healthy habits. Annabel continued to pace at night.

A week or so later, Annabel was in her refuge, the shower. No one bothered her there. No one tried to make her eat or sleep or buy baby stuff or take healthy walks. She liked the water as hot as possible. It was the only time she felt anything. She'd stepped away from the showerhead spray to slather herself with the expensive, aromatic soap that Paulette provided. Using her hands, she soaped her body, her belly, arms, legs, and breasts with the heavenly soap. That's when she felt it. In her left breast. She pressed on it, kneaded it, felt it from all angles. Shit.

She imagined the lump as the pit of a peach. That's what it felt like. It didn't frighten her or sicken her. It only assured Annabel that she was, in fact, a dead woman.

It took another two weeks for Annabel to get around to telling Paulette about the lump. She wasn't sure why she bothered except maybe to subtly torment Paulette with the possibility of losing the baby that Paulette so desired.

"How long have you known?" Paulette asked in a whisper.

"I don't know. It's probably nothing."

"I'll take care of this," said the senior Mrs. Gardener.

A few telephone calls put Paulette in touch with the Women's Health Clinic in Jackson.

On the phone she pressed the number for the critical nature of the problem and managed an appointment for Annabel only two days away.

Paulette and Annabel were assured that the lead apron over Annie's belly would protect the baby from the mammogram. No such problem with the subsequent sonogram. Annabel did what she was told and expressed no interest. The doctor, a breast specialist and surgeon, reviewed the results from the radiologist and told the Gardener women that, for safety, a needle biopsy of the lump should be performed—quickly. They returned the next day. Annabel gazed at the ceiling as the needle withdrew cells from the peach pit.

Of course Paulette fretted during the days they waited for results. James, as usual, was unable to comfort anyone including himself. Annabel was oblivious. The call came. The breast doctor wanted them back for a conversation. Never a good sign. Patients don't go into the office for good news.

The office visit was the next day. Paulette choked and began crying at the word *malignant*. The doctor explained the conundrum. If Annabel were not pregnant, surgery, chemo, and radiation would be in quick order. Those things, however, would seriously, if not fatally, harm the baby.

"You're too far along to terminate the pregnancy," he said. "That makes for very difficult choices for you to make. I know what we need to do for your health. I'm also aware that you've lost your husband and that adds significance to this tiny child. That makes it horribly difficult. I'm afraid that you must decide which way we proceed. We protect your health or the baby's. That's the bottom line. I'm very sorry."

Paulette looked down at her prayer-clasped hands. Annabel thought it odd that the baby took that moment to be so active inside her.

"I'll have to think about it," said Annie.

"Call me. Call your OB when you decide. We shouldn't wait long to determine our course of action."

Annabel felt Paulette's intrusive hovering for the rest of the day. She escaped to her room as quickly as polite after leaving an untouched plate at dinner.

When she had paced as long as her energy allowed, she went to bed and dreamed of Josh. He wore those old jeans that bared one knee and part of his butt. And that was the tee shirt she'd tried twice to throw away before he was deployed. Both times, he'd dug it out of the trash and triumphantly laughed at her. In the dream, he was in a room with glass block walls that permitted a rosy glow from somewhere unknown. Josh sat in a rosewood rocker and held a bundle, something swaddled in a pink blanket. He smiled when he saw Annabel, rose and walked to her. He kissed her cheek tenderly, whispered in her ear, and handed her the bundle—a beautiful, tiny baby girl.

When Annie sat at the breakfast table the next morning and looked at the backyard, she saw the colorful blooms of Paulette's plentiful rose bushes and hydrangeas. She accepted an ample breakfast and helped clean up the kitchen. Paulette saw the peace that had settled over Annabel and was relieved when the girl wanted to see the OB. The conversation proved difficult, however.

Annie told the doctor that she wouldn't have any treatment for the cancer.

"We're going to take care of this baby, then we'll see," she said.

"You're twenty-six weeks now, Annabel. Forty weeks is optimum for the baby, but we can do a cesarean section at thirty-seven weeks. The baby will be fine, and that's what I recommend. I'll contact the breast surgeon. We'll take the baby a little early and then get you immediately into care."

Annabel was transformed with her new mission. She ate. She took walks. She tried to sleep. Paulette exulted. Annabel visited Twentynine Palms in California, the Marine base that had been her home. She didn't know if she'd be able to get there again.

Pamela sat with her at the base coffee shop.

"Are you really okay? Should I go back with you? I can absolutely do that. I miss you."

"I'm better than I've ever been," said Annabel.

At thirty-two weeks, Annie and Paulette sat in Dr. Gooding's treatment room. After checking the baby's heartbeat and anticipated weight, the doctor pushed back the paper gown. Paulette held her breath. She hadn't known that the breast was so swollen and discolored.

"I want to move up the C-sec to thirty-four weeks. We can handle this for the baby and then we can move you forward as quickly as possible," said the doctor.

"Too soon," said Annabel. "We'll wait for thirty-seven weeks. That's the earliest I'm comfortable with."

Paulette saw Annabel shrink in the next weeks. Her natural color faded. Her energy dissipated. Annabel tired and weakened as the days dragged on. Despite her physical decline, she maintained the beautiful serenity that cloaked her.

Annie and her mother-in-law showed up early on the delivery date. Annabel was thin. Dark circles accented her sunken eyes. Paulette and James kissed her as she was sent off to delivery. Annabel was relaxed as the screen was set up between her shoulders and her belly. She accepted the spinal anesthetic and noted the medical personnel working around her, and then the precious sound of her baby's cry. She could only smile and peer into the newly formed fog penetrating the room. She searched for Josh's approval. He stood in the dark corner and smiled at her. He mouthed, "I love you." She responded, repeating his words.

"Ma'am, were you talking to us?"

"No, it was Josh."

Annabel's head was clear by the time Paulette and James stood next to her bed as she held the precious newborn.

"She's so very beautiful," said Paulette. "Do you have a name?"

"Yes. She's Esperanza. It means hope."

The Ride

SALLY P. GREEN

I TOOK A DRIVE with my dad one day in September 1976. He had a convertible MGB and it was a ride that would forever change my life.

We'd moved to Clinton, Mississippi, during one of the hottest summers on record. I was eleven years old, and it was our family's sixth move as my dad climbed the corporate ladder in the executive good ol' boys club. At last, he'd reached the top, Chief Executive Officer. He hauled us along with him like excess luggage, something to be dropped off and dealt with later.

To make amends for moving again, my dad bought my mom a new station wagon and a luxurious home in a beautiful subdivision. The house was a long, split-level ranch, with narrow windows and a wide, manicured lawn. The Bekins moving van was already in the driveway and men were carrying our furniture into the house as we arrived.

We got out of the car and my dad lifted me up and swung me around like I was still two years old.

"Hey, pumpkin! Do you like it? Your old daddy's finally made the big league!" He kissed my cheek and beamed with pride as he surveyed the new house. My brother and I raced inside to claim our bedrooms, knowing the newness of the place would soon wear off.

Being the new kid in fifth grade wasn't easy, but I was getting familiar with the routine by this time and managed to make a few friends. Before long, my teacher figured out I was having trouble seeing the chalkboard and told my mother to take me to an eye doctor. The doctor discovered that I didn't just need glasses, I was borderline blind. I picked out a pair of super-cool, large, square-framed glasses with a fashionable notch cut out of the nosepiece. I marveled on the trip home at how the trees weren't just big green blobs—they had leaves! And the grass wasn't a green mass, it had blades! And the flowers had petals! On and on it went, my mother and brother giggling at my fascination with all things made clear.

I soon found that the kids at school didn't consider my glasses to be very cool. I was pummeled with taunts of "Four eyes!" "Wow, those are some real Coke bottles!" and other put-downs. At first, I was stunned by the insults, but my new friends assured me that I really sort of resembled Lynda Carter on the TV show *Wonder Woman* when she was wearing glasses and pretending to be a regular smart person.

One night, lost in the adventures of a new book, I had stayed up past my bedtime, hidden under the covers reading with a flashlight. I heard raised voices. Were my parents arguing? I turned off the light, got out of bed, and opened the door to my room.

I crept down the hall and peered around the corner into the living room. My dad stood at the bar, pouring brown liquid from a bottle into a crystal glass. My mother sat on the couch, her arms crossed, tears running down her face.

"You promised me you'd stop," she said. "You said if we moved here, it would be a new beginning for us."

"Look, you don't understand what it's like for me," he said. "You don't go to a job every day, like I do. You"—he crossed the room and jabbed his finger in her face—"get to sit around all day, watching your soap operas, gossiping with your little church friends, doing whatever the hell you please, while I'm the one putting up with shit all day long. So, you just shut up and mind your own business!" I noticed his voice slurred on the "s" sounds and he had stumbled while stepping down into the living room.

I blinked in shock. I'd never heard my dad speak to my mother like that. Confused, I silently tiptoed back down the hall to my room. I jumped into bed, pulled up the covers and threw a pillow over my head, trying to shut out the sounds of their voices.

I went to school the next day, pretending it was just another normal day in fifth grade. I never told anyone about the argument I had witnessed. Somehow, I knew it was something you weren't supposed to tell.

One evening, my dad called me to the living room. I watched as he poured a glass of the brown liquid I'd seen him pouring the night he and my mother had argued.

"Come sit and talk with me," he said, sipping the drink. "Mom's at Cub Scouts with your brother. Tell me about your day." He sat down and patted the sofa cushion. I settled in beside him, pushing my glasses up my nose with my index finger, which had become a habit, as they seemed to constantly be sliding down.

So, I told him about Billy Bowen and how annoying he was and that I finished second out of all the girls at Phys Ed that day when we had to run a mile. I made an A on my English test, I said, and we watched a film in Science that showed an x-ray of a skeleton swallowing something liquid. It was gross.

My dad laughed and poured another drink. Then another, and another, lost in his thoughts, no longer interested in my day. As the minutes ticked by, I fidgeted, toying with the hem of my flowered blouse, examining my fingernails and pulling at loose strings on the couch.

"Hey, why don't we go for a drive, just me and you?" my dad said.

I sensed something was wrong with that, but didn't know exactly what. "Okay," I said.

"We can take my MGB and put the top down, that would be fun, wouldn't it?"

I hesitated, staring at the shag carpet rug on the floor. "Yes, sir."

He jumped up, knocking his knee against the coffee table, stumbling and spilling his drink down the front of his shirt. He cursed and wiped at the fresh stain, then looked at me and smiled.

"Sorry, pumpkin. Pardon my language."

We got into the little car, backed out of the driveway, and were soon on Highway 49, heading north toward Yazoo City. My dad hadn't put the top down like he'd said he would.

"I've got an idea. This will be so much fun," he said, looking over at me. "On the count of three, you grab that little lever up there and we'll pop the top on this baby and see what happens!"

"But Dad, we're going, like, fifty miles an hour. Won't that be dangerous?" I pushed my glasses up.

"Nah, it'll be fun! It'll be like a science experiment—physics or something like that. Ready, now? One, two, three!"

On the count of three, I reached up, just like he'd said, and pulled the release lever for the convertible top. My hand snapped away from the lever as wind blasted into the car and blew the top away from my grasp. A whirlwind slammed into my face, whipping my hair around and almost pulling my glasses off. I shrunk down in terror, trying to make myself as small as possible.

As the wind surged into the car, the convertible top made an ominous creaking noise, forced up by the sudden pressure. For one harrowing moment, the car seemed to rise from the road, rubber tires detaching from black tar asphalt. The car slowed, for a split second propelled backwards by the violent burst of incoming air. I heard a horrible tearing sound as the vinyl roof of the car began to split, then cringed as it completely ripped away from the little car, flying off in the wind like a lost kite and landing somewhere on the road behind us.

I screamed, my piercing shrieks of fright mingling with the roaring wind. I don't think my dad heard me wailing as I grabbed at the car door in desperation, afraid I would be the next thing to go flying out of the car. My screams subsided into tears, making my face slippery wet and causing my glasses to slide farther and farther down my nose.

"Woooo hoooo!" he whooped. "Yeah, boy! That was one wild ride, wasn't it!" He looked over at me, his eyes blazing with excitement, his mouth open in an ecstatic grin. He shook his fist in the air and laughed, oblivious to my tears.

After a moment, my distress registered with him and he slowed the car. He pulled over and parked, the MGB listing to the side as two wheels settled into the red dirt on the shoulder of the road and two remained on the pavement. He began stroking my head.

"Pumpkin, what's wrong? Why are you crying? There's nothing to be afraid of. That was exciting, wasn't it?" He paused. My sobbing had dwindled into jerky sniffles and I couldn't stop running my hands around my knees, over and around, over and around, feeling the rough fabric of blue jeans against my palms.

"Hey, I'm sorry if that scared you. I didn't mean for it to. I thought it would be great! It was fun, wasn't it? Aw, come on," he said, nudging me with his elbow. "Wasn't it just a teeny, weeny bit fun?" He leaned toward me, his face too close to mine, holding his thumb and forefinger together to indicate a small amount. He moved them closer together. "Maybe this much?"

I took a deep breath, pushed my glasses up and looked at him. I tried to smile. "Yeah, Dad, that—that was a little fun." I sniffed again, wiping my nose and face with trembling hands.

"I knew it!" He clapped his hands together and laughed. "I knew there was a daredevil in there! That's my girl!" He gave my shoulder several rough smacks and ruffled my hair.

I stared at the floor, mute with shock, until I heard a noise. Snoring? I looked over at my dad. His head was cocked back against the headrest, his mouth wide open and his hands limp across his legs. He had gone to sleep! I reached over and shook his arm.

"Dad," I said. There was no response. "Dad?" Still no reaction. "Dad, wake up! We need to go home! We can't just stay out here on the side of the road. Dad . . . I don't know what to do! Daddy?" He was still and heavy, his snoring deep and throaty. I slumped in my seat.

Mosquitoes buzzed around my ears and the sun began to descend over the cotton fields that lined up to the highway in straight rows like the lines on my wide ruled notebook paper at school. I reached over and turned the key in the ignition, shutting the car off. No point in running out of gas while my dad took a nap.

After thinking about what I should do, I opened the passenger door and got out of the car. I began walking in the direction we had come. It seemed like a long way, but I reminded myself that I had come in second place in the one-mile run in Phys Ed, and I could do this.

When I reached the area where the roof of the car lay in a tangled mess, I walked around, inspecting it. Metal arms protruded at various angles from the ripped vinyl. I picked up one side and realized it was much heavier than it looked. I yanked and pulled and strained until I had moved it off the road, then heaved and pushed until it was more or less rolled up. From there, I dragged it through the dirt and weeds back to the car, a few steps at a time, taking frequent breaks to catch my breath and readjust the heap that had once been the roof of the little convertible. Cars and trucks passed by, and one honked, but no one stopped to help.

By the time I got back to the car, the sky had turned an inky black, smeared with gray-purple clouds. A glowing, yellow moon illuminated the round cotton bolls in the fields and frogs and crickets chirped in an alternating chorale. With a groan, I hoisted the top up and over the side of the car. The metal pieces scraped and screeched along the side of the car and landed with a loud THUMP in the small space behind the front seats.

The noise woke my dad from his slumber. He jumped in his seat, snorting and punching with his arms.

"What!" he yelled. "Who's there?"

I collapsed into the passenger seat of the car and slammed the door. "It's just me, Dad," I said, weariness in my voice, sweat trailing down my back. My shirt and jeans were stained red-brown with dirt from my long haul back to the car with the recovered framework of the roof.

He squinted at me, as if realizing for the first time that I was with him. He twisted around, staring at the spidery contraption sticking up from behind the seat, then at me again, then at the back of the car. He made a

162

noise of surprise, reached back and ran his hand over the jagged scar left by the abrupt detachment of the car's roof.

"Huh. Would you look at that. Ripped clean off! It's gonna cost a pretty penny to fix that. Boy, is your mother gonna be mad at me when she finds out what happened to this car. Well . . ." He exhaled, placed both hands on the steering wheel, and stared straight ahead, as if giving deep thought to the situation. He glanced at me.

"What do you say, let's go home, pumpkin."

I pushed my glasses up. "Yeah, Dad. Let's go home," I said.

He revved up the engine, turned onto the highway, and we headed for home.

Moving the Finish Line

MELANIE NOTO

"THEY GIVE HIM TWO DAYS."

"That's all?" Rosa's ice blue eyes widened, the motion flattening her wrinkles and taking a good five years off her face. She clucked low in her throat. "My goodness. Beatrice must be a basket case."

"She's in his room. Knitting."

"You don't say?" Rosa shoved her purse under her arm and plopped down beside Emily on the low waiting room couch. "She always did like to knit."

"Started with a scarf," Lynnette said with a smirk. Her bobbed salon-colored hair swished as she tossed a devotional guide onto a side table. "It grew into an afghan."

"Now she has a bedspread." Emily closed her magazine and looked at Lynnette. She, Rosa, and Emily had been friends stretching back to 1971 when their boys were in kindergarten together at Aunt Marie's Little Blessings. The school was considered one of the best at the time in their bustling hometown of Jackson, Mississippi. Beatrice and Robert had endured their share of problems, even back then, most caused by Robert's roving eye. Now, he was dying—and Beatrice was knitting herself into a corner.

Rosa settled back against the stained blue cushions. "Knitting calms her nerves."

"I think she's trying to forget." Emily had seen the pain in Beatrice's eyes over the years. She'd tried to hide it, but it was always there. Pain, along with a healthy dose of fury. "Or maybe she's knitting him a burial shroud."

"Oh, wouldn't that be a hoot?" Lynette laughed. "The afghan is bright orange."

"She's always been fond of loud colors, probably because Robert prefers a neutral palette." Rosa lifted her nose and pulled a romance novel out of her purse. "Mind if I read? Takes my mind off his poor soul."

"Poor Robert?" Emily scoffed. "You can't mean that. He brought the heart attack on himself with his wild lifestyle."

Rosa opened her mouth as if to retort, but snapped it shut without doing so.

"Well. I hate to end this fun party, but I need to go." Lynnette bounced to her feet. For sixty-five, she had a helluva lot of energy. Emily envied her. "Ed is expecting me to cook breakfast for supper."

"You have that every Saturday night, don't you?" Emily smiled. Those two had a picture-perfect marriage. "You have for years, even when the kids were home."

"Oh, yes. It's a Wise family tradition."

"Well, for heaven's sake—don't let Robert's impending death cause you to dispense with one of your precious family traditions." Rosa pulled out a cigarette and a fancy silver lighter. Her mottled fingers shook.

Emily's eyebrows flew up. "You can't smoke in here."

"That's right." Lynnette frowned at Rosa. "This is a hospital—and I resent your remark about my family. Everybody grieves in his or her own way. Sticking with tradition eases my mind."

"Oh, please." Rosa rolled her eyes. "I suppose you'll tell me next that Beatrice is pouring her grief into that atrocious orange monstrosity she's knitting."

"That's right." Lynnette lifted her chin. "She is."

Emily tightened her lips. "She's knitting to keep from crying."

"No, she's not." Lynette put her fists on her hips. "Her life with Robert has been holy hell since day one."

"That's right," Beatrice snapped, her words carrying over the annoying whir of the air conditioner. "And it will continue to be, as long as he's still breathing."

"Beatrice!" Lynnette pressed a hand to her heart. "Oh, dear. I didn't see you come in. How is Robert?"

"Hanging on by a thread."

"You should be ashamed," Rosa murmured, looking at Beatrice. Her downturned face turned bright red. She crossed her legs and glared down at her book as if infuriated by the unfolding story.

Emily scooted to the edge of her seat. "Do they give him any hope?"

"He's had an experimental drug." Beatrice pursed her lips. "It's touch and go, thanks to his weak heart valves. Surgery's out of the question. So, who knows?"

"He'll live." Lynette tapped her foot. "His kind always do."

"Not forever," Emily said with a sniff. "No matter what kind of man he is."

"True." Beatrice scowled. "But if he makes it, we'll be making some changes at our house. Important changes."

"Is that what his doctor wants?" Emily wondered what Dr. Jones might ask of Robert. A new diet? An exercise routine?

Beatrice shook her head. "No. Robert cheated on me—again. I've put up with his philandering for years, but no more. I'm tired of looking the other way."

"Don't believe everything you hear." Rosa buried her face in her book.

"Please, Rosa," Beatrice said. "It's true."

"Oh, dear." Lynette's mouth dropped open. She sidled closer to

Beatrice. "I've heard rumors, but I had no idea they were true. Do you have proof?"

"Why, yes. I know everything." Beatrice's nostrils flared. "Well, everything except the brazen hussy's name."

Lynette lifted her eyebrows, while Emily looked away. She wasn't about to tell what she knew. Not with Robert on his deathbed.

"Enough about my scheming husband's extracurricular activities." Beatrice rubbed her weary bloodshot eyes. "I need more yarn."

"Oh, honey. I'll bring you some," Lynette said. "Is tomorrow soon enough?"

"No." Beatrice sighed. "I need it tonight, if I want to outlast him."

"This isn't a race." Rosa raised her head. "Robert is dying."

"Since when are you so concerned?" Lynette eyed her with suspicion.

Rosa closed her book and shoved it into her purse. "Since no one else is."

"Bah. He may be dying, but *I'm* the one in pain." Beatrice sneered. "With him, life has always been a race. First to the finish line in everything. He has to win, no matter the cost. Has to have the swankiest house, the classiest car. The youngest floozy."

"This one is young?" Lynette leaned close. "How young?"

"Hell, I don't know." Beatrice threw up her hands. "Robert's lived his whole life as a race. But now, with death looming, he's suddenly the tortoise instead of the hare."

"Oh, for God's sake, Beatrice. Have some compassion," Rosa said. "He's your *husband*."

"He cheated on me," Beatrice snapped. "My compassion only goes so far—and it certainly doesn't apply to the bitch who brought on his heart attack." Her orthopedic shoes squeaked as she whipped around and stormed off down the hall.

"Whoa," Lynette murmured with a wry twist of her lips. "She's one angry woman."

"She sure is. Wouldn't you be?" Emily rose beside her. "What if you found out Ed had cheated on you?"

"Lazy Ed? Cheat?" Lynette emitted a sharp laugh and brought one well-manicured hand to her mouth. "He doesn't have the balls for that. Never did."

"Hush now. Any way you look at it, it's a sin." Rosa tucked her purse under her arm and pushed herself off the couch. Her knees popped.

Emily stared at her friend in amusement. Rosa was the youngest of the bunch, but she had the worst arthritis. Emily surmised it was because Rosa often acted like a schoolgirl, flirting with men in front of Hank, her beleaguered husband. The man was either a saint or totally blind—especially when it came to her latest fling:

Robert Burnett.

◆

Beatrice entered Robert's hospital room and peered down at her husband with contempt. She had forgiven him the first time, only a month into their marriage, after catching him in bed with his chirpy blond secretary. What a scene that had been. The bitch had screamed, Beatrice had cried, and Robert had sworn he'd never stray again.

The same scenario had played itself out many times over the years, until she had finally become numb to his despicable actions. Or so she'd thought. When she'd learned last month that he had again left the straight and narrow path—and this time, with someone from their church—she had been devastated. But she hadn't found out the name of the floozy who had lured him into bed.

She clenched her teeth. Her bitterness boiled over. Unable to look away from his placid face, she wrapped her hand around the plastic oxygen tube leading to his nose. If she gave it one long, vigorous squeeze—

The door burst inward, and Sue, Robert's attentive young pencil-thin nurse, popped in with an IV bag of fluids in her arms. She paused just inside the door, as if she were surprised to see Beatrice. She looked from them, to the giant afghan piled on the chair in the corner, and back to meet Beatrice's eyes. "Well, Mrs. Burnett. Have you finally finished your knitting project?"

"Oh, no." Beatrice turned so Sue couldn't see her let go of the oxygen tube and slowly lowered her hand. She edged back around and pasted a stiff smile on her face. "But I only have to complete the border."

"Wow. That's one big afghan."

"It's for Robert," she said, knowing exactly what she'd do with the awful orange monstrosity once he passed. She had knitted it to calm her frazzled nerves, but now—

The nurse smiled and stepped over to Robert's IV pole. "That's so sweet. I know he'll appreciate it."

"Oh, I doubt it," Beatrice murmured to herself as she moved away. She picked up the bulky afghan, lowered herself into her chair, and picked up her knitting needles. They gleamed like tiny swords in the meager light from the window.

The nurse bustled around for another moment or two, examining Robert's IV and checking his oxygen level, and then exited the room. A CNA came in almost as soon as she left to check the amount of urine in Robert's catheter bag.

Beatrice spoke to the man but didn't try to make conversation. She was too busy planning. Her mind whirred as her fingers whipped along the border of the afghan. *Orange.* She hated orange. The good thing was, so did Robert.

Her mouth curved in a devious smile. Knitting the afghan for Robert was simple poetic justice—like having him dying, tucked away in his lonely hospital bed with her by his side, rather than frolicking under the sheets with one of his many floozies after racing to some pricey Caribbean resort. He'd done that from time to time. She was sure of it.

Bastard. Her icy fingers flew. She would fix him.

If only Lynette would hurry up with that yarn.

◆

Emily didn't know what to say to Rosa. Her friend perched on the opposite side of the table in Mercy General's revamped cafeteria, devouring a slice of peach pie as if she didn't have a care in the world. Beside her was her latest read, an erotic romance called *Sex on Wheels,* her favorite kind of book to chain-read.

Rosa's surgically smoothed jowls stretched unnaturally as she struggled to chew the pie's tough crust. Watching her, Emily lost her appetite. She set down her fork. Anger washed over her as she thought of what Rosa had done. Unable to keep quiet another minute, she leaned over the table and glared at her friend.

"I know it was you with Robert." She lifted her chin.

Rosa looked up from her plate in surprise. "Excuse me?"

"You heard me." Emily plowed on, eager to confront the witch. "You were with him when he had his heart attack."

"I was *not*." The other woman gripped her fork with white knuckled fingers. "I was at home that night. Alone."

"Don't tell me that, because I know better. You parked your car down the block from Robert and Beatrice's house, where you always leave it whenever she's out and you go over there to sleep with Robert."

"I've never done any such thing."

"Don't bother lying, Rosa!" Emily bellowed with a glare. She was furious with herself for having kept quiet for so long. "I've known about your affair since day one. I went to see Beatrice the day you came back to town and saw you and Robert sucking face in the foyer. You didn't know I was outside, but I was, and I saw him lead you to the back of the house—and into their bedroom. You are despicable. Simply despicable!"

"My goodness. You think—oh, dear. I would *never*." Rosa pressed her free hand to her throat in a theatrical attempt at innocence, something she hadn't known since she was thirteen. "You know me better than that, Emily. You're my best friend."

"Some friend. You stole Tommy Livingston from me back in junior high, and you're still stealing men. Only now, they're married." Emily shook her head. *Once a slut, always a slut.* She edged forward to lessen the chance someone overhearing them. "You left before the ambulance got there, but you were with him. Your antics in bed were probably what triggered his heart attack."

"Your imagination must be working overtime." Rosa picked up a napkin and primly blotted her lips. "You've always liked to make up stories, so—"

"I don't make up stories. You'd better own up to this, or I'll tell Beatrice."

"Don't you dare threaten me you . . ." She gritted her teeth. "You . . . spinster!"

"Oh, please." Emily sat back and laughed. "That's the best you can do? I'm glad Joe died in Vietnam. If he hadn't, you probably would have slept with him, too. Poor Hank. He didn't know what he was getting himself into when he married you, did he?"

"Oh!" Rosa shoved her chair back so hard it hit the table behind her. She muttered a curse, rocketed to her feet, and snatched up her tray. "I don't have to sit here and listen to this. Consider yourself my *ex-friend*."

"That's fine by me. You're nothing but a two-timing hussy." Emily crossed her arms and glared at Rosa until she marched out of the cafeteria. She was acting like a child, but she couldn't help herself. Part of her still ached for the attention of the boy Rosa had stolen back in eighth grade. Her thievery had shattered Emily's self-confidence—and despite her marriage, she had never fully recovered. Damn Rosa for being such a pretty, practiced flirt. Married women shouldn't act that way.

Emily wiped her eyes and stood up. Maybe she should have that little talk with Beatrice after all. That would fix Rosa's little red wagon. Heart pounding, Emily dropped off her tray and headed back upstairs.

To her relief, Rosa wasn't in the waiting room. Maybe she'd gone home. Emily gripped her purse and marched down the hall toward Robert's room. A nurse walked toward her. Gathering her nerve, Emily stopped the woman.

"Excuse me," she said with uncertainty, "but I'd like to visit Mr. Daniels in room five-oh-seven-six. Is that all right?"

"Of course, once either his wife or his other visitor leaves." The nurse bobbed her bleached blond head. "He's only allowed two at a time."

"Who's in there with his wife?" Emily held her breath.

The nurse shrugged. "I don't know her name. I just saw her go in."

"All right, thank you. I'll just stick my head in, to ask if one of them is about to leave. If that's okay." Emily fixed her eyes on Robert's door. The other visitor had to be Rosa, who apparently had a pair of shiny brass balls.

The nurse nodded and continued down the hall toward the nurses' station.

Emily waited until the woman disappeared and then marched over to Robert's door. Fury skittered over her skin like a thousand tiny rodents' paws as she pushed the portal open and wrinkled her nose at the sharp odor of antiseptic wafting out. She paused to allow her vision to adjust to the low light in the room before slipping inside.

Sure enough, Rosa stood next to Beatrice, who perched rigidly on her chair by the window adding more length to that damned afghan. It had to be twenty feet long by now.

Emily allowed the door to drift shut. The dark room reminded her of a tomb, except for the annoying beep of the heart monitor beside Robert's bed. The noise set her teeth on edge. His eyes were closed. He had an oxygen cannula in his nose, and an IV pole gleamed like a sterling silver gallows beside his head.

"You're not supposed to be in here." Rosa narrowed her keen blue eyes. "He's allowed only two visitors at a time."

"The nurse said you were on your way out." Emily turned to look at Beatrice. "How are you, dear? Do you need anything?"

"Only that damned orange yarn Lynette promised to bring—and for the two of you to stop yammering." She scowled at Rosa. "Why are you still here?"

"Well, I never." Rosa stuck her nose in the air. "I was planning to sit with you and keep you company this evening. But I guess I won't."

"I don't need your company." A nasty sneer curled the corners of Beatrice's lips. "Emily is here. You should go home and spend a little quality time with Hank."

"Posh." Rosa sighed. "No time with that man has any quality to it."

"Shame on you." Emily fixed the other woman with a knowing stare. "Hank is your *husband*. He'll feel neglected if you stay here much longer."

"You don't know anything about my marriage. What I've had put up with, or—"

"What *you've* had to put up with?" Emily broke in with a laugh.

"What about Hank? He's a damned saint to have put up with *you* for thirty-five years."

"That's enough," Beatrice snapped. She lowered her knitting and released a weary sigh. "Get out, Rosa. I need to talk to Emily. Alone."

"Fine." Rosa glowered at Emily before spearing Beatrice with her fiery gaze. "I'll pray for both of you." She tossed her gray head and stormed out.

Emily didn't know if Rosa meant she'd pray for her and Beatrice, or for Beatrice and Robert. Either way, she couldn't help but doubt her former friend's connection with the good Lord. He tended to frown upon adultery.

"I must've touched a nerve," Beatrice murmured with a smirk.

Emily sighed. "Yes. She doesn't want us to talk."

"I suppose she has a logical explanation for that."

"She has an explanation, all right." Emily wondered just how much to tell her friend. She met Beatrice's concerned gaze. "But I'm not sure you want to hear it."

"Rosa has always operated on a different plane." The woman shook her head. "She and I have never seen eye to eye on much of anything."

"Have you noticed anything strange about her lately?"

"Not really." She furrowed her brow. "Why? What's she done?"

"I hate to be the one to tell you, but—" Emily bit her lip and peered down at her hands. "She's the one."

"She's the one . . . what?" Beatrice frowned. "Go on. Please."

"Robert was with Rosa the night he had his heart attack."

"Oh. My. God."

"I didn't want to tell you. I debated. But you deserve to know. She's a slut. Always has been. Stealing men is her favorite pastime."

"Robert and *Rosa?*" Beatrice's mouth fell open. Her face flushed tomato-red.

Emily nodded. "Unfortunately, yes."

"Damn him." Her throat jerked. "He's cheated on me for years, you know. I never said anything, because it didn't matter. We haven't slept together in ages. I was afraid of what I might catch. He slept with anything he could get his pecker into. Secretaries, waitresses, friends. I just never figured he'd sleep with *Rosa*."

"Beatrice!" Emily covered her mouth. She was sixty-five years old, and the unexpected mention of a man's private parts still made her blush. Probably because Beatrice was talking about *Robert's* privates and Rosa in the same sentence. Emily did not want that picture etched into her mind. Her cheeks flamed.

"It's true," Beatrice said, her knitting needles clacking like ill-fitting false teeth. "The man has the morals of a weasel in heat."

"I don't blame you for being sarcastic. You've had a major shock."

"You bet I have." She halted her knitting and lifted her eyes to Emily's. "You know, when we married, Robert vowed to be faithful. That lasted all of one month. I should've known he'd eventually stray with one of my friends."

"I didn't know."

"Most folks didn't. I kept it hidden." A familiar ache squeezed her heart. She shook her head. "Thought I'd conquered the hurt, but I was dead wrong."

"I'm sorry."

"Me, too." Tears filled Beatrice's eyes. "Because this one cuts me to the bone. He slept with *Rosa*. Oh, my God."

"She's a man-stealer."

"You can say that again." Beatrice sucked in a shaky breath and peered down at the growing pile of orange on her lap. Orange, like sunshine. A commodity she'd seen too little of lately. Sunshine was for happiness. Not grief, anger, or shame.

A familiar children's taunt echoed through her head: *Robert and Rosa, sitting in a tree. K-i-s-s-i-n-g.* Those foolish words helped to dispel her sadness and allowed an angry blue flame to flare to life inside her chest. A flame so hot it seared her heart. She wished Emily would go home so she could take care of business.

Emily folded her hands.

"Sweetheart . . ." Hoping to prod her friend along, Beatrice dropped the needles into the pocket of her smock, balled up the afghan, and surged to her feet. "I need to be alone for a little while. So, if you don't mind . . ."

"Are you sure?" Emily frowned. "I don't mind staying."

"I'm positive." Beatrice deliberately kept her eyes off Robert, who was still breathing thanks to the damned tube in his nose.

Emily picked up her purse. "All right. You know how to reach me if—"

"I certainly do," she broke in. "I won't hesitate to call if I need you."

"Promise you'll let me know the second anything happens." Emily grabbed Beatrice's hand and gave it a squeeze. "I'll check on you in the morning."

"That would be great." Beatrice squeezed back. "You're a good friend."

"So are you." Emily let go. "Try to get some rest, okay?"

"I'll try." Beatrice plastered on a fake smile. "Thanks for everything."

"You're welcome." Emily smiled. "Oh, and don't forget—Lynette should be back soon with your yarn."

Damn. Beatrice had forgotten about Lynette. She'd have to work fast.

Coughing to mask her annoyance as she walked Emily to the door, she hugged her friend and ushered her out into the hall. Once the portal whooshed shut and Beatrice was once again alone with Robert, she turned toward the hospital bed where he lay still as death. The nurse would be in soon to take his vitals.

Desperate to get the job done before the woman came in, Beatrice crept across the cream-colored tiles to stand beside her husband. His eyes were closed, and his face was slack. Even so, wrinkles bunched around his mouth like a series of tiny parentheses. His jowls trembled with every breath. He looked so *old.*

"The race is almost over," she whispered. "For you, anyway."

She pulled several antiseptic wipes from the container by the bed and carefully wiped down the oxygen tube where she'd squeezed it earlier in the day. Then she wrapped another one around the tube and fisted it in her right hand, pinching it closed with her thumb and forefingers. All she needed now was time.

The heart monitor kept up its steady beat—until Robert's mouth fell open. His eyes rolled back, and he gasped like a landed fish. The monitor faltered. Erratic beats filled the air. Erratic beats pounding the truth into Beatrice's soul.

She tightened her hold on the tube. Her nerve endings tingled, and she became aware of Robert, twitching. A loud wheeze rattled his chest. Cool air spewed from the overhead vents and dried the perspiration on her forehead. She shivered.

The beeps grew farther apart. Robert's face grew slack.

Footsteps pounded down the hallway. Forcing herself to remain calm, Beatrice took out one of her knitting needles and pierced the tube where it met the tank.

The door flew open.

She released the tube and returned the needle to the pocket of her smock. Turning away from the bed, she wiped her eyes with a wad of tissues.

"Thank God you're here," she said to the nurse. "He . . . he stopped breathing. I didn't know what to do."

"Step aside, please." The nurse eyed the monitor and checked the tubes. A frown marred her brow. "I don't understand what—"

"He was fine just a second ago." Happy the nurse was confused, Beatrice backed away from the bed. Her heart pounded. She hoped the woman wouldn't discover the hole in the tube until much later. "Nurse, I—"

The monitor's shrill, piercing beeps coalesced into one long squeal.

"He's coding!" Her face pale, the nurse snatched up the phone and called for help. Then she began chest compressions, awkwardly pushing on Robert's thick chest with both hands. "Come on, Mr. Burnett. Come on. Damn it."

Just let him go! Sick to her stomach, Beatrice tiptoed around the bed.

A bevy of hospital personnel poured through the door. A nurse dragged in a defibrillator. A doctor loped in and grabbed the paddles. They and several others surrounded Robert, poking and prodding him before ripping open his hospital gown.

"Clear!" the doctor shouted. Everyone stepped away from the bed as he rubbed the paddles together, then pressed them to Robert's bare chest. Electricity jolted through him. His back arched off the bed.

The squeal blipped, but resumed its annoying cry. Robert dropped back onto the bed. Still unconscious. Beatrice choked back her glee.

The doctor upped the amperage and yelled, "Clear!" before shocking Robert again. No luck. The doctor's face reddened as he pressed the paddles to Robert's chest a third time, but Beatrice's husband simply flopped back onto the bed like a dead fish, his pale, flabby body already growing cold.

The doctor glanced at the nurse, then peered up at the clock on the wall. "Time of death," he murmured with a deep sigh. "Eleven twenty-two P.M." Beatrice pressed her hands over her mouth and prayed for forgiveness. The nurse turned. "I'm so sorry, Mrs. Burnett."

"You did everything you could." Beatrice lowered her hands and crept toward Robert. She forced a waver into her voice. "Oh, my poor dear."

The healthcare workers slipped from the room one at a time. The defibrillator disappeared. Finally, only Beatrice, Robert, and the doctor remained.

"His heart was in bad shape after the heart attack," the doctor said.

"I know," she said. "You showed me pictures. I'd hoped he'd recover, but it must have been his time."

"I thought he was strong enough to allow his heart to heal."

"Apparently not." Beatrice swallowed, hard. Her husband's cheeks had an eerie gray tint, and his eyes were closed. The odor of death surrounded him. Nausea bubbled up her throat. She wanted the doctor to leave.

He walked over and took her hand. She didn't look up. She couldn't. Tears of relief had flooded her eyes.

"Would you like to have a few moments alone with him?"

"Y-yes, please," she murmured, wiping moisture from her lashes. "If you don't mind. I'd like to say goodbye."

"Of course." He squeezed her hand, released it, and turned toward the door. "Let me know when you're done, and I'll send someone in to prepare his body. You might want to gather his things."

"I will. Thank you." She nodded and waited for him to leave. Once the door closed behind him, she took a deep breath.

Robert is dead. She braced herself, expecting grief to pummel her as the realization set in, but instead she relished the relief running through her veins. Relief, tempered by a tiny thread of guilt that wound its way around her wounded heart.

I'm a murderer. Swallowing hard, she looked out the window into the night. *Wait—no. Robert was dying. I simply moved the finish line.*

Beatrice scurried over to her chair, picked up the afghan, and spread it over Robert's prone form. She started to tuck the orange monstrosity around her philandering husband when the door burst open. She turned away from the bed as Lynette plunged into the room cradling three skeins of bright orange yarn. Her friend stopped short and gaped at her.

"Oh, hon." Her friend sobbed. "They . . . they told me about Robert. I'm so sorry."

"Yes, he's gone." Beatrice pulled the afghan over her husband's face. "So, unfortunately, I have no more use for the yarn."

"It's all right. I'll call Rosa and Emily." Lynette dumped the yarn into a chair and took out her phone. "They'll both want to know. Especially Rosa. Robert's heart attack really upset her."

"I'm sure it did." Beatrice muffled a snort and shooed her friend away from the bed. "Go on, now. Please. I need some time alone with him. I'm sure you understand."

"Oh, of course you do. I'm so sorry." Her face wreathed in sadness, Lynnette turned and slipped out the door without another word.

Beatrice turned back to her husband's shrouded body. "The race is over now, Robert," she whispered with a smile. "*I* won."

He, of course, didn't answer.

She reached into her pocket and touched her knitting needles. They were cool against her fingertips. A smirk tilted her lips.

"Guess who's next?" Her words lingered in the air. She curled her lips in a brittle smile. "That's right, dear husband. *Rosa,* the husband stealer."

Elvis and Linda Lou

JP LUBY

In 1961 I was a junior at Yazoo County High School. Linda Lou was a sophomore.

Turned out we had both signed up for glee club, which met on Tuesdays and Thursdays in the auditorium. We were lined up on the bleachers to rehearse for the upcoming Christmas program. Tenors stood behind the altos, and to my delight, I somehow ended up directly behind Linda Lou.

As we concluded "Silver Bells," she turned around, and with a red lipstick smile, said, "On that last note, you sounded just like Elvis Presley!"

While our music teacher, Miss Harrington, worked with the soprano section, Linda Lou turned once again. "I just love Elvis!"

Then, with uncharacteristic boldness, I sang, "I . . . I'll have a blue Christmas without you . . ." into her curly raven hair.

She whirled around and chortled in her singular deep Southern accent, "Don't get carried away—it was just that one note!"

The first time I saw Belinda Louise Underwood was the first day of second grade. My classmates and I were following our soon-to-be second grade teacher, Miss Blaine, to our new classroom, but our procession came to a halt when Anne Alice Atkinson dropped her coin purse, scattering her life savings. As she methodically gathered up the coins, I happened to be positioned in front of the door to room one-twelve.

My first grade teacher, Mrs. Fisackerly, was in there gently prodding tearful mothers from their mournful children. I smiled—crying is what *little* kids do, not us older, wiser second graders. Then I noticed a girl in a blue dress gazing out the window.

I concluded that her mother had left and she was probably crying. But then, as if I had called her name, she turned, and her blue eyes looked directly into mine. She wasn't crying; she was smiling.

Harris Devlin jolted me from my trance by nudging me forward— Anne Alice's coins had been secured. As we proceeded down the hall, I was oblivious to everything and everyone. My mind was still saturated by that smile.

I had a crush, and I didn't even know what a crush was. I did, however, find out her name—Belinda Louise Underwood, or Linda Lou, as everyone called her.

A few days later I overheard some girls in the cafeteria talking about "the new girl." She and her parents had just moved to Yazoo City from out of state. Her family moved a lot because her daddy worked for a big company that sent him all over the country.

I didn't catch another glimpse of Linda Lou until several months later one windy March morning as the kids in my class lined up on the sidewalk to go back inside after recess. Miss Blaine directed me to go fetch Marshall Porter, who was lingering once again on the merry-go-round. As I zipped past the slide and the swings, I nearly ran into a girl hanging upside-down on the monkey bars. It was Linda Lou.

Though I think I blushed at the sight of her light blue panties, I also recognized her smile, even upside-down.

"Belinda Louise Underwood! You straighten yourself up right now!" Miss Blaine had noticed her, too.

Both boys and girls could play on the swings, the slide, and the merry-go-ground—but not the monkey bars: girls wore dresses in the 1950s.

Miss Blaine's distinctive nasal whine got me moving again, and I negotiated my way around the blue-eyed, blue-pantied girl to collect Marshall from the merry-go-round. As he and I caught up with the rest of our group, I saw Linda Lou skipping over to her class's line as it started inside the building.

Linda Lou had smiled at me *again.*

I saw Linda Lou a number of times over the next couple years, but always from a distance—and, in elementary school, boys didn't mingle with girls anyway because, hey, girls had cooties. I didn't think Linda Lou did, though I never told my friends this.

It also didn't help that, at that time, my family lived about six miles outside town, and when children weren't at school they were expected to help around the farm. Plus, Linda Lou's family went to a different church. And then to top it off, her family moved away just before I started sixth grade.

For a time I was quite beside myself, though I didn't know why. I got into trouble a lot, with my folks wondering what'd gotten into me. But time passed, and sometime in the ninth grade I became aware there were other girls at school and I seemingly forgot Linda Lou for a while.

But at the beginning of sophomore year, I saw a familiar face in the hallway one day just before lit class—it was Linda Lou! Her family had moved back to Yazoo City—for a while, anyway.

I was older now and nowhere as shy as I used to be—but around Linda Lou, I was still in the second grade and a playground away. One day I went for broke and sat across from her at lunch in the cafeteria. I tried to make small talk before several of her girlfriends materialized to visit and chat, and I quickly became a third wheel. Linda Lou was polite, but I finished my sandwich and picked up my tray.

Besides glee club, we shared just one class the rest of my high school years—geometry—where our young, red-headed teacher, Miss Callihan, had taken it herself only a few years prior. My desk was second in the row by the windows, while Linda Lou's sat in the middle of the room.

One extremely hot day in May, Miss Callihan had given us a test on chapters ten and eleven. There were no air conditioners, and forty-eight teenagers generate substantial heat. The open windows and oscillating fans only seemed to evenly distribute the humidity.

It suddenly occurred to me to turn and glance at Linda Lou. Normally I would have ignored such a notion and not chanced the consequential embarrassment; however, nothing related to Linda Lou had ever been normal. My eyes darted from Miss Callihan, who was grading papers, to my test paper. I just had to turn and look at Linda Lou.

One more quick glance. Miss Callihan was totally focused on her papers.

Slowly, furtively, I turned my head to my right. My peripheral vision hazily encompassed other students using their rulers and protractors. Linda Lou, however, was slowly fanning herself with her test paper. Our eyes met. She blinked, then smiled, as she continued fanning herself.

It couldn't have been more than five seconds when I heard Miss Callihan gently clear her throat. I quickly faced forward. But her eyes were not unkind, and I think I saw a faint smile.

I made up my mind to try and talk with Linda Lou after school that day, even though I stood a good chance of missing the bus, but I didn't care. After the last class, I quickly gathered my books from my locker and made my way down the hall past the other students toward Linda Lou's locker—where I stopped dead right in front of the chemistry class door.

Linda Lou was smiling and talking to Thomas.

Smiling and talking—and holding hands. With Thomas.

Thomas Parker Hammons, who, *surprise*, was a jock. A Troy Donahue look-alike—tall, green eyes, blond—he always wore expensive clothes and English Leather. I found out later Linda Lou called him "Tom Parker."

I made the bus.

My Aunt Lida Pearl was a devoted Elvis fan. She would press her ear to the radio and cry whenever an Elvis song came on. And one Friday evening, she insisted I accompany her to see his newest movie, *Loving You*, which was playing at the Dixie picture show.

As we stood in line at the concession stand before the movie started, I spotted Linda Lou and Thomas strolling through the lobby.

My aunt and I entered the auditorium with our Cokes and popcorn, and she happened to pick a couple of seats just three rows behind Linda Lou and Thomas. I don't remember much about the movie, but I do recall that Linda Lou had her head nestled against Thomas's shoulder for most of it. And, when Elvis sang "Loving You," she slowly lifted her head and kissed him.

It had taken a while, but I finally realized my crush on Linda Lou was a one-way street.

Our graduation ceremony was perfunctory. I vaguely remember marching down the aisle as Mrs. Harrington played "Pomp and Circumstance" on the school's aging piano. Brother Isonhood, a Baptist preacher, mouthed a prayer. I gave the salutatory address. The choir sang "Dreams for Sale." Our principal, Mr. Abernathy, soberly reminded us to ". . . make something of ourselves."

Linda Lou would never graduate from our high school, however, because her family had moved yet again just before the holidays. But that was okay. It was over and done with.

Since the first of that year, I had been tentatively seeing Susan Mussberger. She was cute, brunette, slightly taller than I, and first-chair clarinet. I say "tentatively" because we had occasional spats. But we always somehow made up. This happened so much that folks said it was like we were married. And seven years later they would be proved right.

After garnering a BA in English from Mississippi State University, I eventually returned to the Delta and taught for thirty-five years—and in some of the same classrooms I'd shared with Linda Lou. I hadn't heard much about her since high school; however, at our third class reunion, Harris Devin, a proud Ole Miss Rebel, had brought his yearbook, *The Reveille*, and while browsing through it, I came across some photos of Linda Lou!

Her family must have moved back to Mississippi, or, at least, she'd come back to Mississippi to attend Ole Miss. Looking through the pages,

I saw that she had been selected a beauty. Her face covered an entire page, and although her smile was subdued, her solemn beauty was still captivating. Someone mentioned she'd married an Ole Miss alumnus.

One day sometime later I was bathing my Shih Tzu in the backyard when Judith, my six-year-old granddaughter, brought me the phone. It was my cousin Karen.

"Did you hear about Linda Lou Underwood?"

◆

After a brief service at St. Luke's Methodist Church, I proceeded to Cedar Grove Cemetery about ten miles northeast of Yazoo City on Graball Road. It was an old cemetery with intriguing tombstones in the oldest sections. A few of the original cedars still survived, but most had surrendered their spaces to magnolia and pin oaks.

As I drove, reminiscences of my schooldays flooded my mind. I had rarely seen Linda Lou away from school. Although we lived only a few miles apart, our religious, economic, and social circles had unfortunately not overlapped. And then every summer I was sent to visit with my grandparents in Attala County. It was all just *stuff* that happened along the way, but that is how life goes.

Six months later, I drove back to the cemetery. It was Christmas Day, and we'd had a light, dusty snow, unusual for Mississippi. A stiff breeze wafted the snow around her tombstone. As my gloved fingers traced Linda Lou's name etched into the granite, I reflected on the smiles, the brief conversations, the moments.

I sat on the stone bench for a few minutes. Then I sang "Blue Christmas" to her.

Every note.

The Thornton Line

LINDA RAITERI

S HE HAD A VISION of a ballerina—a doll with articulated joints, like a marionette, but who could maintain any position it was put in.

She worked on the sketches during the long winter evenings while her husband Dan relaxed in the big house with Karl and Elvira. Oblivious to the cold wind swirling snow outside the one-room cabin, unmindful of the chill that seeped in under the door and numbed her toes and the tips of her fingers, Diana sketched and erased and sketched again, joyfully, patiently, silently.

◆

Before Dan, she had not felt this kind of joy—the joy of bringing an idea, a glimmering vision into reality. She had met him at the University gallery where a few of his drawings were on exhibit. They began talking and found that they didn't need complete sentences to communicate. A word, a phrase would do it.

On their first date, Dan Thornton took Diana Simmons to the

waterfront where they climbed to the top of an abandoned warehouse. They sat cross-legged on a gravel and tar roof. Under the slender silver crescent of the new moon, his voice rising soft as the night, he named her an Indian Princess, a witch, a moonlit high black swan. As Jupiter reached to embrace the moon in the silent firmament, she called him Daniel—God is my judge—and gently stroked his face.

In the autumn, they married. They threw their few belongings into a VW bus and Dan, unable to adjust to the rhythm of Diana's driving, drove them to Montana where they apprenticed themselves to Karl and Elvira Kruger who made wooden toys in their small country workshop.

Mrs. Kruger set them down at the trestle table in front of a dancing fire and served them hot apple pie and spiced tea. Mr. Kruger cleared away the empty plates and laid out the plans for three new toys. He lovingly smoothed the papers in front of Dan and Diana who wrapped their arms around each other at the end of the evening and strolled silently to the cottage where they would live. Each held an image of the two of them living contentedly to old age surrounded by the things they loved and the toys they would make.

Before they went to bed, Diana unpacked. The oriental fan that Dan had given her she placed open on a shelf. She found a niche for the radio they had received as a wedding present. She placed the small Art Nouveau lamp she had given Dan next to the bed. "If only we had a dog," one said. "And a cat and a goat," the other answered. The last thing either heard before going to sleep was the other whisper, "I love you."

In the middle of the night, Diana awoke shivering. As the objects in the room began to take shape, she remembered with extraordinary joy where she was. She peeked one toe and then another out from under the comforter and, squinting her eyes in anticipation of the cold floor, set her feet gingerly on the rag rug. She slipped her shoes on and scurried across the room to turn up the heater.

There seemed to be too much light in the room and as she glanced out the window, she saw snow falling in giant white rushes against their new home. She paused at the window in wonder at the utter silence snow contained.

Every morning they bundled up and walked to the big house where Elvira had steaming oatmeal or pancakes or eggs and biscuits waiting. Then Karl, Elvira, Dan, and Diana went to the workshop where they worked side by side carving and sanding and painting the wooden toys.

During the long blue-white winter they seldom saw anyone other than their new family. Dan and Diana slept late on Sundays while the Krugers went to church. Sometimes they went to the nearest town for a movie or to pick up a few paperbacks. Sometimes they drove out along this road or that road to see what enchantments they could find in this, to them, unknown territory.

In the spring, when the first leaves began to bud, Karl took them to the shops where his toys were sold. By summer, when the trees were in full bloom, he sent Dan and Diana out to make deliveries and get new orders. Over dinner, they told each other about the sales they had made that day and the characters they had met. They were in a different motel room every night and the only people they saw twice in the same day were each other.

Back in the cozy warmth of the Kruger household with winter approaching and the hubbub of their production season, Dan and Diana fell back into the rhythm of working together. In the evenings, Diana helped Elvira with the dishes then retired to read or work on her ballerina.

First she drew the figure wearing a tutu, hair pulled up and held in place with a tiara. Then she sketched all the ballet positions she could remember. She worked out a possible way to join the knees to the thighs, the feet to the ankles, the wrists to the forearms to allow flexibility yet resist the gravity that would pull the doll out of position.

When she showed her sketches to Dan asking if he thought it was a good enough idea to present to Karl and Elvira, he told her it would never work and even if they did make something like it, it would never sell. "Who," he said, "would want a doll with all those ugly holes in her legs?" Slammed by a crimson shame, as though the voice of God had boomed, "WHO do you think you are?" Diana folded up the sketches. She hid them in a drawer down under her sweaters.

But after dreaming about the ballerina every night for a week, she took the sketches to Karl. As the four of them sat at the trestle table drinking coffee after dinner, she pulled out the sheets of paper. Karl chuckled. "I'd wondered when you'd be bringing a design to show us."

Karl spread the sketches out on the table. Elvira scooted closer to examine them. Diana explained what she wanted the figure to do. Leaning over the plans, tracing the detail of the joints, Karl said, "This is a good beginning. I think . . ."

"Listen to this," Dan interrupted, flinging his arms and knocking over two cups of coffee, drowning Diana's sketches. "Oops." He smiled his straight across smile. "I've got this great idea for an alligator."

◆

No longer did Diana and Dan explore the countryside on weekends. Dan secluded himself in their cottage copying the plans for the toys they had made for the Krugers. "It's time," he announced to Diana one day. "It's time for us to begin work on The Thornton Line."

"But Karl said we could begin production on the ballerina. We've worked out a way to joint her. You know that."

Dan put his arm around her. With his other hand he lifted her chin as though she were a pouting child. "Diana, Diana. We came up here to learn the business so we could start the Thornton Line. We agreed. You can make the doll later."

He stood over his sketches tapping the plans with his pencil. "We can get jobs and work on the toys at night." Beaming his straight across smile, he winked at her. "We can do it. As long as we're together, we can do anything."

And so they packed up the VW bus and headed south to Mississippi, back home to the house in the woods Diana's grandmother had left her. Diana got a job in a shop in Jackson and Dan in a shoe factory. They agreed they would make five sample toys to show area merchants. Diana immediately began work on the ballerina.

While Dan worked in the garage workshop, Diana whittled at the kitchen table, shaping the arms and legs of her dancer, chiseling out the sections where the joints would be, working meticulously to get this first one just right.

She came home from the shop one day and wanting to do just a little more work on the ballerina before starting dinner, she reached to the top of the cabinet where she kept the treasure. The pieces for the dancer were not there. As she dug deeper into the cabinet and searched any possible place she might have left her, Dan ran in, excited about his own work.

In the workshop, he showed her a wooden figure and a sketch of a toy soldier. The legs and arms were jointed so they would stay in any position in which they were placed. Diana's eyebrows furrowed. "Where did you get the jointed limbs?"

"They were on top of that old cabinet in the kitchen. I figured they were leftovers. You know, something we brought back from the Krugers."

He handed her the soldier. "Look at what he can do. Will you make a uniform for him? I've made his hat and his drum. All you'll need to do is make the pants and tunic."

◆

During their second year of production—they had quit their day jobs— the journalists found them. Pictures were taken of Dan and Diana surrounded by toy ships and sharks and dolls and horses. Their painted brown bungalow, hidden by trees from the road, delighted both the writers and the photographers. Stories were headlined: Husband and Wife Team in Toyland; photos captioned: Mr & Mrs "Santa Claus" Thornton in their gingerbread house. They put words in Diana's mouth: Mrs. Thornton says if you see an elf looking for work, just send him out to Hollycroft Rd.

Dan was quoted more and more often in the articles. He was articulate, energetic, and whimsical, yet quite serious about his venture with the toys. Dan's voice was rich and resonant. Diana sometimes put her hand on his back when he spoke so that she could touch the sound of his voice resonating through his wiry frame.

The more Dan talked, the less Diana had to say. When she disagreed with him about a detail of a new toy, he waved his hands in front of him as though he were trying to capture her words before they got to his ears.

But holding a finished toy, a kite or a wooden truck, or one of the dolls fully clothed and lifelike was an exquisite joy for her. She caressed each one before packing it in shredded paper, mentally blessing it, and wishing it a good home. She was bewildered that she and Dan were not like the Krugers—loving and gentle and happy with each other. When they were first together, it was as though each had found their missing half. The other would make them whole, make them round. But she had grown smaller, narrower, thinner, the thin crescent of her barely escaping at the edge of his eclipsing sun.

Usually quiet and soft-spoken, Diana became taciturn. Journalists began referring to her as Dan's helper. "Words," Dan said when she complained, "Words are cheap."

Ideas for new toys no longer came to her. She made costumes, upholstery, saddle blankets. And then, too, they were on a schedule. Dan was always asking her why this or that sewing project wasn't finished. He didn't stay to hear her silence.

It was the silence of mourning, deep and wordless. Encapsulated, bereft of influence in the human world, Diana took to wandering the twenty acres of woods. Her dog and her cat and her goat were her only companions.

Under the shelter of the oaks and maples and dogwoods, her bewilderment left her. Her mind emptied itself of memories and forebodings. Her restlessness dissolved as she felt the earth cushion her feet, as she learned the secret names of the broom corn she gathered, the goldenrod she vased, the passion flower twining through the marsh mallow, the belladonna rising black berried by the pond. She found joy in the growth of new saplings, the witch hazel, the tiny as yet unknown shoots peeking out from humus.

Because of the pleasure they gave her, she named each of the trees she walked under. She called them after the old gods and goddesses. She wished to be resolute as they were—straight and strong despite cold and snow and ice, despite summer winds and storms.

She gathered muscadine and mulberry and elderberry explaining to each how she would use their fruits. But not out loud; she no longer had the words.

She read books about love and forgiveness, books that said love was the lesson to be learned on earth. She prayed that her heart be not hardened and resolved to love Dan for his joy in his work and his sparkling eyes. Though he had taken all her words from her and shaped them in his own image, she told herself that he loved her as well as he could.

She asked herself, after Dan had voiced her thoughts in the very words she was thinking, what she needed words for. His words, exploded, erupted, flowed into the long winter nights filling the spaces around them. And he was no longer angry with her, not since she began following his exact instructions and offering nothing of her own.

"Our life moves smoothly now," she silently addressed the oak she had named Hera. "I've kept my part of the bargain. See how the Thornton Line grows and prospers?" She touched the tree asking, "Do you feel the touch of my hand? Do you see me?"

One bitter January night after a roast beef dinner in the warmth of the Kiwanis Club where Dan had given a speech on the joy of being a husband and wife toy-making team, after driving home through the sudden and treacherous winter ice storm which had turned the county into a delicate fairy land of glittering branches and sharp pinnacles of glacial grasses, after he had parked the VW and begun picking his way up the slope toward their gingerbread cottage, an ice-laden oak limb fell on Dan pinning him to the frozen ground.

He called out to Diana. She struggled to free him, but the limb was too heavy. She looked to the center of the great oak where the full moon shot a circle of light and silently rebuked it. "Hera, that's not fair to Dan. He's a living being as you are." Then shook her head and called herself "Fool." The tree was not to blame. It was ice and gravity that had pulled the limb down. Yet, there was something in the shadows as the winter wind blew, something not quite revealed by the full moon's light.

In the house, everyone she telephoned was busy talking to someone else. Finally, she heard a ring.

"Hello."

"Whooh," she said. "Whooh," like the sound of blowing out a candle.

"Some kids …" she heard as the phone was slammed back into the cradle.

She ran through the falling snow and knelt beside Dan. She frantically kissed his cheeks, his eyes, his forehead.

"Get away from me! Is someone coming? Who did you call?"

She mimed an answer.

"Stupid woman! This isn't a game. Open your mouth and talk." He hadn't noticed that she hadn't said a word in months.

She made walking motions with her fingers, balled her fist and knocked at an imaginary door.

"Hurry then. Get somebody."

She climbed over the fallen limb and ran to the main road. Wind blew the snow into her mouth and eyes. She trudged miles through the snow-white silence to reach the next farmhouse. With every step, she prayed Dan would give her back her words.

◆

When Diana returned with the neighboring farmer, she found Dan frozen dead, words dribbled out of his mouth and ears and eye sockets.

She picked up the blue words and the red and green and yellow words, leaving the sword-sharp grey ones, the ones she did not want to make her own.

She took them to the house while the farmer attached his plow to the fallen limb. She put water in the pot for coffee. She stared at the words all laid out before her on the kitchen table.

And when they thawed, she ate them.

Jake's Detour

CHARLOTTE HUDSON

J AKE TOMLIN burst through the sliding doors of the Mercy Medical
Center emergency room. "This girl needs a doctor—now!"

All eyes in the waiting room whipped from the television screen to the
panicked man cradling a limp and bleeding child, followed by a distraught
woman.

A nurse scurried into the waiting area. "What's going on out here?"
Her first glance at the scene answered her question. She hurried the man
with the child and the woman into the nearest exam room and called out
for the desk clerk to get a medical team stat.

Moments later two doctors and another nurse appeared, flanking the
bed where the little girl lay motionless. Within seconds they had triaged
her and rushed the bed into the hallway toward a surgical suite.

One doctor hung back to inform the woman they were taking the
child to surgery to determine the extent of her injuries. After she signed
some documents, he escorted her to the surgical waiting room and told

her she'd get a status report as soon as possible.

Jake zipped and unzipped the pocket of his leather jacket as he paced the floor in the empty exam room where only moments before he had placed the young girl on the bed.

A nurse stood in the doorway. "Sir, could you come with me? We need this exam room for a patient."

The nurse's voice snapped Jake back into reality, ceasing his rhythmic pacing. "Oh, I'm sorry . . . I just . . ."

Back in the waiting room, Jake asked the lady at the desk, "Could you tell me where I might find the mother of the girl they just took to surgery?"

The bottle-blond clerk smiled at the bearded man and directed him to the waiting room on the second floor.

Wondering what he would say to the girl's mother, Jake rushed to the elevator and around the corner to his dreaded destination.

When he reached the waiting room, Jake felt like he was moving in slow motion, pulling his heavy feet from the door to where the woman sat, dabbing her eyes with a soaked tissue. She seemed to wear her sadness on the outside like a heavy winter coat.

Jake crouched in front of her. Shaking his head with palms up, he said, "Ma'am, I'm so sorry. I didn't see her. I *swear* I didn't see her. She was in my path, and my bike hit her before I knew what happened." He shivered as the scene replayed in his mind.

The woman folded her hands in her lap. "I know you didn't mean to hit her, sir. It was an accident."

Jake rubbed his hands along the sides of his faded jeans and wondered why he felt so guilty since it *was* an accident.

The woman continued. "Gabrielle jumped out of the taxi ahead of me. I told her to wait, but she was so excited about the toy store. She ran ahead of me and into the middle of the street. It wasn't your fault."

It wasn't your fault were good words to hear, yet a two-ton burden pressed on Jake's chest. He needed to hear the right words from the doctors.

Jake sat in the chair next to the young woman and offered his hand. "I'm Jake Tomlin, and I'm sorry to meet you under these circumstances."

"I'm Marianne Kerns," she said, shaking his hand.

Jake fixed his eyes on hers, red from crying. "I live in a neighborhood with children, and I'm used to watching out for them. They're always chasing balls into the street. I just can't believe I didn't see Gabrielle."

"She's full of life, that child, and quick on her feet. Her impulsive nature gets her into a lot of trouble." Marianne wiped a tear with the back of her hand. "Today her impulsivity got her into serious trouble."

Gabrielle and I must have been cut from the same cloth, Jake thought, *because Impulsive is my middle name.*

He checked his watch. It was 5:30. "Can I call someone for you?"

"No," Marianne shook her head, her auburn locks bouncing. "I have no family here. Gabrielle and I moved here just last month."

"Then may I get you some coffee?"

"No, thank you."

She pulled a lipstick from her purse and dabbed it on her lips. "Do you live here? I'm still trying to learn my way around the city."

"I used to," he said. "Not now, though. Just passing through. Actually, I wouldn't have taken this route had the detour from the bridge construction on I-93 not forced me to." He gazed out the window. *I was hoping to pass through this place as quickly as possible.*

◆

Three and a half hours passed. Jake brought burgers, chips, and sodas from the hospital deli. He and Marianne ate a few bites and flipped through pages of *Outdoor Life* and *Southern Living*, waiting for a report on Gabrielle.

At 8:45 a doctor walked into the room, his surgical mask pulled down under his chin. "I'm Dr. William Snyder."

Marianne and Jake stood. "I'm Marianne. This is Jake." They all shook hands.

"The surgery went well. Gabrielle has a broken arm and leg, which will slow her down for a few weeks while she's lugging the casts around. But they were clean breaks and should heal fine."

Dr. Snyder ran his hand through his salt and pepper hair. "What

197

concerns us is her head trauma. We're going to move her to NICU and keep a close watch on the swelling of her brain. We inserted a drain and a saline IV to pull off the fluid."

He motioned for them to sit as he eased into a chair across from them. "For the next 72 hours we'll keep her heavily sedated to let her brain rest. Then we'll wean her off the sedation to see where she stands."

The doctor looked at them through compassionate eyes. "In the meantime, you two get some rest. There's nothing you can do."

Clearly, Dr. Snyder thought they were Gabrielle's parents. He shook Jake's hand again and patted Marianne's shoulder, then smiled. "We promise to take good care of Gabrielle. I know you want to look in on her."

He looked at the wall clock. "Follow me. You can leave your phone number at the nurses' station, in case they need to reach you."

Jake saw the panic on Marianne's face when Dr. Snyder said *in case they need to reach you.*

He followed Dr. Snyder and Marianne down the familiar halls that led to the NICU and whispered a silent prayer: *Lord, please heal this little girl. Lord, please.*

Jake noticed a few changes since he was last at Mercy Medical. The cafeteria had been remodeled, and bright blue signage with arrows made navigating the halls easier. Artwork was now hung along the passageway to the NICU, a path Jake knew well.

Maybe it was there all along, he thought. *I was sleep-deprived back then; maybe I just didn't notice it.*

When they reached the stark stainless steel doors at the entrance to the unit, a shiver ran down Jake's spine. It took all the courage he could muster to walk through those haunting doors. The last time he'd encountered them rushed back into his memory—not something he wanted to remember.

Hoping he wouldn't be recognized in his full beard and leather jacket, he walked on.

Jake heard a familiar voice from the right side of the unit. Dr. James Middleton was speaking to family members outside a patient's room. Jake turned his face away and remained silent, fearing that his voice wouldn't be as unrecognizable as his appearance.

Soon after his arrival in Boston, Jake discovered that a southerner's accent from south Mississippi stood out like a sore thumb. He knitted his brows.

If only being teased about his accent had been the worst thing about his time at Mercy Medical Center.

◆

Fall term of Jake's third year of his neurosurgical residency was seared into his memory like the brand on one of his grandpa's prized Brahman bulls, specifically, the Friday night before Thanksgiving.

He wasn't on call Thanksgiving weekend and planned to go home to Hattiesburg. His mother was cooking the traditional southern holiday feast, and all the family would be there. Jake's long-term plans changed after that fateful Friday night, when his future career took a major detour.

◆

Jake followed Marianne and Dr. Snyder into Gabrielle's room. He gasped when he saw the number on the door. In his mind's eye, the child he saw lying in that bed was not Gabrielle—it was Andrew Jacobson.

Andrew was an adventurous 6-year-old. The day his family moved into their new house in a Boston suburb, he decided to slide down the banister from the second floor. Halfway down, Andrew toppled off and slammed onto the foyer floor.

He was rushed into surgery as soon as the ambulance reached the ER. Once he was assessed, a team of doctors, neurology and orthopedic, was summoned to the OR. Jake scrubbed and waited for Dr. Middleton, the attending physician, to arrive. The orthopedic team went straight to work on Andrew's broken bones and finished in record time, ready to turn the patient over to the neuro team.

Jake checked the clock on the wall again. *Where was Middleton?*

All the ORs were filled, leaving a shortage of attending physicians. Chuck Mason, a neurology resident, rushed over to Jake. Clearly, Jake knew by the look on his face that Chuck was thinking the same thing he was. *If Middleton doesn't come on, this kid's not going to make it.*

Jake thought of Andrew's parents in the waiting room, and without considering the consequences, he shot a sidelong glance to the assistant. "Scalpel."

Jake then began a desperate attempt to save Andrew's life.

Twenty-five minutes into the procedure, Middleton rushed into the room, gave Jake a "go to hell" look, and snatched the scalpel from his hand.

Andrew lived six days.

Dr. Middleton, Chief of Neurosurgery, severely reprimanded Jake and denied him entrance to the OR for three months, at which time his status would be reconsidered.

Middleton's severe reprimand didn't compare to the punishment Jake gave himself. He returned to Mercy Medical after Thanksgiving break and withdrew from medical school, forfeiting his scholarship. Though his parents tried to convince Jake to remain in school, Dr. Middleton offered him no encouragement.

Since that day in November six years ago, Jake had wandered aimlessly, not knowing how to fill his days. His Harley became his only companion, and he'd ridden thousands of miles in search of a meaningful way to live out his life.

He was 12 years old when Mrs. Crowder, his seventh grade social studies teacher, had invited professionals to career day. By the time Dr. Joseph Foster, a local surgeon, left the podium, Jake was convinced that he would become a surgeon. *His intent was to save lives, not to take them. He had taken the Hippocratic oath wholeheartedly.*

◆

"Jake . . . Jake, it's time to go," Dr. Snyder called out, pulling Jake out of his trance and pointing both Marianne and him toward the door of Gabrielle's room.

Relieved to see no sign of Dr. Middleton in the NICU, Jake followed Dr. Snyder and Marianne into the hall.

After 72 hours, Gabrielle was weaned off sedation, and the neurological tests began, which she passed with little effort.

The fluid on her brain, though diminished, was still a concern. Dr. Snyder said the next 24 hours would determine whether they would have to take Gabrielle into surgery to make a flap in her skull and remove fluid from her brain.

◆

Every day at seven A.M., Jake arrived with breakfast in a McDonald's sack. The sixth day he entered the NICU waiting room as Dr. Snyder was telling Marianne of Gabrielle's improvement and the plan to move her to the step-down unit. When Dr. Snyder walked away, Jake recognized the confusion on Marianne's face.

The morning sun cast a shard of golden light across the floor. "Here, have some breakfast," Jake said, "and I'll explain in layman's terms what Dr. Snyder just said."

As Marianne set her coffee on the table beside her chair, Jake saw a calm wash over her face. *She must wonder how a biker knows medical terminology.*

Jake wondered the same thing—*Who am I? And more than that—where am I headed?*

Marianne tossed the empty cups and wrappers into the trash can just as a nurse came to take her to the room where Gabrielle had been moved.

Marianne motioned to Jake. "Come meet Gabrielle."

Jake was anxious to meet the little girl who'd brought him back inside the walls of Mercy Medical Center—the one place he never wanted to again enter.

When Gabrielle caught first glance of Marianne, Jake saw pure joy on her round, freckled face. Her auburn curls were spread haphazardly across the pillow, and her hazel eyes exuded delight when her mother kissed her cheek.

Marianne held her daughter's hand. "Gabby, I want you to meet Mr. Jake Tomlin, the kind man whose motorcycle you ran in front of."

Giddy, Gabby said, "You ride a motorcycle? I love motorcycles!"

Marianne straightened Gabby's curls and said, "Gabby, don't you think you need to tell Mr. Tomlin something before asking him about his motorcycle?"

Gabby tucked her chin to her chest with apparent remorse, and said, "I'm sorry I ran in front of you. Did you wreck your motorcycle?"

"Now that you're all right, everything is okay," Jake chuckled. "No, the bike wasn't damaged. Just my heart—because I was worried about you, Gabby. You must never run ahead of your mother into a busy street again. Promise?"

Gabby smiled, holding out her little finger for Jake to latch onto. "Okay, I pinky promise. Can I ride your bike?"

"Let's get you well first, and then we'll talk to your mother about a bike ride. Okay?"

"Okay!"

Before he left, Jake told Marianne to call him if she needed anything and that he would be back tomorrow with breakfast.

When Jake approached the nurses' station he saw and heard the familiar face and voice of Dr. Middleton. He pulled down the brim of his cap and hurried to the elevator.

◆

A week later, the day Gabby was discharged, Jake rode the elevator up to her floor. His arms were loaded with flowers for Marianne and a large stuffed owl for Gabby—a reminder to be wise and to not cross busy streets alone.

As Jake stepped off the elevator, his view was blocked by the flowers, and the elbow of someone stepping into the elevator accidentally knocked the owl from his arm. As both Jake and the newcomer knelt down to retrieve the owl, Jake's cap fell off.

Now standing face to face with the other man, Jake swallowed hard and said, "Excuse me."

Though he hoped his beard would be a sufficient disguise, his piercing blue eyes—that until now had been hidden by his cap—and his southern accent gave him away.

"Jake Tomlin!" Dr. Middleton said, wide-eyed. "Where are you going? No—a better question is where have you been?"

Both questions were ones that Jake had rather not answer. But before he could say anything, Dr. Middleton, in his familiar demanding tone, said, "Unload your arms and come to my office. You know where it is."

What Jake *knew* was that he was under no obligation to follow Dr. Middleton's orders. But he replied, "Give me ten minutes."

On the way to Gabby's room Jake asked himself: *Why did I comply to his command? I don't want to rehash the past. He kicked me out of the OR and now wants to know where I've been. How can he think that's any business of his?*

In the room with Marianne and Gabby, Jake gave them cab fare for the trip home, exchanged contact information with Marianne, and promised Gabby a bike ride on a safe street when she was well and her casts were off.

◆

In the Chief of Neurosurgery's outer office, Jake said, with hesitation, "I'm Jake Tomlin, here to see Dr. Middleton."

The administrative assistant smiled, and Jake knew it was because of his accent. "Oh, yes, he's expecting you." She picked up the phone and announced, "Jake Tomlin is here."

Jake's hand froze on the doorknob. While he was thinking of turning and walking away, the door opened.

"Come in, Tomlin, and have a seat."

Both men offered their hands in a shake.

Jake settled into one of the blue leather chairs in front of the massive hand-carved desk, remembering the first and the last times he'd sat there.

His hands folded on the desk, Dr. Middleton asked, "What brings you to MMC?"

Jake sensed the formidable shimmer in his cool, blue eyes. He placed his cap on his lap and told the story of why he was there.

"Oh, yes, that's the little girl that was in NICU. It was touch-and-go with her the first few days."

Jake stared at his cap. "I know. I was concerned about her condition."

"I know what you mean. It's tough being a doctor. Sometimes knowledge is a curse. You know what they say about ignorance being bliss."

Dr. Middleton stepped to the mini-fridge in the corner of the office and took out two bottles of water, placing one on the edge of his desk in front of Jake. "Speaking of being a doctor, I've always hoped you went on to finish medical school and were practicing."

Jake took a long drink of water and felt a vein pulsing on his forehead.

Dr. Middleton continued. "I knew you were going to be an exemplary doctor—one I had hoped to keep here at Mercy."

Jake sat speechless, his ears burning. *He sits here now and tells me how confident he was in my ability. Where was he when I needed his encouragement? It's one thing to be tough on medical students to prepare them for the real world; but it's another thing to squash their self-confidence . . . or even worse, their self-worth. Who does he think he is up on his ivory throne telling me what a good doctor I would have been?*

Jake swallowed hard. Angry words seared his tongue, and he spat them out. "So why didn't you tell me of your confidence in me the day I came in to resign from medical school?" He slammed the water bottle on the desk.

"Well—"

Jake interrupted him. "No. I beg your pardon, sir, but it's my turn to talk today."

Dr. Middleton leaned back in undivided attention, pulling his hands off the desk onto his lap.

Jake continued. "Dr. Middleton, I know today, just as I knew *then*, that I made the wrong decision—a terribly wrong one—one that may very well have caused the death of that child. But you were unavailable, as were all the other attendings, that day."

The doctor put his elbows on the desk and rested his chin on his folded hands. "You're right. We were extremely short-handed in surgery that day."

Jake felt heat surging under his collar. He stood and paced the floor. "Now, I'm going to ask you a question I've wanted answered for six years."

Standing in front of the desk, he planted his palms on the cool mahogany and locked eyes with the doctor. "In your professional opinion, Doctor, do you think Andrew Jacobson would have lived had I not started the surgery?"

Dr. Middleton stood, walked to the window, and stared out. After a long moment of silence he abruptly turned toward Jake. "The chances of the child's survival would have been slim to none if you hadn't done what you did for him."

Without speaking, Jake walked toward the door to leave.

"Jake, it was hard for me to reprimand you that night because I thought you possibly saved the boy's life on the table. Even though he died later, his death was not caused by anything you did. His parents had time with him they probably wouldn't have had."

Jake turned and glowered at Middleton in a frozen stance.

"Then—"

Again, Dr. Middleton walked to the window, and this time he didn't turn facing Jake.

Jake sensed that he couldn't.

Arms folded across his chest, he stared out the window. "The hardest part of my job here at MMC is not the difficult surgeries or the countless hours spent in the classroom teaching medical students. It's the times I'm forced to follow policies and procedures laid out by administration when it adversely affects students' futures."

After a long exhale, the doctor continued. "My contract clearly states that if a student does anything that goes against the policies set before them while under my supervision, I must reprimand—and possibly suspend or even expel—them. I didn't write the rules, Jake, but I have to abide by them if I want to continue practicing and teaching here."

When Dr. Middleton turned to Jake and gently motioned for him to sit, Jake saw sincere remorse on his battle-weary face.

Slowly Jake walked back and slumped into the chair.

With moist eyes fastened on Jake, Dr. Middleton said, "Jake, I've prayed for a long time that our paths would cross again."

And all that time I was praying that we would never meet again, Jake thought.

The folder that Dr. Middleton took from his desk drawer and slid toward Jake was confirmation that the good doctor had not only prayed for a chance meeting; he'd also trusted that it would happen.

Dr. Middleton came around the desk, stood beside Jake, and pulled a pen from his pocket. "Jake, I don't know what you've done with your life since you left medical school or what your financial standing is, and I don't care to know. The one thing I do know is that you'll make an outstanding surgeon."

That said, the doctor took his checkbook from the inside pocket of his starched white lab coat. "Because I believe in your ability as a surgeon, I want to pay your tuition to finish your residency."

With dropped jaw, Jake's eyes darted from Dr. Middleton to the folder on the desk.

"This is a simple contract," the doctor said, opening the folder. "All I ask in return for my check is that you sign this document, agree to complete your residency in neurosurgery at MMC, and remain on staff here for at least seven years after graduation. If you choose to go somewhere else for a fellowship, we can work that into the deal."

Dr. Middleton placed the pen on the contract and stepped back. "I'm planning to retire in five years. As Chief of Neurosurgery, I feel duty-bound to line up a stellar group of surgeons for the department before I leave."

Dazed, Jake looked up from the contract and said, "So you—"

"Yes, Jake, I knew all along what a fine doctor you could be and have regretted your dropping out of medical school and forfeiting your scholarship."

Still stunned, Jake stared at the contract.

"You don't have to sign it now. Take it with you, read it, and let me know your decision within a week."

Jake looked up at the doctor. "Why would I need to think about this for a week?" He scribbled his signature and closed the folder.

Jake stood and embraced his mentor. "Thank you, Dr. Middleton, for a second chance at my dream."

With a handshake and a grin, Dr. Middleton said, "See you in class and the OR, Doctor Tomlin."

The Quicksand and the Dead

JIM R. ANGELO

NATE WAS PACING THE FLOOR, waiting on Sally to finish dressing so they could meet their friends at Hook's Tavern and Grill, an ancient nightspot on old Highway 80 between their rural Vicksburg home and Bovina.

"C'mon! What's taking so long? You tryin' to primp for somebody? Ain't nobody lookin' at you. Let's go!"

Nate always insulted his wife, whether in public or private. It made no difference—at least, not to him. Sally was a striking woman, as tall as her husband, and deserved none of his comments. It was no secret that more than one man had made a serious pass at her, thinking she could be seduced because of her husband's behavior. But even though she was married to the biggest philanderer in the county, she refused to sink to his level.

"I'm almost ready," she said. Sally had learned to avoid confrontation with her husband and had the bruises to prove it.

She knew Nate was anxious to get to Hook's because he often made late-night plans with women—single or married—who hung out there, made them almost under Sally's nose when they were there together. He would usually return to the bar after dropping Sally off at home, under the pretext of meeting a friend for another drink.

"You got a problem with that?" he would say, more as a threat than a question.

"No," she always replied, never looking directly at him when he spoke that way. There would be no argument. Besides, every minute without Nate was a blessing.

Sally knew Nate and knew him well. When returning home from late nights out, he reeked of other women's perfumes. The smells were not always the same, but they all had that same cheap undertone. If he was attracted to those women, what did that say to Sally about herself? Her self-image and confidence were zero.

"Get your butt out here now and let's go!" he yelled just as Sally walked out of the bedroom into the front room of their small, modest home.

"It's about time. You know it's always packed on Friday nights. Joe and Nell are waiting on us. You wearing that flowery thing again?"

She did not reply. Her mind was somewhere else.

◆

Hook's existence predated the Mississippi bootlegger days and came to depend on behind-the-building moonshine sales at the outset of Prohibition. Indeed, in the '60s and earlier, it was Warren County's place to go for white lightning and other alcoholic beverages, surpassing Rankin County's more notorious Gold Coast.

When national Prohibition and Mississippi's dry laws were repealed, the tavern prospered, and the joke was that everybody got richer except the folks who sold brown paper bags. But Hook's had another, albeit surreptitious, reputation. It was known to be a pick-up spot and that was what attracted Nate to it.

When they arrived, Nate wasted no time scanning the room for his next late-night encounter as he and Sally strolled up to the table where their friends sat.

"Hey, guys. What's going on?" Joe said.

Sally and Nell hugged and then talked about what they had done that day as Nate and Joe ordered some drafts for themselves and wine for their wives.

"She gets on my nerves," Nate said to Joe. Turning his back to his wife, he continued: "She always wears that dress when we go out. Sometimes I wonder why I married her. Look at her."

"Aw, man—you don't mean that. Sally's pretty."

Their wives, talking with each other while listening closely to their husbands, heard every word. Nell was embarrassed for her friend. "Just two little boys talking, honey," she said. It doesn't mean anything."

Sally knew otherwise but remained silent. They had all heard this kind of talk from him more times than anyone cared to remember.

"Yeah," Nate continued, "I told Sally that when I die I don't care about being buried next to each other. I want to be buried in my truck, you know. Just a small funeral and me in that truck. That's what I want."

Throughout the evening, Nate kept looking past Sally's shoulder at a woman who was sitting alone and staring back, smiling at him. He gave her an almost imperceptible nod—Sally pretended not to notice—and announced it was time for Sally and him to go home. The couples said their goodbyes and departed.

Once arriving home, Nate, as usual, said he had to run out for a couple of hours. Sally said nothing.

Sally was awakened just after two A.M. by Nate's F-150 racing down the half-mile gravel driveway, then slamming its brakes, scattering pebbles onto the porch as it fishtailed.

After the engine remained on for several minutes, Sally got out of bed and went outside to see why her husband hadn't turned off the ignition. As she approached the truck, she could tell he smelled as always after one of his late-night ventures: that all-too-familiar reek of alcohol and cheap perfume. He had passed out and was slumped onto the passenger side of the seat, leaving the engine running.

The last time this happened, Sally had tried to awaken him and get him inside—and had suffered for her efforts. That wouldn't happen again.

Sally stood by the truck for a long time, thinking and looking down at Nate.

Finally she opened the passenger door and pulled him partly out of the truck—his head hanging off the seat—then calmly walked to the storage room and returned with a plastic drop cloth and a metal pipe. She nudged him with the pipe, but he remained motionless, barely grunting.

Sally wrapped the cloth tightly around his head and all the physical and mental abuse she had suffered came to mind. With each memory, she struck his skull with all her strength, the pipe clenched in both hands.

She was a strong woman; he was dead after the first blow.

Sally threw the pipe on the floorboard, got in the driver's seat, and drove across the field and away from the house. Recently, she had discovered something about a mile away, something she had never heard anyone mention and, for whatever reason, decided to keep to herself. It was a quicksand pit—and it was about to be put to good use.

At the edge of the pit, Sally stopped and got out of the vehicle. She placed a heavy stone on the gas pedal, put the truck in drive, and watched it lurch forward and into the pit. As it slowly submerged, the sound of the engine abated until there was only silence. Nate and his coffin disappeared into the quicksand, and in a few minutes the surface was quiet again.

Nate's burial wish was fulfilled.

Sally hiked the short mile back to her home, washed the pipe rust off her hands, and went to bed.

◆

Monday morning, Sally sat on her porch, coffee cup in hand. It was the first time she was able to do so without being yelled at or having to do something for her abusive husband. Those days were gone.

Since the house was a half-mile from the main road, the first sign of an approaching vehicle was a cloud of dust swirling toward the front yard. It was Nate's friend, Joe, who drove up next to the steps leading to the porch.

Joe was talking as soon as he exited his truck: "Sally, where's Nate? He didn't show up at work today and Mack is really chapped. I tried to cover for him but I got chewed out."

"Couldn't tell you, Joe. Maybe he fell in a hole. You know how he hates it when I 'nag' him." Sally barely avoided a smile. "Why don't you ask one of his girlfriends? They see him more than I do."

Joe managed a weak smile and tried to pretend he didn't hear. "Well, when he shows up, let him know I came by. See ya."

"Say 'hi' to Nell for me."

A week later, Sally decided it would be a good idea to visit the sheriff's Grove Street office in Vicksburg. She approached Deputy Maggie Welch and told her she wanted to file a missing person's report on Nate.

"Why'd you wait so long to come in?" Maggie asked, when Sally told her Nate had been missing for several days.

"You should know."

Maggie could only nod in agreement. She had been married to Nate less than a year before calling it quits.

"We'll be in touch," said Maggie, as Sally left the office and walked back to her car.

Several days later Sally answered a knock on her front door. It was Maggie and another deputy, Bill. "Hi, Sally," Maggie said. "May we come in?" But Maggie didn't sound like she wanted to come in.

Sally motioned them in. "How about some coffee? What brings y'all here?"

"No thanks. Let me get right to it, Sally—I'm sorry to tell you this, but we found Nate. I'm afraid he's dead."

Sally blinked. "What? What are you talking about? What happened?" She reached for a chair and dropped onto it.

"Well, two hunters were on the edge of your property and noticed some brush that looked like it had been driven over. They followed the tire tracks and found a quicksand pit a mile or so from here. So, they called us."

"Quicksand?" She felt the two deputies' eyes fixed on her.

"Yeah, a big pool," Maggie said. "They were afraid somebody might get trapped in it and figured we could do something to fence it off. Then, the sheriff had the idea to use that fishing radar gadget of his and see if he could find anything in there. He was just playing around, but, boy, he got a helluva surprise. Nate's truck was just below the surface."

Sally took a deep breath. "What about Nate? Where was he?"

"He was in the truck . . . I'm sorry, Sally." Maggie cleared her throat. "At first, we figured he accidently drove into the pit but now it looks like he was dead before then."

"When did all this happen?"

"We found the truck yesterday."

"Yesterday? Why are you just now telling me?"

"We didn't want to say anything until we knew more. And . . . there's something else."

Sally froze. The two deputies stared at her.

The other shoe was about to drop. Sally knew she was doomed. Should she confess and get it over with? Before she could say anything, Maggie continued:

"It looks like he was killed and then driven into the quicksand. It's too early to know for sure, but we think—excuse me for saying it—it might have been a jealous boyfriend or husband. I'm sorry."

Sally's heart was pounding. She did her best to appear upset.

"Is there anything we can do for you?" asked Maggie.

"No, thank you. I-I'll be okay."

◆

Maggie was back the following day, this time alone. "I want to show you something," she told Sally. "Don't speak; just listen. When Nate's truck was pulled out of the quicksand, Harold from the towing service and me were the only ones there. He recognized the drop cloth from helping Nate paint your garage last summer."

Sally froze, wide-eyed with surprise, but Maggie eased her onto a kitchen chair.

"Look, we figured out everything," Maggie continued, holding open a large potato sack. In it were the bloodstained drop cloth and metal pipe.

"Harold's wife was one of Nate's conquests way back when Nate and I were married. Harold never found out until recently—after he helped with your garage, obviously."

Maggie looked Sally in the eye and said, "I'll take care of this. Harold's not talking, that's for damn sure. Nobody else has to know anything. The bastard got what he deserved."

"I . . ." Sally's voice trailed off.

"See you later," Maggie said, and hugged Sally on her way out the door. "Take care of yourself."

Several days after Nate's cremation, Sally walked out to the pit, urn in hand. She stood there a moment, then threw the sealed vessel as far as she could. She watched it sink, and after it was gone she turned away and walked home.

The Garden Club

JOHN M. FLOYD

Rudy Tullos was in love with his neighbor. Her name was Karen Pennington, she was staying the summer with her aunt and uncle next door, and she was eleven years old. To be exact, she was eleven and a half—two months younger than Rudy. Which was a good thing: it meant he wasn't dating An Older Woman.

Then again, they weren't actually dating, he reminded himself. What they were doing, and had been doing since her arrival here in Mississippi three weeks ago, was just sort of hanging around together. Going fishing, playing checkers, riding bikes. Or at least that's what Karen was doing. Rudy was more or less tagging along and going through the motions. And looking at her. He felt certain he could spend hours on end doing nothing but looking at her—and the more he did, the more hopelessly lovesick he became.

On this particular day, as Karen Pennington sat beside him in the wooden swing on his front porch, Rudy decided he'd like to try something a little different. Specifically, he'd like to convince her to walk with him along the path beside the creek, and even more specifically, he'd like to steer her to a spot under the big oak tree halfway down the path. The oak tree with all the mistletoe in the top branches.

As he sat and tried to formulate the right way to phrase such a suggestion, she came up with one of her own.

"Want to play *Monopoly*?"

Rudy blew out a sigh. *He who hesitates,* he thought.

"Why not?" he said, with a shrug. At least with *Monopoly* he was sure what he was doing. And he could still look at her.

Rudy went upstairs to fetch the game box while Karen wandered to the living room and dropped into a chair to wait. When he came back he found her staring at a point on the floor near the doorway to the dining room. Puzzled, he followed her gaze, then understood. On the carpet between the coffee table and the open door was a big, ugly stain. Even though it was close to two feet in diameter, it wasn't terribly noticeable— it was just a dark gray spot on a lighter gray floor—but Karen had noticed it anyway. It was in the shape of a circle with a couple of splashes on each side, making it look like the planet Saturn. "What's that?" she asked, pointing, as Rudy plopped down cross-legged on the floor and spread out the game board.

He glanced at the strange-looking spot on the carpet, then started counting out the play money. "It's a long story," he said.

Karen waited a moment, watching him. When he didn't elaborate, she said, "Did your mom spill something there?"

"Not exactly. What kind of man do you want?"

She frowned at him until she saw he was holding out a handful of little metal tokens. "Oh. The top hat, I guess."

Rudy placed it on the board and selected the race car for himself. His man was always the race car. "You can go first," he said, handing her the dice.

Her eyes were still on his face. "Aren't you going to tell me what happened?"

"I suppose. If you really want to know."

She stared at him, waiting.

"It was a Garden Party," he said.

◆

He began the story with an observation: He had never really understood why they were called Garden Parties. Nobody in Morgan's Hollow even had a garden, at least not the kind you see on TV, or in the fancy magazines. The gardens this far south of the Mason-Dixon were several long rows of peas and okra and butterbeans. Still, the ladies of the town called their organization the Garden Club, and their little gossipy gatherings were named accordingly.

They were dull affairs, these parties, Rudy thought that day as he looked down at the proceedings from his hiding place at the top of the stairs. A dozen stiff and proper ladies, all gussied up and staring down their powdered noses at everyone else, were milling about the living room and dining room like corralled cattle and murmuring to each other while they munched odd-looking little goodies laid out in bowls and platters on every flat surface in sight. Rudy found it hard to believe that his mother had invited them here in the first place.

Well, that wasn't quite right. What he found hard to believe was that they had accepted the invitation. His mom had wanted to join the exclusive group—or at least to be in some way acknowledged by them—for most of her adult life. The truth of the matter was, he and his mother and little sister were from the Other Side of the Tracks, so to speak, and until now had been consistently and pointedly ignored by the "finer" citizens of Morgan's Hollow. That bothered Rudy not one bit, of course—the children of these particular folks were no fun anyway. But his mother wanted their acceptance, and always had.

Ever since his father had run away three years ago and left them with next to nothing, his mother's irrational desire to be a part of the Garden Club had grown into an obsession. Hardly a day went by that she didn't go all dreamy-eyed and mumble something about "that fine and dignified group of ladies." Rudy snorted under his breath. His mother, so smart and level-headed about most everything else, was horribly mistaken about that, he thought. The only thing these women wanted today, the only reason they were here at all, was to snoop around and peer into corners and eat the tiny cookies and sandwiches and make fun of Dorothy Tullos and her simple lower-class existence.

The one exception was a woman named Edith Garland. Mrs. Garland had recently moved down here from Memphis. In fact she was the new doctor's wife, and had defied the rules this afternoon by bringing along some goodies she and a friend of hers had made, to help out. Rudy didn't know her personally, but he was a pretty good judge of character, and from what little he'd seen so far he figured she was the only one in the gathering today, besides his mom of course, who was worth a damn.

Once, a few minutes ago, Mrs. Garland had caught him peeping at them from the top of the stairs and had winked at him slyly.

As Rudy sat there thinking these thoughts, a prunefaced old woman named Maude Ogletree rose from her chair beside the window, marched over to his mother, and stood there looking at her from three feet away. Dorothy Tullos, who was busy gathering up some of the used plates and glasses, turned to find the old woman blocking her way to the kitchen.

"Excuse me," Rudy's mother said, with a smile, and started to go around her. Maude Ogletree simply moved to the left a step, just far enough to again block the way. The two women stared into each other's eyes for a moment. "Is something wrong, Mrs. Ogletree?" his mother asked, her hands full of dishes.

"I'm afraid so," the old lady said, in a cold voice. "You seem to have missed the mark a bit, on those balls."

Dorothy Tullos frowned. "I beg your pardon?"

"Those things over there on the cabinet, in the little blue bowl. They taste a bit like sausage balls, but not quite." Mrs. Ogletree raised her head and thrust out her chin like the Wicked Witch of the West. "Personally, I wouldn't feed them to my dog."

Surprised and blushing, Rudy's mother pressed her lips together and took a slow breath. This kind of thing had been going on all afternoon. "I'm afraid you'll have to speak to someone else about that, Mrs. Ogletree. They aren't mine."

The old woman gave her a stony look. "Indeed," she said. "And who else would have brought food here, may I ask?"

"I believe Mrs. Garland brought them." Dorothy Tullos paused, then added, "Maybe she feeds them to *her* dog." After another smile, she tightened her grip on the dishes and trudged past Mrs. Ogletree to the kitchen door.

The old lady's eyebrows, which had shot up at the mention of her distinguished neighbor, swooped down again. Her gray head swiveled in a slow arc, searching the room for Edith Garland. Even from his distant vantage point, Rudy Tullos could see the sudden gleam in Mrs. Ogletree's eye. And he knew what she was thinking. Mrs. Garland, as the new doctor's wife and the most recent member of the Club, might at last be a lady deserving of Maude Ogletree's valuable time and attention.

After a moment the old woman spotted her, and on the way across the room detoured to the cabinet to pick up the bowl of sausage balls. With the container in hand, Mrs. Ogletree strode over to stand beside Dr. Garland's wife. As Rudy watched, the old woman interrupted with an upraised finger the conversation Edith Garland was having with several of the other ladies, and during the awkward silence started ranting about how wonderful Mrs. Garland's little sausage balls were. Every few seconds Mrs. Ogletree would pause and pop another one into her mouth. Yum, yum. Rudy's mother had noticed also, he saw, and she sighed tiredly before turning back to the dining-room table to set out another plate of cookies.

To Rudy's pleasure, however, the good doctor's wife seemed unimpressed with the old woman's performance. After a long, lip-smacking dissertation by Maude Ogletree about everything from her Confederate ancestry to her bank account, Edith Garland excused herself and glided away, leaving the old biddy standing there alone, chewing on the last of the balls. And though Rudy didn't hear all of Mrs. Garland's parting remark, he caught enough to hear her say the sausage balls were, regretfully, none of her doing—but she was glad Mrs. Ogletree had enjoyed them.

The old woman stood there a minute, stunned and blinking. The little blue bowl, empty now, was replaced on its cabinet so loudly it almost broke. Fuming, Mrs. Ogletree stomped back across the room, mumbling to herself and rubbing her mouth with a napkin.

At about that same time, Rudy was struck with an idea. An idea so simple and so brilliant it made his insides tingle just thinking about it.

Slowly he rose to his feet and crept down the stairs. After a moment he caught his mother's eye and weaved his way over to where she stood, between the living-room coffee table and the doorway to the dining room. As he approached his mom, Mrs. Ogletree apparently noticed him, and came over also.

"Mrs. Tullos," she announced, "I'm afraid we don't allow children at our gatherings."

Both Rudy and his mother turned to stare at her. "Mrs. Ogletree," Dorothy Tullos said, when she had regained her composure, "this is not just a child. This is my son, and this is my house." To Rudy she said, in a quiet and unsteady voice, "Rudy, honey, this is Mrs. J. L. Ogletr—"

"I repeat," the old woman said, louder this time, "children are not welcome. He must leave at once." She stamped her foot hard on the carpet to underline this last word.

Everyone there had overheard them by now, and most were gathering around. Several of the women's expressions were cold and aloof, but a few showed open concern.

One lady said, "But, Maude—"

"Shut up, Nell," Mrs. Ogletree snapped, without turning. "Leave now, young man," she said to Rudy. "And do not return until our meeting is finished. Do you understand?"

Dorothy Tullos, her pretty face reddening, opened her mouth to reply, but Rudy cut her off. "I'm leaving, ma'am," he said politely. "I just came for my eggs."

Everyone looked at him. "What, honey?" his mother said. For the moment her anger was sidetracked.

"My eggs," he repeated. "Tommy wants 'em back."

There was a puzzled silence. "Rudy, what do you mean?"

Rudy smiled his most innocent smile. "I mean the eggs Tommy and I cut out of his dead turtle yesterday, Mom. They were in a little blue bowl on the cabinet . . ."

◆

Karen Pennington sat and stared at him for a long time.

Finally Rudy blinked and focused on her. "Sorry," he said. "I told you it was a long story."

"I think it's fantastic," she said, in a hushed voice. The look on her face made it clear that she was seeing Rudy Tullos in an entirely new light. "It's the absolutely coolest thing I ever heard."

He just shrugged.

She turned to look at the big gray stain on the carpet. "So she did that? Mrs. Ogletree?" Her voice was faint, almost a whisper. She seemed awestruck.

"That's just some of it," he said. "Mom scrubbed most of it out, the next day." He thought for several seconds, remembering. "But it was something to see, all right. Soon as I said the words 'the little blue bowl,' the old lady just pulled the plug. Mom and I ducked and missed the worst of it, but poor Mrs. Polk got covered head to toe, and Miss Russell and Mrs. Bennett and Mrs. Watkins got a pretty good soaking, and they were five or six feet away. A couple of ladies tried to run and slipped down in it. Pretty gross." He shook his head, smiling at the memory. "I never saw anybody throw up like that except the little girl in that exorcist movie."

Karen didn't seem to know what to say. She was still looking at him as if he had just waved his cape and pulled a white rabbit out of the *Monopoly* box.

"Well," he said, with a glance at the board. "You want to roll first?"

She stayed quiet. Rudy could hear the growl of old Mr. Burnley's lawnmower two doors down, and the crunch of gravel as a car rumbled by on the dirt road. The smell of honeysuckle floated in through the open window.

"Karen?" he said.

She had tilted her head a bit, watching him. "Why don't we go outside?" she asked, in that low, strange tone.

"Outside?"

"Yeah." A tiny smile played at the corners of her mouth. "We could maybe take a walk down the path. You know, the one beside the creek?"

Their eyes held, then he shrugged again. "Okay. If you want to."

Rudy closed up the game box and walked with her across the living room. Before following her through the doorway, he paused a moment, smiling, and turned to study the big gray Saturn-shaped spot where his little sister's dog had wet the carpet last month.

Imagination, he said to himself, *is a terrible thing to waste . . .*

Contributors

Jim R. Angelo
Jim Angelo earned his B.S. and Ed. Spec. degrees in Mathematics Education from Mississippi State University and his M.S. degree in Mathematics from The University of Southern Mississippi. He is a former mathematics teacher and soccer coach, having worked in public education, youth soccer leagues, and Belhaven University. He also worked as a supervisor and planner at Delphi Packard in Clinton, Mississippi. He started writing short stories two years ago and received an honorable mention for his entry, "Suspended," in the 2017 November/December "Mysterious Photograph" contest of *Alfred Hitchcock Mystery Magazine*. Jim is a current resident of Brandon, Mississippi, where he lives with his wife Susie.

Marion Barnwell
While teaching writing and literature at Delta State University, Marion Barnwell co-founded *Tapestry*, a faculty literary magazine. She compiled and edited the anthology, *A Place Called Mississippi*, and co-authored *Touring Literary Mississippi*. She was invited to the Sewanee Writers Conference for her one-act play, *Rats!* Her short stories have appeared in *Christmas Stories from Mississippi, Fireflies in Fruit Jars, Mad Dogs & Moonshine*, and *The RavensPerch*. She co-edited *Fannye Cook: Mississippi's Pioneering Conservationist*.

Lottie Brent Boggan
Lottie Boggan began writing feature articles for *The Northside Sun* in the 1980s and continues to do so. Her first novel, *Victory Ridge* (retitled *Redemption Ridge*), won first place in the Division of Novels in the Eudora Welty Film and Festival. Through the years she has won other awards and competitions for her novels, short stories, and essays. She is co-author with Judy Tucker of three short story anthologies: *From the Sleeping Porch*, *Fireflies in Fruit Jars*, and *Mad Dogs and Moonshine*.

Janet Brown
A native of Illinois, Janet Brown is the published author of numerous articles, short stories, and poetry, plus four published novels including the recent *Deadly Visits*, published in April 2019 through Dogwood Press. She holds a BA and MA in English literature, was a writer and editor for SIU-Carbondale, and taught creative writing at ASU-Arkansas. She is the winner of an Eppie and twice winner of the Eudora Welty fiction award for the novel. She has traveled extensively, but considers Mississippi her home.

John M. Floyd
John Floyd's work has appeared in more than 250 different publications, including *Alfred Hitchcock's Mystery Magazine, Ellery Queen's Mystery Magazine, The Strand Magazine, Mississippi Noir, The Saturday Evening Post*, and *The Best American Mystery Stories*. A former Air Force captain and IBM systems engineer, he is also an Edgar Award nominee, a three-time Derringer Award winner, a three-time Pushcart Prize nominee,

and the recent recipient of the Edward D. Hoch Memorial Golden Derringer Award for lifetime achievement. His seventh book, *The Barrens*, was released in fall 2018.

Chuck Galey

Chuck Galey grew up in a small farm town in the Mississippi Delta. He has illustrated more than seventy educational books and sixteen children's picture books, one he authored. He writes short stories in addition to his other creative work. When not working in his Jackson studio, he presents exciting school programs that inspire and astonish students. His programs, listed on the Mississippi Arts Commission's Teaching Artist Roster, encourage students to be creative in reading, writing, and art. He also reviews children's picture books for *Parents & Kids Magazine*. His website is www.chuckgaley.com.

Sally P. Green

Along with her husband and son, Sally P. Green is happy to call Vicksburg, Mississippi, home. She has Bachelor of Science degrees in Finance and Information Management, and after a career in insurance, now devotes most of her time to volunteer projects involving church, community, and her son's school. In her spare time, she enjoys reading, drawing, and writing stories. She is also an award-winning artist, most recently having been chosen by Wyatt Waters as one of a select group to exhibit artwork at the 2018 Cedars Juried Art Show in Jackson. She has also won People's Choice, First Place, and other awards at Vicksburg Art Association shows. Her business, The Painted Paper, produces cards and prints that feature Mississippi's unique architecture, animals, flowers, and people.

Sherye Simmons Green

Sherye Simmons Green's writings reflect her journey of faith and explore the inner landscapes of the heart. A former Miss Mississippi, she has enjoyed two careers: business and education. She has written an inspirational novel, *Abandon Not My Soul,* and a devotional essay collection, *Tending the Garden of My Heart: Reflections on Cultivating a Life of Faith,* and more than sixty-five articles for magazines, newsletters, and newspapers.

Wendy Harms

After studying science at Mississippi State University, Wendy Harms changed gears and spent several years developing a passion for writing. She is a member of the Pennin' and Grinnin' writing group. She and her brilliant college classmate, Jason, are the parents of two wonderful children, Emily and James. Although she's made stops at many towns across the state and now resides in Madison, her home is Causeyville, a small community in Lauderdale County, Mississippi.

Brent Hearn

When he's not dreaming up monster stories for his day job, Brent Hearn writes plays, fiction, and comedy. His work has appeared online in publications that specialize in the well, that's certainly . . . different; onstage at various theaters across Mississippi; and onscreen promoting an assortment of companies and organizations that will sell you a car, sell you the insurance to cover it, and harvest your organs when Bubba Ray decides his F150 is gonna beat that red light like it cussed his dog.

Contributors

Charlotte Hudson

Charlotte Jones Hudson, a native of Forest, MS, has lived most of her life in Byram and Brandon, Mississippi. She earned a degree in elementary education from Mississippi College. She and Bill, her husband of forty-two years, have two married children and two grandchildren. In addition, she has a stepdaughter and a stepgrandson. She and Bill recently moved to Petal, Mississippi, where their son, daughter-in-law, and grandchildren reside. She enjoys spending her time with family and friends, crafting handmade greeting cards, writing, and reading.

Daney Kepple

(September 6, 1945–March 5, 2016)

Daney Kepple, was a writer, reader, and an advocate whose devotion to each of these passions intersected in her work and writing. She retired in 2007 from Rhodes College as the director of communications and previously served as Vice President of Chandler Ehrlich, a marketing and branding firm. She graduated from Ole Miss in 1970 and spent most of her life living in Memphis, Tennessee. She also led a writers group with devoted members Linda Raiteri, Diane Thomas-Plunk, and Stephanie Swindle Thomas, who submitted on her behalf and whose work is also featured in this anthology.

JP Luby

JP Luby, Mississippi's 1990 Teacher of the Year, is a retired educator. He lives in rural Yazoo County, where he rescues animals from dumpsters and maintains a no-kill chicken shelter. His children's poetry was published in *Beat the Drum: Independence Day Has Come*, and his story "Snow" was published in *Jabberwock Review*, the literary journal of Mississippi State University. He is currently writing a collection of essays, *Ruminations on Immortality and other Vagabond Notions*.

Chuck McIntosh

Chuck McIntosh has written three feature-length screenplays and one short film, which he produced and directed for the film-festival circuit. He has also illustrated over twenty children's books and written and illustrated two comic books. He publishes a weekly cartoon called *The Friday Chuckle*. He is the Director of Communications for the Mississippi Department of Finance and Administration. He has spent over forty years in broadcast and non-broadcast film and video production, advertising, corporate, and non-profit communications. His producing and directing have won two Telly awards. He and his wife live in Madison, Mississippi.

Frederick Charles Melancon

Frederick Charles Melancon is a native of New Orleans. Currently, he lives in Central Mississippi with his wife and daughter. He has taught creative writing classes at Mississippi College and Hinds Community College. And, yes, it was his daughter who broke the toy crane in the back of the bookstore.

Melanie Noto

Melanie Noto is a multi-published author of romantic suspense and an avid reader.

Writing is more than an escape for her—it's a way of life. She grew up in the Deep South listening to tall tales and penning stories about her cats. Now she writes gripping stories of suspense, love, and mystery with the help of her furry little feline muses. Learn more about her and her books at www.melanieatkins.com or connect with her on Facebook.

Linda Raiteri

Linda Raiteri's work has appeared in literary journals as well as in publications such as *The Memphis Flyer, Number: A Quarterly Journal of the Arts, Memphis Magazine, Southern Living, The Commercial Appeal, National Forum: the Phi Kappa Phi Journal*, and *The Memphis Downtowner*. Journalism gives her the opportunity to explore and photograph the reality of people and places that she may not have otherwise experienced. Fiction and poetry allow her to shape, order, and arrange other levels of reality. She lives in Memphis.

Nicolas Smith

Nicolas Smith lives in Brandon, Mississippi, and is currently writing a novel.

Kyle Summerall

Kyle Summerall is the author of "Juke" (*Thuglit: Last Writes*, 2016), as well as "What Came Before" (*Good Works Review*, 2018), "Mud Bottom" (*The Flash Fiction Magazine*, 2016), "The Surface" (*WritingRaw*, 2015), and "Beaten Path" and "The Dragonfly" (*The Dilletanti*, 2014 & 15). He won the award for Excellence in Creative Writing from East Mississippi Community College and placed each year in Mississippi University for Women and Men's college magazine, claiming first place his senior year. He lives on the Gulf Coast, while his writing focuses more on central Mississippi where he's from. He hopes to follow in the footfalls of those who've also called the South home, like Larry Brown, Ron Rash, William Gay, David Joy, Barry Hannah, and Michael Farris Smith.

Stephanie Swindle Thomas

Originally from Memphis, Tennessee, Stephanie Swindle Thomas is a writer, photographer, and former Beale Street musician. Her family has been scattered across Mississippi for four generations, and she has many fond memories of making music and sharing meals across the state. She is currently the Public Relations Specialist for Penn State's College of Arts and Architecture, and leads a writers' group in State College, Pennsylvania.

Janet Taylor-Perry

Like many of her characters, Janet Taylor-Perry is a history buff and loves anything of historical significance—from old cars to old cemeteries. Her writing continues to receive 4- and 5-star reviews, with her novel, *Broken*, finishing in the top 20 at the Faulkner competition and her most recent release, *Spirits' Desire*, winning the Preditors and Editors award for novel in "other" genre. She holds a B.S. in psychology from the University of Southern Mississippi, a Master of Arts in Teaching from Belhaven University, and gifted certification from Mississippi College. She's a native Mississippian from Laurel, mother of five, educator, author, editor, entrepreneur as the owner of Dragon Breath Press, and a person who has overcome great obstacles and still holds on to her faith. Her website is www.janettaylorperry.com.

Contributors

Diane Thomas-Plunk

A Pushcart Prize nominee, Diane Thomas-Plunk was also recognized by NPR when her entry was designated a "favorite" in the Three-Minute Fiction contest. She participated in the 2017 Mississippi Book Festival and recently in the Bookstock author festival in Memphis, Tennessee. Her story "Cassie's Chair" was a finalist in the Nivalis 2016 short fiction competition, and she wrote the foreword to Lydel Sims' re-publication of *Assignment: Memphis*, now in bookstores. More than a dozen of Thomas-Plunk's short stories and poetry have appeared in *Deep South Magazine*, *Belle Rêve Literary Journal*, *The Dead Mule School of Southern Literature*, *Steel Toe Review*, and *China Grove Magazine*. She is now at work on the sequel to her first book, *Opal*. She was born and raised in Memphis.

Judy H. Tucker

Mississippi native Judy H. Tucker has published with University Press of Mississippi; Algonquin Books of Chapel Hill; Pelican Publishing, Gretna, Louisiana; and Quail Ridge Press, Brandon, Mississippi. Her stage plays have garnered a Fellowship from Mississippi Arts Commission, National 1st Prize from Daughters of the American Revolution for Historical Plays, 1st Prize from Memphis Mid-South Writers Association, and selection of her work for presentation at Shakespeare Summer Workshop, Montgomery, Alabama. Locally, her plays have been staged at Jackson's New Stage Theatre, Fondren Theatre Workshop, and Brick Street Players in Clinton.

Johnny Lowe

Originally from Vicksburg, Mississippi, Johnny Lowe has worked in advertising at agencies in both California and Mississippi; as the editor of a trade magazine for Abbott & Hast Publications; as a copy editor for University Press of Mississippi; as a comics letterer for various publishers, including Boom! Studios, Devil's Due, Image Comics, and Wildstorm; and as a ventriloquist.

Made in the USA
Columbia, SC
13 July 2019